HARD BLUE EMPTY

DWIGHT HOLING

Hard Blue Empty

Dwight Holing

Print Edition
© Dwight Holing 2023

Published by Jackdaw Press
All Rights Reserved

ISBN: 979-8-9866978-4-0

For More Information, please visit dwightholing.com.

See how you can **Get a Free Book** at the end of this novel.

For the Waorani

PROLOGUE

Logan Riggins didn't always see the road to extinction as eight lanes wide. His horizons never extended beyond climbing in Yosemite and his cares were limited to making sure he wasn't hammering a piton in a lightning storm. Logan never felt more alive than when his face was pressed against a sheer wall of granite with nothing around him but the hard blue empty.

The buzz that came with cheating death had something to do with it. He'd seen other climbers crater and escaped the same fate more than once. The closest was when a young guy he was teaching to lead fell on the final pitch up Lost Arrow Spire. Logan was belaying him from a ledge no wider than his feet. When his grigri failed to put the brakes on the kid's plummet, he grabbed the nylon rope with both hands despite the risk of being pulled off. The speeding line burned through his palms like a heated blade before he could stop it. Then he held fast as the young climber yo-yoed sixty feet below. When Logan hauled him up, the rope was slick with his own blood.

Everything changed the day Sarah Newton walked into the cramped art gallery he ran in Berkeley. She glanced at the color blowups of snowfields reflecting sunsets and pen-and-ink draw-ings of towering rock walls with climbers reaching for the top. Picking up a basket woven by a Miwok artisan, she said, "My mistake. I thought Wild Things would be a women's clothing boutique."

One look into her green eyes that sparkled as bright as an alpine lake shot with sunlight had Logan falling harder than a free climber with sweaty fingertips. "No, you're in the right place," he said before she could U-turn.

He grabbed a pair of carabiners he'd left on his desk and dangled them from his ears. "See, jewelry." Then he guided her to a rack of shower curtains hand-painted by a local artist. "Look, the latest in formal gowns, straight from the runway in Milan. I can order them in any size you want."

Sarah's laugh matched her eyes and Logan fell even harder.

By the time she left, he'd sweet-talked her into going to Yosemite that weekend. They spent the night on the valley floor watching bright points of starlight dance as a full moon arced over the silvery granite headwalls and Bridalveil Fall thundered. When the sky paled with the new morning, their sleeping bags were zipped together and Logan and Sarah's arms and legs were entwined tighter than the limbs of the cottonwoods that lined the banks of the clear, cold Merced River.

Logan had never felt more alive—even more than when he free-soloed every inch of the 2,900-foot nose of El Capitan. Sarah moved into his place after they got back. They were married on the top of Half Dome as a trio of bluegrass musi-cians who'd scaled the granite monolith with their instruments strapped to their backs played love ballads followed by Irish jigs.

It didn't take much for Sarah to convince Logan to change the direction of Wild Things even though it meant changing himself. He could no sooner refuse her than a rope frayed by an arête could halt a fall. Action photos of rock climbers and plein air landscapes were returned to their creators. Bedroom sets and coffee tables replaced Indigenous carvings and clay pots. The front window display was given over to kitchenware and coordinating placemats and napkins.

"Tastes change," Sarah told him. "It's not about keeping up. It's about keeping ahead."

She did just that by marketing home goods and housewares under their own label. Sarah oversaw a team of designers while Logan traveled to Asia to negotiate manufacturing deals. They opened new retail outlets across the country to handle the demand. Sales doubled after they launched an online storefront. Wild Things kept right on growing day after day, month after month. Each year brought Sarah and Logan new opportunities and the riches that came with them. They had to hire a team of personal assistants to manage their public appearances and the media frenzy surrounding their meteoric stardom.

A climbing podcast broke a different kind of story. The host talked Logan into giving him an interview at the base of Indian Rock, a stack of gray rhyolite in the hills behind Berkeley that local climbers used for keeping in shape between expeditions to the Sierra and beyond. The podcaster made a raw comment about how Logan had turned his back on the climbing community, how Wild Things relied on child labor to make linens, how shipping furniture around the world was fueling climate change, that the only thing he climbed these days was in and out of private jets and luxury automobiles.

Logan was seething as he challenged the host to a race. As they scrambled up the rock, he admitted to himself he was indeed out of practice, but with each crack he jammed, each nub he pinched, each edge he toed, he seemed to rediscover who he once was, what he once loved. He reached the top first.

The sun was melting into the Golden Gate as the two sat with their feet dangling over the side. Logan was transfixed by the freeway below where the glow of bumper-to-bumper headlights and taillights wavered the same as stripes on a windblown flag.

"I'm as stuck as those nine-to-fivers," he said. "I used to see routes to the summit. Now all I look for is the bottom line."

"Why don't you quit?" the podcaster prodded while keeping the microphone hot. "With all the money you've made, you could start saving mountains in addition to climbing them."

"Maybe I will," Logan said.

The pod aired and prompted others to dig for more. A gossip show streamed an even juicier tidbit: Logan's dissatisfaction with the boardroom had begun in the bedroom. Sarah confirmed it when she filed for divorce, claiming her husband had been unfaithful and cited his affairs with catalog models as proof. Logan never refuted her charges nor did he refuse her demand that he sell her his share of Wild Things.

Three hours after signing the papers, he was on a plane bound for the Andes vowing to summit every peak in the chain or die trying, and no one heard from Logan Riggins again.

1

The fog followed the ebb tide out of the Oakland Estuary. A ferry departing Jack London Square blasted its horn, prompting a flock of seagulls to give chase in case a commuter bound for San Francisco tossed a half-eaten muffin over the side. Jess Parks rode the freight elevator down to his street-level boat shop in a three-story brick building and rolled up the overhead door. An old man pushing an overflowing shopping cart with a scruffy dog riding on top stopped.

"Morning, Carl," Jess called to him, handing over a container. "Isabella made pesto pasta last night. There's a sausage for Kelp too."

"He'll like that. Won't you, boy?" Carl gave the dog a pat. "We been keepin' an eye out like I told you we would. Ain't nobody gonna get the jump on you again. Not with Kelp and old Carl around."

"I appreciate that, but, remember, you got to take care of number one first. You don't have to sleep on the street. Meals, showers, and a bunk are waiting for you at the Seafarers' House whenever you want. You're entitled to them. You put in the years and paid your union dues."

"I did, didn't I? Same as your granddaddy done." Carl's blue knit watch cap bobbed like a troller on rough seas. "Ain't no port we never got to, ain't no sea we never sailed on. I'll try and remember to do that, but sometimes it's hard with all the other stuff I gotta remember. Like him bein' gone and you takin' over, and me and Kelp keepin' an eye out so you don't get jumped again."

Carl balanced the container of leftovers beside the dog and shoved off, his mutters keeping time with the shopping cart's front wheels that squeaked and skidded each time they struck a bump.

Jess left the overhead door open for fresh air and stepped back inside. He ran his palm along the orange hull of a sixteen-foot sea kayak resting on sawhorses. The bow was marred by a gash just above the waterline. Two nights earlier he'd been paddling *Pursuit* on the estuary as part of his rehab when a party boat piloted by a drunken skipper swerved into his lane.

It would've been a lot worse if he hadn't pulled off a massive sweep stroke and veered hard to port. Three months earlier, Jess wouldn't have had the strength to do it. At six months, he wouldn't have been paddling at all, not from a bed in the trauma unit at Highland Hospital following emergency surgery to repair the close-range gunshot wound in his shoulder.

Jess began mixing epoxy resin with hardener in preparation for applying a final coat to a fiberglass patch. He was picturing the moment he finished the repair and launched *Pursuit* back into the estuary for a paddle. Miss another day and he'd have to find a gym with a rowing machine. Muscles, he chided himself, use 'em or lose 'em.

The sound of footsteps made him look up. It wasn't Carl bringing back the container, but a short man who wore a size-too-big long-sleeved white shirt buttoned at the neck and leather sandals. His obsidian hair looked as if it'd been cut with blunt scissors after a bowl was placed on his head. Two thin lines were tattooed across his nutmeg-brown cheeks. A green parrot feather was struck through his left earlobe. The unusual look didn't command Jess's attention as much as the scabbarded machete hanging from his shoulder.

"Can I help you?" he said.

"Park?" the man said in heavily accented English.

"Not in front of the entrance, please. I need to be able to get my customers' boats in and out. On either side is OK."

"You. You are Park?"

"Oh, my name. Yeah, with an *s*. Parks. Jess Parks. And you are?"

"Dabo." Noticing that Jess's eyes were locked on the machete, he said, "You want to look?" He gripped the handle and drew the blade. The shop's hanging fluorescent lights made it gleam. "I made it. It is very sharp."

"So I see. And the scabbard, did you make that too?"

"From caiman skin. A caiman with big teeth."

"I take it you bit him before he bit you."

Dabo grinned.

"How can I help you?" Jess said.

"I am waiting."

"For what?"

"My friend."

"Who's your friend?"

A car door slammed out front. "Me," a voice called from the sunlight. "Hello, Sparks. Long time."

The nickname gave Jess a jolt. He got an even bigger one when Logan Riggins stepped inside the boat shop. In the seven years since he'd last seen him, crow's wings had taken flight at the corners of his steel-gray eyes and there was more salt than pepper in his hair. Other than that, he looked as fit as ever.

Jess stuck out his hand, and when the man fifteen years his

senior gripped it, he felt the raised scar on his palm, a blunt reminder of how he owed Logan his life, not only from having saved him on Lost Arrow, but when he was floundering on the streets with no direction home. Logan had given Jess one by hiring him on at Wild Things and teaching him how to climb.

"What happen, you run out of mountains?" he said.

"Turns out I only needed to summit the first one," Logan said. "When I reached the top of Cotopaxi and looked east, there was nothing but green as far as the eye could see."

"The same color as your ex-wife's," Jess almost quipped, but said instead, "The Amazon."

"It was the only thing big enough for me to get lost in. I hiked down the mountain, wandered around, and finally found what I was looking for."

"What's that?"

"A purpose."

"Which is?"

"Saving it."

"That's a tall order."

Logan shrugged. "You know how it is, Sparks. The higher the rock, the better the view from the top."

He scanned the boat shop, taking in a demasted twelve-meter wooden sloop on a trailer, a vintage Chris-Craft Riviera shiny with a fresh coat of mahogany stain, a pair of antique wooden rowboats that were the last survivors of a fleet of Lake Merritt rentals.

"I always figured you'd wind up taking over your grandfa-ther's business. How I knew to come here to look for you."

"He died a couple of years after you left. There's still a need for restoration work and not many shops left that do it."

"Good for you for keeping his legacy alive. What about this other job you volunteer for, Alameda County Sheriff's Search and Rescue?"

That gave Jess another jolt of surprise. "How do you know about that?"

"Even the Amazon gets satellite Internet now, spotty as it is. I may have pulled a Percy Fawcett, but I keep an ear out for Bay Area news, especially when it's about a friend who received a mayor's commendation for taking a bullet and saving a cop's life." He chinned at Jess's shoulder. "Will you be able to climb again?"

"We'll see."

"Must've hurt."

"Like getting struck by a rock kicked loose by the climber above you."

"What are you doing for rehab?"

Jess ran his palm along *Pursuit's* sleek hull. "Paddling this first thing in the morning and again at night. But you didn't travel four thousand miles to check on my health. Why did you really come back after all these years?"

"Remember the first rule of climbing?" Logan said.

"Trust your gear, your partner, but, most of all, trust yourself."

"The other one. Someone needs a hand, you reach first and ask why second. Dabo and his people need help."

Jess stuck out his hand.

Logan shot Dabo a grin. "See, I told you we could count on him." He glanced at his watch. "We're late for a meeting. Ride with us and I'll explain on the way."

"Who's the meeting with?"

"The head of CaliCo."

"As in CaliCo Energy?"

"They plan on drilling for oil in Dabo's homeland. I'm going to talk the CEO out of it and Dabo is going to give him that." He nodded at the machete.

"Give as in ..." Jess mimed swinging it.

"It's his people's tradition to exchange gifts with enemies first before going to war. Dabo is Tarani, the smallest tribal group of the Waorani people who live throughout the Amazon in Ecuador. Tarani, Toñampare, Quenahueno, Zapino, no matter the tribal group's name or what part of the rainforest they call home, all Waorani people share something in common besides speaking Wao."

"Land is life," Dabo chanted, brandishing the machete. "It is not for sale. We fight for it. We die for it."

"Come on, let's ride," Logan said.

A rental car was parked out front. Dabo got in the back seat and Jess took shotgun. Logan drove the same way he did when they used to go to Yosemite—fast, skilled, and with the windows always rolled down, no matter if it was summer or winter, daytime or night. He steered them north and soon they were on the same stretch of freeway that he'd looked down on from Indian Rock years before and decided to seek new horizons.

"Tell me about CaliCo and Ecuador," Jess said.

"Sure thing. CaliCo's one of the last of the independent oil companies," Logan said, changing lanes with only a glance at his side mirror. "Jim Buckle is the CEO. The company was founded by his great-grandfather, a dry holer from West Texas who moved to Bakersfield and hit a string of gushers."

A car honked as Logan cut in front of it. "I met Jim a few times back in the day at Bay Area Business Council meetings. He puts on the aw-shucks for the cameras, but holds a master's from Stanford Business School and makes more money than a tech VC. He believes his family was put on earth to drain every drop of oil on the planet. He wants to do that in Ecuador."

"Then why's he going to listen to you when you ask him not to?"

"Because he listens to money, and I can offer him a way to

make a better return on his investment than bushwhacking through the Amazon."

"How?"

"You'll find out when I explain it to him, but before we get there, I need to tell you what Dabo and I are hoping you can do for us."

"Name it."

"Put your search and rescue skills to work and help him find his little sister. He has reason to believe she lives in Oakland."

"Mintaka," Dabo said from the back seat. "*Mintaka* means blue macaw in English. She has been gone a long time. Our mother is sick and wants to see her before she dies."

Jess turned to look at him. "Her name's Blue Macaw? That's beautiful. Where did you learn English? You speak it very well."

"Father Banana taught me. Spanish also."

"Father Banana? Is that some kind of, well, deity for your people?"

Logan answered first. "No, Father Banana is what everyone calls him because he has chronic jaundice from so many bouts of hepatitis. His real name is Father Bernardo. He runs a Catholic mission near the Tarani homelands."

Jess asked Dabo why he thought his sister lived in Oakland.

"Our mother got a letter from her. It was the first we heard from her since she disappeared a few years ago. She sent it to Father Banana and he brought it to our mother by dugout."

"On the Caiman River, that's where your village is?"

"Tarani do not have one village. We have many. We go from one to the next with the season and animals."

"Tarani live as they always have," Logan said. "They're hunter-gatherers. They're also one of the last tribes in the Amazon ever to be contacted by the outside world."

Jess asked Dabo if his sister wrote where she was living.

"Only on the envelope: 365 Box. Oakland. California. USA."

"That was the return address," Logan said. "I couldn't find it on Google. Box isn't even on a good old-fashioned AAA folding map." He made another lane change.

"Can't say I've heard of it either," Jess said. "But there are hundreds of streets in Oakland. Could be one of those little alleys only a block long. What about a zip code?"

"The return didn't have one."

"Do you have the envelope and letter?" Jess asked Dabo.

"My mother kept it. It was all she had of Mintaka."

"Can you tell me what she wrote? Like, what's she doing up here? Does she have a job, and if so, what is it? Does she live alone or is she married? Kids in school? Is she living in a house, an apartment? Knowing things like that would help."

Dabo dipped his head. "All Mintaka wrote was, 'I am sorry. I cannot come home. Please forgive me.'"

"That's it?"

Dabo nodded.

Jess wanted to ask him what she'd done and why she left, but the sadness in his face stopped him. "The number and street should be easy enough to track down through the Alameda County Sheriff's database and mapping app I use for search and rescue."

"Good," Dabo said. "I must find Mintaka and take her home. There is not much time before our mother walks past the giant anaconda and greets the old ones."

2

______

Logan pulled off the freeway in Richmond and took a frontage road that followed the San Pablo Bay shoreline. The air coming through the car's open windows carried the egg stink of a nearby oil refinery's cracking plant that neither the briny scent of the bay nor the feral aroma of mudflats could mask. They pulled into a freshly asphalted parking lot festooned with banners stamped with CaliCo's multicolored plaid logo.

"The company has been cleaning and restoring some wetlands they fouled from a ruptured pipeline at their refinery," Logan said. "They turned it into a nature preserve and are holding a dedication ceremony today."

He led the way past information kiosks displaying zoo-like posters of birds and animals. Servers dressed in safari costumes were offering snacks and drinks from wooden trays. The ones heaped with cheese and crackers weren't nearly as popular as those holding plastic flutes of mimosas. A woman wielding a tablet intercepted the trio.

"Welcome to CaliCo Bayside Wildlife Preserve. May I have your names, please?"

Logan gave her his.

She started swiping the screen. "Hmm. I don't see it on the list of invitees and project partners. How do you spell it?"

He told her.

She hmmed again. "Perhaps you're listed under your company."

"Not for a long time."

The woman appeared flustered. She looked at Jess and Dabo. "How about you?"

"I am Dabo," he replied.

"Is that your first or last name?"

"My only name. Tarani only need one."

She switched her gaze to Jess. "Two names. Jess Parks, but I won't be on your list. I'm with them."

A man appeared at her side. He wore a tan hunting jacket with rifle cartridge holders above the pockets. It wasn't a rental like the costumes worn by the other staff. His eyes shifted behind the yellow lenses of shooting glasses and then remained fixed on the scabbarded machete.

"Do we have a problem?" he said.

"These guests aren't on my list, Mr. Hunt." She swiped the tablet's screen again.

Logan took a step toward Hunt. "Logan Riggins. Our acceptances must've gotten lost in email. We just flew in from Ecuador."

"Ecuador?"

"That's right. Where the oil is. Where CaliCo wants to be." He gave a smile. "And you are?"

"Lyle Hunt. Head of corporate security."

"Pleasure, Lyle. Now where's old Jim planted himself?"

Hunt's stony expression remained unchanged. "While we can make an exception for you not being on the list, we can't for the weapon. You'll have to lock it inside your vehicle."

"And deprive Jim of receiving a ceremonial gift from all the good people who live where he wants to drill?"

Logan shook his head and quickly walked away with Jess and Dabo hurrying to keep up. They passed a pond that was ringed by pickleweed and eelgrass. A pair of common mud hens paddled in the dappled shallows, their squat silhouettes like greasy smudges on the water. Redwing blackbirds perched atop quivering bullrushes. Reverb caused by someone speaking too close to a microphone acted the same as a shotgun blast, spooking the birds and sending them squawking, screeching, and flapping.

The trio reached a clearing where a pale man in a black business suit stood on a podium holding a cordless mike. He issued a mirthless smile and started over.

"Good morning. Welcome. My name is Pius Wheedling, executive vice president and general counsel of CaliCo Energy. It is my honor to acknowledge a few of our esteemed guests."

He announced by name the district's congressional representative, state senator, and the heads of various California agencies. As the audience gave each a round of polite applause, Jess turned around. Lyle Hunt was standing close behind him.

Wheedling cleared his throat. "Now, please join me in welcoming CaliCo's chief executive officer and chair of the board, C. Jamison Buckle."

The applause grew louder as a man in his early fifties with silver hair and glacial blue eyes strode to the front. After smiling for the TV cameras and photographers, he shooed Wheedling away who was trying to hand him a prepared speech.

"No need for that, Pius. This place speaks for itself." The clapping started all over again.

Buckle went on to praise public-private partnerships, level-headed conservationists, a streamlined permitting process, and his own company's commitment to clean energy and sustainable development. Waving at the pond, his voice boomed, "Who says oil and water don't mix?"

The CaliCo chief posed for the cameras and then waded into the crowd to shake hands and slap backs with the confidence of a candidate running for office who knew he had a ten-point lead in the polls.

Logan waited until the crowd polished off the mimosas and began to thin before approaching him.

"Hello, Jim. Still punching holes I see."

Buckle turned from a coterie of business executives he was holding court with and mustered a grin to mask his surprise.

"Well, well, well. Look what the tide washed up. Logan Riggins as I live and breathe. What was it you set out to try to do all those years ago, break the world record for walking around the world? If this is your finish line, let me be the first to congratulate you. I'll even put up a plaque to mark your feat."

As Buckle started to turn back to his guests, Logan said, "You have a minute to take a little walk? I want to talk to you about the oil lease tracts in Ecuador you're planning to bid on."

Buckle's left eyebrow arched. "What makes you think I am, and more to point, why do you care?"

"Because that's where home's been for the past several years."

"You don't say? Your feet get stuck in all that mud down there and you couldn't keep on keeping on?"

A few of the onlookers laughed.

"I want to share with you an alternative to drilling that will prove more lucrative for CaliCo and its shareholders. Give me a couple of minutes and I'll explain how it works."

Buckle waved dismissively. "I appreciate you thinking of my pocketbook, but I have a pretty decent track record running the company as it is. Take a look at our current stock price and you'll see I know what I'm doing when it comes to finding oil and bringing it to market."

"My plan will earn you more for leaving it in the ground. The savings in legal costs from not having to fight lawsuits and all the PR help you won't need to pay to gloss over destroying the Amazon will more than make up for any short-term profits."

Buckle's gaze turned frosty. "CaliCo runs a clean operation. We create thousands of jobs, pump millions into local economies, and usher people who've been living in grass shacks into the modern age." He locked eyes with Lyle Hunt and gave him a nod. "Now, if you'll excuse me, I don't have time for Fantasyland. I live in the real world and have a real business to run."

Hunt put his hand on Logan's shoulder, but he shrugged it off.

"It's no fantasy. It's a real business solution to the real-life nightmare happening down there when drillers come in. Land gets stolen from people, the rainforest is reduced to smoking black stumps, and birds fall out of the sky from all the fumes."

The head of security tried to grab Logan's shoulder again as Buckle's smile tightened.

"Where do you get off being so holier-than-thou? All the sweatshops you ran in Asia churning out your cheap furniture? You fouled half of Guangdong Province with all the toxins your factories spewed."

"Those were third-party manufacturers and you know it. I ripped up their contracts once I found out. I ran a clean business."

"You mean your wife did. Sarah was always the brains of the outfit. Look how she took you to the cleaners. I've seen her in action. We serve together on the boards of a half-dozen companies and foundations. While you been playing Tarzan, we've kept the Bay Area economy humming and its cultural resources sparkling. This Saturday night we'll be raising five million dollars at a gala for the Oakland Arts Foundation. You want to make a real difference? Rent a tux and come to the Grand Hotel and see how the grown-ups get it done. Don't forget to bring your checkbook."

Logan dipped his shoulder to throw off Hunt's attempt to grip it again. Jess moved in to keep the security chief from throwing an armlock around Logan's neck, but Dabo moved even faster. He stepped between Logan and Buckle, bowed, and held out the scabbarded machete.

"Please, take this. It is a gift from the Tarani. Spare our homeland. Thank you."

A TV crew caught wind of the confrontation and was scurrying over. Buckle saw them coming. He nodded at Hunt to let go of Logan and then took the machete from Dabo. Holding it up for the camera, he made a show of admiring its craftsmanship.

"It's an honor to receive this on behalf of CaliCo Energy. We're all committed to sustainable development and protecting trees and animals and Indians too, whether it's here at our new wildlife sanctuary on the Bay or wherever we go to find the fuels that keep America safe and strong and the world a better place."

He waved goodbye to the cameras and hangers-on. With Lyle Hunt leading the way, Buckle marched toward a line of SUVs idling in the parking lot. He handed the scabbarded machete to Pius Wheedling who was hustling to keep up.

"Have this put in my golf bag. I'll give the boys a laugh when I pull it out on the course and pretend it's a lob wedge."

3

———

Logan didn't say a word as he drove back to Oakland. Jess and Dabo followed his cue and stared out the windshield. When they pulled to stop in front of the boat shop, Logan said, "I never thought it was going to be a cakewalk, but at least now we know what we're up against. Don't worry. I'll figure out a new route."

"I know," Dabo said.

"When can you start tracking down Mintaka?" Logan said to Jess.

"Right away. Do you need a place to stay? You're welcome here."

"Thanks, but I booked us rooms before we left Ecuador."

"Which hotel?"

"The Grand."

"Did you know Sarah was chairing a gala there before Buckle told you?"

Logan shrugged. "Couldn't change now even if I wanted to. I prepaid for a week when I made the reservation."

"Have you talked to her since you moved to Ecuador?"

"Only through lawyers and emails. I tried calling her once or twice, but getting a connection is always a challenge, and, well, Sarah travels a lot."

Jess didn't try to hide a grimace. Shortly after Logan and Sarah married, she made it clear she had little tolerance for his climbing buddies and the kids he was trying to introduce to wilderness pursuits. Eventually, she fired Jess and ordered him to quit hanging around.

"Seven years is a long time gone," Logan said. "Sarah and I may not agree on much, but we do on one thing, and that's we're both better off having split. She got to run the business the way she always wanted and I got what I needed."

"What's that?" Jess said.

"Freedom to be me."

"If you change your mind, I have room for you and Dabo here."

Logan looked up at the narrow brick building. "Three whole floors and it's just the boats and you all by your lonesome?"

"Not exactly. I live on the top and rent out the middle floor."

"To?"

"A tenant."

"Someone who pays you actual rent in real money?"

Jess nodded.

"What's your tenant do?"

"She's an artist and teacher."

"She, huh? Sculptor or painter?"

"Neither. Performance artist. She choreographs different types of dance to different sounds and either performs them live or films it and puts it online. Japanese butoh. Modern. Hip-hop. I couldn't name them all. The soundtrack? Everything from indie to jazz to clanging from the shipyard."

"And people pay to see that?"

"They line up."

"Why do I think you're always the first one?"

"I appreciate art, even if I don't always understand it."

"But you appreciate the artist even more."

"What do you want me to say?"

"Nothing. You already did." Logan laughed. "What's she teach?"

"Dance at schools and community centers. Kind of like what you were doing for kids with camping and climbing."

"I like her already. Dabo and I'll go get settled at the Grand and later you can invite us over to meet your tenant. What's her name?"

"Isabella."

"Is she Ecuadorian by any chance?"

"No, Italian on both sides. Her ancestors came from Tuscany."

"I've been there. It's beautiful. Sarah and I spent a belated honeymoon in a hill town called San Gimignano. Has all these tall towers made out of stone. You know what I thought when I saw them?"

"You could free climb them."

"See, after all these years, you and I still think alike. The only thing I needed was a little chalk on the fingertips. No rope necessary."

Jess opened the door and was halfway out when Logan said, "I have a better idea. Isabella's an artist, right? Bring her to the gala. Buckle said it's a benefit for the Oakland Arts Foundation. That includes everybody from the art museum to the symphony to a dancer pirouetting to a steel drum made out of an oil barrel. I'll leave two tickets for you at will call. Dabo and I'll meet you there."

"Then you do want to see Sarah again."

"Actually, Jim Buckle. This will be another opportunity where I can buttonhole him. I told you I needed to find a new route. He might be less willing to tell me to shove it in front of an audience of wealthy progressives. It is the Bay Area, after all."

"I've never worn a tux, much less owned one," Jess said.

"Don't worry about it. Buckle and his ilk will be the only ones wearing them. No matter if it's in Oakland or the Amazon, clothes are either a way to blend in with your tribe, declare yourself chief, or scare your enemies. You should see how the Tarani dress when facing down an enemy."

Dabo trilled. "With spears and blowgun darts dipped in frog poison."

"See you there, Sparks." Logan gunned the car and sped off.

Jess let himself into the building, but instead of going back to patching *Pursuit* or rebuilding the damaged deck on the demasted sloop, he slid open the wooden picket safety gate to the freight elevator and rode it up. He kept an ear out as he passed the second floor, but all was quiet. That was to be expected. Isabella rarely went to sleep before the wee hours. Since she'd moved in, he learned to fall asleep to the echoes of different types of music and whatever sounds she'd recorded and was mixing downstairs.

His floor had solid brick walls on three sides and steel-framed windows in the front. Jess made a fresh cup of coffee in the ship's galley-like kitchen and sat down at an old chart table that doubled as his desk. He looked out at the Oakland Estuary. Across the water was Alameda Island. To the right was the Port of Oakland and all the cargo ship terminals where container cranes operated day and night. To the left, marinas and private boat slips lined both sides of the estuary's shoreline all the way to Coast Guard Island. It was his turnaround point when paddling *Pursuit* as part of his rehab routine.

Jess opened his laptop and searched for Box Street, Box Avenue, Box Boulevard, Box Place, Oakland, California. Getting no hits, he tried the surrounding cities of Alameda, San Leandro, Piedmont, Emeryville, and Berkeley. Still nothing. Finally, he searched on variations of the spelling. Bock. Bocks. Bach. Back. A big fat zero.

The chair creaked as Jess leaned back and looked out the window again. He drank the rest of the coffee. Dabo said he'd learned English from Father Banana, but that didn't necessarily mean Blue Macaw spoke it. Maybe an acquaintance had written the letter for her. If the writer had gotten the return address wrong, Blue Macaw wouldn't have known.

The more Jess thought about it, the more he realized he didn't know anything about Dabo's little sister. Why did she leave home? How long ago? Did she go straight to California or come overland via Mexico like many migrants from Central and South America did? And why was she sorry? Why did she need forgiveness? Why couldn't she go back home?

"I need to know more about you, Blue Macaw," he said. "I need to talk to your brother."

Jess typed in the VPN for Alameda County Sheriff's. A few clicks took him to the database the Search and Rescue team of volunteers used to pinpoint addresses and locations. It came complete with maps and 3D satellite and drone imagery showing terrain, elevation, and everything from ponds in parks to culverts beneath roads that people could fall into or be stuffed.

Not everyone the team searched for was lost or an accident victim. Oakland PD and Sheriff's used them on kidnappings and homicide investigations. Homeland Security, FBI, and DEA did too. No matter the agency, the pay was always the same. Another big fat zero.

Jess kept clicking keys, but Box Street and the spelling variations he'd come up with didn't trigger a thing except a bar called Box Cars down by the Coliseum and a mixed martial arts club named The Fighter Box in the Fruitvale District. Both were beyond long shots, but he made a note of their addresses anyway.

He was rinsing out his cup when the elevator began to rattle and hum. It went down a floor and then came back up. The wooden picket safety gate juddered.

"Did I leave my moka here?" Isabella said, blinking as she looked in the direction of the galley kitchen.

Jess pointed at the stovetop espresso maker. "It's on the rear burner."

Isabella put a hand to her forehead to shade her eyes. Silver bracelets on her wrist tinkled like wind chimes. "How do you expect me to see anything in here? You keep it so bright."

"It's called daylight. Those are called windows. You should open your blackout curtains sometime."

He made her an espresso while Isabella kicked off her flats and sat on the couch, hooking one leg beneath the other. She wore a sweatshirt with the neckband cut off. Her hair was a nimbus of curls.

Jess brought over a cup and sat beside her.

"How come you're not downstairs working on your boats?" she said.

"I am working. Something for an old friend."

"Who's your friend and what's the job?"

He told her about Logan Riggins, how they met, why he'd gone to Ecuador, and what he was doing back in California.

"That's sweet. He catches you shoplifting and when he asks your name, you're so frightened, you get tongue-tied and say it all together. *Jessparks. Jess Sparks.* Then he gives you a job and teaches you how to climb rocks."

"Technically, I wasn't stealing, only borrowing. I was riding my bike past his gallery and got a flat. The door was open and I needed something to take the tire off so I could patch the inner-tube. No one was around and so I took a letter opener off the desk. Logan was in the back and heard me. As for my name, I had a little speech impediment back then."

"You don't stutter anymore."

"No, I lost it."

"How?"

Jess was about to explain how everything changed the first time he got on the rock, how once he started climbing, he left all his fear behind, the fear that had paralyzed him after his parents' sailboat capsized off the Farallon Islands and their bodies were never recovered, how he was held in a youth detention center for months while Child Services determined whether his grandfather was fit enough to care for him, how he used to get the shit kicked out of him by the bangers who controlled the neighborhood.

Instead, he said, "Logan will tell you he calls me that because I climb so fast I make sparks fly off the granite."

Whenever Isabella smiled, it was always with her eyes and lips. "Tell me more about Dabo and Blue Macaw. I love her name. I can see her flying over the treetops."

"Sure, what little I know."

When he finished, she said, "I'd like to meet them and learn about Tarani music and dance. Maybe they could show me. Maybe even let me film them. I could show it to one of my classes. The kids would love it. What do you think?"

"I don't know. I don't know a thing about their culture, traditions, or beliefs. You'd have to ask them."

Isabella finished the espresso. "Of course, and if they say no, then I'll understand. But I'm of the mind that cultural arts are even more powerful when they're shared. Respected, yes, always, but shared, definitely. They teach us about ourselves and others. They tie the world together a little tighter so we're less willing to unravel it. Javanese shadow puppets, Caribbean stilt dancers, *Swan Lake*? Dance is a kind of Esperanto for the world.

The more I can share that with children, the better off their future will be."

"Sounds like you're writing a book on your theory."

Eyes and lips smiled again. "Maybe I am."

"Fair enough. What are you doing Saturday night?"

"Why?"

"There's a fundraiser at the Grand for the Oakland Arts Foundation. A big gala. Logan and Dabo are going so they can talk to the CaliCo CEO. Logan said he'd leave me a couple of tickets."

"A gala? Then there's sure to be dancing after the dinner and speeches."

"Most likely."

"That's perfect. I've been looking for an opportunity to try out something I've been working on."

"Given it's a black-tie fundraiser, the music and dancing could be more traditional than you're used to."

"We'll see about that."

Isabella put the espresso cup down, leaned forward, and slid her hand beneath Jess's shirt, reaching up past his chest toward his shoulder. Her fingertip found the scar tissue that had grown over the hole the bullet had drilled.

"How's your physical therapy routine coming?"

"Still stalled out until I can get *Pursuit* patched and back in the water."

"You can't think of doing anything else?"

"Joining a gym with a rowing machine."

She traced the scar, making circles. "Oh, I think we can come up with some exercises better than that. Why don't you start stretching your shoulder by pulling those curtains."

4

———

It was past six o'clock when Jess Parks called the Grand Hotel and asked for Logan Riggins. He answered on the third ring.

"Did you get a line on Mintaka?"

"Not yet. The database and mapping app came up empty. I made a couple of calls too. Guy I know at Oakland PD's central dispatch ran a check of street names in every police beat. No Box."

"How many beats are there?"

"Thirty-five spread across five areas, but some of the beats are subdivided. My boat shop? It's in Area One, Beat One X, *x* as in x-ray. Across town on the border with San Leandro? That's Area Five with Beats Thirty-One X, Y, and Z."

"Is the list of streets up to date?"

"Right down to a who's who of interest living on each block. Every law enforcement officer—including us on Search and Rescue—knows the streets where you need to keep both eyes wide open, especially the ones in the back of your head, if you get the call to roll there."

Logan asked Jess who else he talked with. He told him about

the librarian at the public library's main branch who used to date his grandfather.

"She runs the history room. It has maps going back to gold rush days. Old photos and drawings too. If there was ever a Box Street, she'd know, even if it got renamed. Lot of Oakland streets have over the years. East 14th Street was changed to International Boulevard. Tupac Shakur got a few blocks of MacArthur named after him. He lived here back in the day."

"What's your next move?"

Jess smiled to himself. Same old Logan. He'd never said, "You're not quitting and turning around, are you, Sparks?"

"I need to talk with Dabo and learn more about Blue Macaw. Who she is, what she looks like, or at least what she looked like when she left. What she likes to do. Dance. Music. Sing. Sports. What she likes to eat, drink. How she likes to dress. Anything like that."

"You sound more like a detective working a case than a searcher rescuer."

"We're often brought in to ask the same kind of questions cops do because people will tell us more. It's a trust thing, like what firefighters and EMTs have going for them. We're not there to arrest anyone, only find and rescue them."

Logan asked for an example. Jess took a deep breath. "A couple years ago four teens went missing. One of the kids had taken the family's minivan without permission. Oakland PD and FBI kept coming up empty. Search and Rescue got the call because someone figured a fresh pair of ears might help. First thing I did was go to the family with the minivan."

"What happened?"

"I knocked on the door and the dad answered. Said I wanted to hear what he had to say. Just him. Not the mom or the little brother or sister. Said they'd suffered enough. We went in the backyard. He did the talking and I did the listening. Within a couple of minutes he's complaining that the cops are treating it like his son's some kind of monster, that he'd coerced the other three and was either holding them somewhere or had murdered them, buried their bodies, and ran off to Mexico."

"What do you say to something like that?"

"I let him know I didn't care what his son did or didn't do. All I wanted was to find him and bring him home. He started talking about how great his kid was, how he got straight As and was head of the high school astronomy club, how he'd always been shy but finally worked up the nerve to talk to a girl in his science class and ask her out."

Jess was seeing it all over again. "Something about the astronomy club struck me. I remembered reading about a recent planetary event. I asked the dad to show me the kid's room. It was covered with photos of meteors and constellations he'd taken himself. The dad was proud of them. I asked him how the kid did it. Through his telescope, he said, his son's pride and joy. He'd worked weekends cutting lawns and washing cars to save up for it. I asked him to show me the telescope. It wasn't there."

"That's it," Logan said. "They were out looking at stars."

Jess nodded. "I searched on stargazer websites. There was a conjunction of Saturn and Venus on the night the four disappeared. That's when two planets are really close together."

"I've seen that while climbing. The night sky is a nonstop light show. It's always changing." He paused. "Reminds me that people change too, even the ones you fell in love with."

Jess let it go without comment. "The Saturn-Venus conjunction was what I'd read about. A chat room talked up the best places to see it. Didn't matter where in the country it was, the common denominator was someplace away from city lights."

"He took the girl to look at it to impress her, didn't he?"

"And his best friend and her best friend too. It was a school night and they knew their parents wouldn't let them be out late, so they made a plan to sneak out and meet at midnight. He took the keys to the minivan and picked them up."

"How did you figure out where they went?"

"I used the Sheriff's special map apps and imagined myself as a teenager. There was a spot in eastern Alameda County that was the furthest away from any major light source, but less than an hour's drive from the kid's house. They could get there, see the planets, and be home by dawn before they were missed."

"Smart."

"It's farmland out there and bisected by a big irrigation canal. We searched and found fresh car tracks on the canal's dike. Access to it is usually blocked at the blacktop, but the gate was pushed open and rocks placed as a doorstop. The lock had been cut, most likely by fishermen going after catfish. The aqueduct is full of them."

"I don't like where this is going."

"Sorry, but you asked. Anyway, there was no moon that night, which made viewing the conjunction easier but driving harder. The kid must've thought the dike was a dirt road leading into a field where he could set up his telescope. The van nose-dived into the canal. We found it at the bottom. They couldn't open the doors against the pressure of the water. The kid tried breaking a window with his prized telescope. He made spider-webs, but it was too late."

Logan's exhale sounded as if he'd been punched in the stom-ach. "You've seen some heavy shit."

"Goes with the job."

"A job that doesn't pay."

"It did that time in its own bittersweet way. I knew the father and the other parents wouldn't have to go through life wondering what happened to their children, wake up in the middle of the night imagining an even more horrific death."

"I don't know. I'd rather fall off a rock than drown."

"So, is Dabo there? I need to talk with him."

"He's asleep. By the time we checked in and rode the elevator up, he was dead on his feet. We have connecting rooms. He went straight to bed, lay down with his clothes on, and was snoring in seconds. Can't blame him. We've been traveling nonstop for three days."

"Jetlag, huh?"

"Dabo's never been on a plane before, much less an international flight, but, yeah, he was too keyed up to close his eyes. He sat next to the window, nose pressed to it the whole way even when we were flying above the clouds and through the night."

"Let him sleep. I'll talk to him tomorrow."

"Tell you what, let's meet for a bite now and I'll tell you what I know about Mintaka. That way you'll have a jump on tomorrow."

"Don't you get jetlag?"

"No time for it. Too much to do."

"Want me to come to the hotel? There's a restaurant downstairs."

"How about Hannigan's?"

"I'll see you there."

Hannigan's was a waterfront institution, an old haunt of Jess's grandfather. It was the kind of joint longshore workers could count on getting their thermoses filled no matter what time of day or night a ship pulled in, no matter what kind of liquid they ordered. His grandfather had taken him there for dinner twice a week every week after his parents died.

The only thing Irish about Hannigan's were the faded shamrocks pinned to the wall behind the bar and a corned beef special offered on Saint Paddy's Day that nobody but an out-of-towner would order. The Lau family had owned it for as long as anyone could remember and the menu reflected their heritage with the dishes favoring Sichuan and Cantonese. Even the steak and eggs came slathered with chili garlic sauce or sweet-and-sour, diner's choice.

Logan wasn't there when Jess arrived. Madam Lau, the family matriarch, was hunched behind the cash register matching order tickets to receipts and checking them off with a pencil. She wore a black dragon jacket with red piping and her bouffant updo was held in place with lacquered chopsticks used as hairpins.

"You want the usual?" she said without taking her eyes off the paperwork.

"I'm waiting for someone," he said.

"We're not a bus stop." If Madam Lau had said it once, she'd said it a thousand times. She waved her pencil at a corner table without looking up.

Two cargo container crane operators with tattooed forearms sat at the bar eating short ribs and washing them down with schooners of beer. An older Chinese American couple slurped wonton soup at a table near the back. Three hipsters wearing earbuds watched reels on their phones.

Logan kept Jess waiting twenty minutes. When he pushed through the door, he greeted Madame Lau with a loud hello. "Remember me?"

That prompted her to look up. She shook her pencil at him. "Aren't you supposed to be dead?"

"I missed you too."

Madame Lau clucked. "You want the same thing you always ordered when you were alive? Numbing chicken, sizzling rice soup, and a bottle of Tsing Tao."

"Seven years and you haven't forgotten a thing."

"I haven't forgotten I told you not to marry that girl after you brought her here. Miss Better Than Everyone didn't like my food and told you not to leave a tip. I heard she took you for everything in the divorce."

"I should've listened to you."

"Like you should've listened when I told you to hire my cousin in Xiaoxiang to make your furniture at a big discount."

"I did hire your cousin."

"You hired the wrong one." Madame Lau eyed him and then her expression softened. "You back looking for a new wife? I will introduce you to my other cousin's daughter. You want to see her picture? Very pretty." She reached into her coat pocket and pulled out a phone.

Logan waved his hands. "No thanks. I learned my lesson."

Madame Lau clucked again and then jabbed her pencil in Jess's direction. "I suppose he'll have the same as you."

"Of course he will."

"Still the little brother. Some things never change."

She switched to Cantonese and called out their order and then went back to checking receipts. A waiter scurried over and set two bottles of Tsing Tao on the table. Logan picked up one, Jess the other. They clinked bottles and both took long pulls.

"Why is it foreign beer tastes better?" Logan said. "You know my favorite? Club." He rhymed it with cube. "It's brewed in Quito."

Logan drank some more. "You ever try beer made from manioc? It's called chicha. Every tribe in the Amazon brews it. The women make it. They take the root of the manioc, peel it, then wash it and boil it. Once it's soft, they chew it and spit the mash back into the pot. That's the secret to good chicha. It's left to ferment for four or five days. When it's done, they drink it by the bucket. Even the kids are nursed on it."

"Haven't tried it because I've never been to South America," Jess said.

Logan winked. "We'll have to see about getting you down there real soon. The first time I attended a feast at Dabo's village, the men got drunk and started a spear-throwing contest. At each other."

Jess asked him if he'd met Blue Macaw there.

"I've never met her. She was already gone."

"Did anyone tell you why?"

"No one knew, not even Dabo. That's another tragedy of the rainforest to go along with all the others. Indigenous women disappearing without a trace. While some run away to marry a man from another tribe or to live in the city, the majority get taken."

"You mean kidnapped?"

"Not for ransom like you think. Indigenous people living in the rainforest don't have any money. No, the girls and women are taken and raped. Few victims are ever found. Bodies dumped in a river or jungle don't always surface."

Logan sighed. "Predators in the rainforest aren't limited to wildlife. You have your drug traffickers, poachers, illegal miners and loggers, pirates preying on riverboat traffic, and private security forces who work for the oil companies and are above the law. Life is cheap, laws are few, corruption rife, and violence rampant."

"Doesn't the government do anything to stop it?"

"There's the occasional investigation and maybe even an arrest, but it's always for show. The government has a long history of treating the Amazon and the tribes that live there as a major pain in the ass. Protecting them would get in the way of business."

"What business?"

"Oil. The state owns everything in the ground. The business of extracting it is all-powerful, all-untouchable. Has been that way since the mid-sixties when it was first discovered in the Amazon. Bananas used to be the country's leading export, but now it's oil. Seventy million barrels flowed to the US last year, most of it going to California refineries. China takes even more, like eighty, ninety percent of it."

The waiter came back with a platter of chicken smothered in a thick sauce of red chiles, peppercorn, garlic, ginger, and soy. A fumarole of steam rose from a bowl of scorched rice topped with prawns and tomatoes.

Logan pinched a prawn with his chopsticks. "There's long been talk about a connection between oil drilling and missing Indigenous women. Gangs of sex traffickers prowling the rainforest, snatching native girls, and selling them to the oil camps to keep the drillers whistling while they work."

"Only talk, not proof?" Jess said.

"Most camps operate deep in the rainforest and have guards to keep people out. If anyone's tried to document what goes on inside, they didn't live to tell about it."

"But if Blue Macaw was taken, then somehow she escaped and made her way to Oakland. Does she know how to read and write Spanish or English?"

"Probably both since she lived for a while at Father Banana's mission the same as Dabo did. He told me his little sister was always quicker than him when it came to learning."

"Did Dabo search for her?"

Logan nodded as he chewed the prawn and washed it down with beer. "As best he could in the Tarani homelands. He traveled as far as Coca, which is the nearest city of any size. Turns out going there set him on a path to becoming an advocate for Indigenous peoples' rights."

"How so?"

"He met some Waorani from other tribal groups who were living there. They'd started a campaign to lobby the government to clean up oil drilling pollution and stop the takeover of their ancestral lands. A bunch of lawsuits were filed against the state and oil companies. Litigation has gone back and forth for years. Waorani have come a long way in the fight, including putting a winning initiative on the ballot to prevent additional drilling in Yasuní National Park. It was a big victory, but a lot more like it are needed."

"Is that where you met Dabo, in Coca?"

"Yeah. I bought a place on the Napo River to use as a base for exploring the rainforest, but everywhere I went I kept seeing damage from oil drilling. I heard about the fight being waged from Coca and went to see if I could help. Dabo and I hit it off. Don't let his quiet demeanor fool you. He's very fierce when it comes to fighting injustice."

"How old is he?"

"About your age. He's married and has two children."

"He started early."

"Not for his culture."

"And Blue Macaw? How old is she?"

"A few years younger. There's a sibling or three between them."

"What do you know about her?"

"Only what Dabo and Father Banana have told me. She's smart, brave, very athletic, and curious."

"Sounds like the right ingredients for wanting to see what's on the other side of the road. Maybe Blue Macaw wasn't taken. Maybe she was one of the ones who moved to a town and then to a city and then all the way to the US." Jess ate a prawn. "Dabo and his people are fortunate you found them."

"Other way around."

Logan put down his chopsticks. "I need to tell you about the deal I'm trying to sell Jim Buckle on. It's more than keeping drilling out of the Tarani homelands. I'm trying to protect a swath of rainforest twice the size of the entire Bay Area. Twelve thousand square miles of utterly spectacular, incredibly diverse tropical wilderness.

"It's unlike anything I've ever seen. Gigantic trees that reach right up through the clouds and beyond. I know because I've roped up and climbed to the top of some. The view? Better than the one from the summit of Cotopaxi. Braided rivers with pink dolphins swimming in them and four different types of macaws at every mineral lick. I've seen both spotted and black jaguars. Harpy eagles are as common as bald eagles in Alaska."

"Sounds beautiful."

"It's more than that. It's primeval. Otherworldly. Magical. And that's not a word I use lightly. You'll have to come down and see for yourself. I'll buy you a ticket and be your guide."

Logan pushed his plate away. "I have a lot riding on this, Sparks. More than a lot. I have everything."

"What do you mean?"

"I put the money I made from selling Wild Things toward protecting it. Every penny. And don't believe what you've heard that I sold it for a pittance. I did okay. Better than okay. A lot better. I put it all up as a guaranty in a debt-for-nature swap deal I've been trying to swing."

"What's that?"

"Swaps have been around for a while. A nonprofit brokers a deal between an undeveloped country that took a big loan out from a developed country. The developed country agrees to forgive a portion of it in exchange for the undeveloped country agreeing to preserve wilderness as a way to help address climate change and protect biodiversity. It's usually an easy sell since most of the time the undeveloped country is going to default on the loan anyway."

"You started a nonprofit?"

Logan nodded. "Rainforest Now!"

"And what's the guaranty thing?"

"Since Rainforest Now! didn't have a track record, I had to put up my own money for a surety bond that guarantees the swap. If Ecuador doesn't honor its commitment to protect the land, I get stuck with the original debt and the bond goes to pay for it."

"How much money are you talking about?"

"Think of a number with lots and lots of zeros at the end."

"But you must've thought the swap would go through."

"I did and it was a done deal until a team of botanists visited to search for never-before-seen plants to help document how special the place is. It was all a con. They were actually prospectors. They set off explosives to create seismic waves for mapping and located a big oil reservoir beneath it."

The waiter brought the check. "Once Ecuador found out about the oil, it reversed course and announced it would lease tracts for drilling to the highest bidder. If that happens, the swap defaults and I'm left holding the bag."

"What makes you so certain CaliCo will win the bid?"

"Because Buckle has been spending a lot of time down there ingratiating himself with the state oil company. My guess is he's been doing it through payoffs. Plus he's scared off the competition. Nobody else wants the hassle or expense of drilling there. That's why I need to convince him to take a stand against it. If he does, then Ecuador will take the easy route and go ahead with the swap and eventually designate the area as a national park."

"But you said they've been drilling in national parks."

"True, but maybe the new law prohibiting drilling in Yasuní will pave the way for more protection."

"Buckle didn't seem too interested when you said you could save him more money than he could make drilling."

"That's because he didn't know how much it's going to cost him. You remember the poker games we used to play when we were stuck at base camp in Yosemite waiting out storms? I have a lot of aces up my sleeve and I know I can beat Buckle no matter how many hands it takes."

They got up, said goodbye to Madame Lau, and walked outside. The air was turning moist as the fog blew in.

Jess said, "I'll swing by the hotel in the morning to talk to Dabo about Blue Macaw. See you then."

"Probably not. I have an early start. Breakfast meeting in San Francisco and a full schedule of face-to-faces with my Rainforest Now! team and other advocacy groups. Every day from here on out is packed. I'll let Dabo know you're coming."

"Tell him he's welcome to join me while I check out a couple of places that came up in my search. They're crapshoots, but you never know. If one pays off, Dabo should be there."

"You'll find Mintaka. I'm counting on it. See you at the gala."

5
———

Jess rose at dawn, filled a travel mug with coffee, and went downstairs to put the final patch on *Pursuit's* damaged hull. Once the fiberglass dried, he sanded the repair and the kayak was ready for paddling. He would've carried it down to the estuary right then but searching for Blue Macaw came first.

After locking up, he walked to his truck, half-expecting to find Carl asleep on the sidewalk. There was no sign of the old salt and his dog. Though Jess hoped he'd taken his advice and moved into the Seafarers' House, he knew it was unlikely. Pets weren't allowed and Carl would never consider abandoning Kelp even though it meant sleeping on the street and surviving on handouts and throw outs.

It was a short drive to the Grand Hotel. Dabo was standing in front.

"I hope you haven't been waiting long," Jess said.

"No, I always wake before *naenke*. That is our word for sun. I go and touch the river here. It is salty and much colder than the Caiman River."

"That's because it's an estuary. Tides bring water from the

ocean through the Golden Gate, all the way across San Francisco Bay, past the Oakland waterfront, and then back out again. No caimans in it though."

Dabo flashed his toothy grin. "You made a joke. I like jokes."

Jess crossed Broadway and steered south. "Logan told me you've been living in Coca."

"Yes. I am working to protect the land and animals and spirits my people share it with."

"Protect it from oil drilling and logging and poaching."

"And *cowori*, our word for outsider. Drilling and logging hurt the land and river, but cowori kill us. They bring disease and evil. Our people have no protection against them. We warn our people to stay away from cowori, but it is not easy because cowori give people food, clothes, and pots and pans. Then they make our men work and our women—" His gaze cast downward and he no longer grinned. "If we say no, they kill us."

"Logan said you're a very fierce advocate for human rights."

"All Waorani people are fierce. Now the Tarani must be even fiercer because the oil company comes for our land."

They rounded Lake Merritt and cut across the city toward Fruitvale Avenue. Traffic was heavy. The sidewalks were bustling.

"And your wife and children? Do they live in Coca too?"

"No. It is too crowded, too far from home, too full of cowori."

"You must miss them."

Dabo nodded.

"Boys or girls or both?"

"Son and daughter." He struck his chest with his palm. "They are my light. I carry them here always. My wife also. Her name is Nimu. Star in Wao is *nimu*. I see her every night when I look up."

"Tell me about your sister," Jess said.

"She is smart. And pretty and fast. Very fast. She always beats me when we run. Climbs trees faster also. Only thing I am faster than her is paddling a dugout. Mintaka goes slow because she is always looking at birds and monkeys." Dabo's grin returned.

"One day, Mintaka found a baby anteater. Hunters killed its mother. Mintaka made milk from powder that Father Banana gets for Tarani mothers. She fed it to the anteater with a bottle. Then she showed the anteater how to find ants. Termites also. Mintaka dug in the dirt and let the ants crawl on her fingers. She licked some and then put her finger with ants on it in the anteater's mouth. Mm. The baby anteater grew big." He stretched his hands apart. "Mintaka called it our word for moon, *Apaika*."

"Why do you think she left the homelands?" Jess said.

"I do not know. I only know it was a mistake."

"Do you mean she made a mistake by leaving or she left by mistake—that she didn't mean to go?"

"I think she made a mistake. Why she wrote in the letter she was sorry and asked for forgiveness. Why, I do not know. But I forgive her. Our mother forgives her. I will tell Mintaka that when you find her. I will tell her all Tarani people will forgive her and to come home, to live like Tarani do because she is Tarani no matter what she did, what happened."

It wasn't the right time to ask Dabo if he thought his sister had been taken and escaped or had left in search of a new life. He needed more time with him to win his trust.

Jess turned onto Fruitvale Avenue. The traffic slowed. He looked for the mixed martial arts club that had come up in his search. According to the address, The Fight Box would be in the middle of the next block. As soon as he saw an empty parking spot, he pulled in.

They got out and walked across the intersection. Jess found the right building, but the windows were soaped out and a For Lease sign was posted in the window.

"It was always a long shot," Jess said to Dabo. "Do you know what that word means?"

He nodded. "It is when you see a wild pig across the river and must throw your spear very far."

When Jess saw the corners of Dabo's lips fighting to stay clamped, he laughed. "Now, that's a good joke."

They started to walk back to the truck when Jess saw a sign in the upstairs window of a stucco building across the street. Urban Rez: Intertribal Resource Center was spelled out in lettering that evoked American Indian art.

"I'm not sure what that place is or what it does, but it's worth checking out."

They climbed the stairs. The floor had a row of offices. Urban Rez was between a law office and an accountant's. Jess twisted the doorknob and entered a room with hand-painted murals covering the walls. One was a scene of ancient American Indian men and women harvesting mussels on a rocky shore. Another listed the two hundred different tribes that lived in California. Ohlone, Miwok, Chochenyo, Karkin, and others native to the Bay Area were highlighted in red. A floor-to-ceiling shelving unit displayed baskets, carvings, and stone tools. Feathered dreamcatchers and shell-and-bone mobiles hung from the ceiling.

A stocky man with shoulder-length hair sat a desk behind a laptop. He looked over the screen at Jess and Dabo.

"Can I help you?"

"I am Dabo. I am looking for my sister. Her name is Mintaka. Blue Macaw. Can you help me find her?"

"Welcome, Dabo. I'm Benny Guerrero. Who are your people? You look and sound pretty south of the border. Am I right?"

Jess said, "He means you don't appear to be from North America."

"I am Tarani," Dabo said. "Our home is on the Caiman River."

"That's in the Amazon, in Ecuador," Jess added.

"Long way," Benny said. "Around here, that feather in your ear would be from a red-tailed hawk. Maybe an osprey or heron. Depending on your people."

"Who are your people?" Dabo said.

"Ohlone."

"But your name, Guerrero, is Spanish."

"Blame that on California's first governor. He ordered the extermination of every Indigenous person living in the state. Hundreds of thousands were murdered. Our people had to pretend to be Mexicans to survive."

"It is the same in Ecuador. I like your Spanish name because it means warrior."

"A'ho, brother. Now, have a seat. Tell me more about your sister."

Dabo explained the letter and the return address and Jess said how he was able to use the Alameda County Sheriff's database—all to no avail.

"The letter proved my sister is alive and was not killed back home like other Tarani women," Dabo said.

"I hear you. Native people here have missing sisters, mothers, and daughters too. It's the old White man way come back again of committing genocide."

Jess said, "Are there any particular social media sites Native people around here use?"

"All of them plus every tribe has its own website."

"I was thinking we could post a message or ad or something."

"Bad idea."

"How come?"

"Because of what you said. Blue Macaw, she's been here,

what, maybe a couple of years, maybe longer? And you don't know how she got here from Ecuador? Odds are she's here illegally. If she does have a green card, it's probably a fake. You don't want to call attention to her. ICE will hunt her down and stick her in a cage until they deport her."

Dabo looked to Jess for an explanation, but Benny answered first. "US Immigration and Customs Enforcement. They're federal cops and have a reputation for being hard-assed and hard-hearted. They even separate kids from their parents when they're conducting roundups."

"Where do people like Mintaka?" Dabo said. "I will go there and ask if they know her."

"I wish it was that easy. There're twenty thousand Native people living in the Bay Area, six hundred thousand in the state. California's Indian Country, brother."

Jess said, "But you're talking about North American Indians in the Bay Area, right? What about Indigenous people from Latin America? Are there specific neighborhoods they live in or places they hang out?"

Benny picked up a smooth black rock the size of the bowl of a soup spoon and rubbed his thumb in the shallow. He noticed Dabo looking at it.

"It's an Ohlone talisman that was found at a sacred burial site not far from here. My ancestors made it."

Dabo dipped his head and then looked skyward and spoke in Wao. After he finished, he translated. "I ask if it is powerful for your people, then let it be powerful for mine."

The Ohlone nodded. "Right on. Okay, you might try this little bodega down on Foothill. It's called Altiplano. I hear it's popular among South Americans in general. I don't know if that's true for Indigenous. But if you go there, be careful what you say. They might mistake you for undercover ICE. And definitely watch your back. Mara Salvatruchas control some of the blocks down there."

Dabo asked if they were a tribe.

"They're a tribe, all right. Salvadorean criminals better known as MS-13. Trust me, you don't want to mess with them." He raised his chin at Jess. "You know who I'm talking about, don't you?"

Jess nodded. They were on the who's who of who to look out for on the Oakland PD's beat map.

"Thank you," Dabo said.

"No problem, that's what we're here for. I'll ask around too. If you need anything else, give me a call or drop by. Hope you find Blue Macaw."

Jess and Dabo drove to Foothill Boulevard. The Altiplano was bookended by a nail salon and a check cashing store. Posters of Brazilian and Argentinean soccer stars and their teams competed for space on the walls. A neon beer sign that spelled out *El futbol va mejor con Cristal* hung behind the bar.

They took seats on stools covered in brown and white cowhide. The bartender eyed them suspiciously before coming over. He had a hooked nose and wore a brown fedora. His skin was as dark as Dabo's but without the tattoos.

"It's very quiet here," Jess said.

"Most people are still at work," he said. "What'll you have?"

Dabo grinned. "Chicha."

The bartender's fedora waggled. "Jungle juice? Forget it. The ABC would pull my license."

"Alcoholic Beverage Control," Jess explained automatically. He asked the bartender if he had Club, pronouncing it the same way Logan had.

"Can't get it. No one imports it. Cristal's better anyway. It's from Peru." He fished two bottles out of the refrigerator, opened them, and sat them on the bar.

Switching to Spanish, he asked Dabo where he was from. "I am Tarani," Dabo said. "What people are you?"

"Peruvian," he replied.

"What tribe? Peru has more tribes than Ecuador."

"Quechua. Near Cuzco. The Sacred Valley."

"Quechua people live in Ecuador also. In the mountains at Riobamba."

"Never been." He turned to Jess and peered down his nose. "I'm a US citizen. Been here ten years. Naturalized. Do you need to see proof?"

"Why would I?"

"Because you're ICE. You guys try all sorts of things."

"I'm not. Nor is Dabo."

"Sure you're not."

"Got a phone? Look me up. Jess Parks. I run a boat shop down on the estuary."

"Then why are you here? Don't tell me you were passing by and happened to get thirsty at ten in the morning."

"Benny Guerrero at Urban Rez suggested it. We're looking for Dabo's sister. She wrote a letter saying she was living in Oakland, but the return address is wrong. Their mother is sick and wants to see her before she dies."

The bartender put both hands on the bar and leaned forward. Copper bracelets encircled his wrists. "I don't know a Benny whatever his name is and Urban Rez sounds made up. Finish your beers and get out."

"Please," Dabo said. "I must find Mintaka. Somebody must know her."

The bartender frowned. "Sisters, mothers, daughters, they don't come to places like the Altiplano. Only men do. They come because they thought they'd only be up here for a year to make enough money to take home to their family, but one year turns into two and two into ten. So they come to drink and ease the pain of not seeing their little ones grow big, to feel their wives' legs wrapped around them in bed. Now beat it. *Lagarse!*"

"We are all far from home. I am staying at the Grand Hotel. Please, call me if you hear something."

Jess took out his wallet and put two twenties beside the still-full bottles.

"One will cover it," the bartender said.

"Keep it." He jotted his phone number on a napkin. "Her name is Mintaka. It means blue macaw. If you learn of anything and can't reach Dabo at the Grand, give me a call or send a text. Day or night. I'll make it worth your while."

The bartender didn't make a move to pick up the twenty-dollar bills or the napkin, and so Jess and Dabo left without saying another word.

6

———

Valet parkers at the Grand Hotel were running full tilt to keep the line of cars delivering gala attendees from stacking up and blocking Broadway. Jess and Isabella avoided the crush by walking the few blocks from the boat shop to Jack London Square and hailing a pedicab.

They picked up their tickets from a will call table and headed into the ballroom. It had been transformed into a 1930s-style supper club. Crystal chandeliers hung over scores of round banquet tables covered in starched white linen tablecloths with place settings for eight. The rear of the room was modeled after a speakeasy. Bartenders were mixing cocktails and pouring champagne.

Logan Riggins stood alongside Dabo and a tall brunette. He beckoned Jess and Isabella to join them.

"You must be Isabella," Logan said. "Sparks confessed he's your number one fan. He wasn't only talking about your art."

"He did, did he? He told me why you call him Sparks. Thank you for not nicknaming him Sparky."

They both laughed. Logan said, "Have you met Dabo?"

"Not yet. *Waponi*, Dabo."

"You speak Wao," the Tarani said and bowed.

"Only the word for hello and thank you. Since they're the same, it made it easy. The rest? Not so much."

"I will teach you."

"And this is Mattie Voss," Logan said, touching the arm of the tall woman with brown hair. "We met in Ecuador when she was on a fact-finding mission with a US congressional delegation. Mattie was chief of staff for a congresswoman from LA. Now she runs political campaigns and is helping Rainforest Now!"

"Logan told me you combine dance with sound and video," Mattie said. "It sounds fascinating. Where can I see your work?"

"A couple of venues in the Bay Area, but mostly at the schools where I teach dance. I have a channel as well. I'll send you the link."

"You should consider putting a plug for Rainforest Now! on it. We could also talk about using your next performance as a headliner for a fundraiser and awareness builder. We need all the help we can get if we're going to stop oil drilling there."

Logan grinned. "See why I hired her? Mattie never misses an opportunity to further the cause."

Isabella said to Dabo, "The red paint on your face, it's made from achiote seeds, right?"

"Yes. I mix it with water. How do you know?"

"I've read what I could find about Waorani culture and traditions. I understand face painting is done for a lot of reasons."

"Yes. Sometimes to make Tarani look fierce to the enemy. Sometimes for celebrating and ceremony. Like when a boy become man. Most of the time we do it to make change."

"What do you mean by that?"

"Tarani share the forest with animals and spirits. We are them. They are us. I paint a jaguar on my face, I become a jaguar. Have jaguar strength. Have jaguar speed. Do you understand?"

"I think so. Why did you paint your face tonight?"

"All those things. Celebrate. Be fierce. Be strong like a jaguar."

"And do women paint their faces too?"

"Yes. In Wao, jaguar father is called *menye waempo*. Jaguar mother is *menye baada*. Now you know more Wao to speak."

"And dancing, do both men and women dance at ceremonies and celebrations?"

"Most of the time, but sometimes not."

"What about music? Do you play instruments? Chant, sing?"

"Sometimes all night. We play drums, flutes, and whistles." He trilled. It startled the people near them.

"Would you show me a Tarani dance tonight? If it's forbidden, I understand."

"Yes. I will dance. Would you like to dance with me?"

"I'd love to!"

"Here comes Jim Buckle," Logan said.

The CaliCo CEO entered the ballroom arm in arm with a woman who looked at least fifteen years his junior. He wore a tuxedo with a calico-patterned cummerbund. She had on a long lavender gown.

"That's his wife, Clare," Logan said.

The corporate lawyer, Pius Wheedling, and security chief, Lyle Hunt, trailed close behind. A woman in a sleeveless sheath dress the color of polished emeralds that matched the green in her eyes followed.

"Sarah," Logan said stiffly.

"Sarah Newton," Jess whispered to Isabella. "His ex."

"She's stunning," Isabella said.

Sarah joined the Buckles, and the trio threaded through the crowd, pausing for handshakes and air-kisses. Buckle and Sarah basked in the recognition and congratulations while Clare wore a fixed smile. They finally came to a halt near Logan and Dabo.

"Been a while, Sarah," Logan said. "Jim, Clare. Quite the shindig you're putting on."

"I see you brought your Indian friend," Buckle said. "I trust you brought your checkbook too."

"Always willing to support a good cause." Logan glanced at the crowd watching and listening. "Tell you what. I'll cut a check for a hundred grand right now if you do the same for Rainforest Now!" Logan turned to the onlookers. "That's a nonprofit based in Ecuador dedicated to protecting the Amazon home of my friend Dabo here. What do you say, Jim? Both are good causes."

Buckle's smile was anything but happy. Jess looked at Sarah. He hadn't seen her for years, but, like Logan, she looked as fit as ever. She wasn't smiling.

"Tonight is the Oakland arts community's night," Buckle said good-naturedly. "The trees down yonder can wait."

"No, they can't. Nor can the people who live there or any of us standing right here. We all depend on the rainforest. It's the planet's lungs."

Buckle's eyes narrowed. "I've never heard of your group. Is it even registered as a nonprofit? If it isn't, then not a single penny given to it is tax deductible." He grinned at the crowd. "I can assure you the Oakland Arts Foundation is legally registered. So, tonight give generously. The artists will thank you and so will your tax accountant."

People chuckled.

"I've heard of Rainforest Now!" a woman in a black and gold dress said. She was standing next to a man in a tuxedo. "Our son interned with them in Ecuador during his gap year. Naturally, we were very concerned about his safety when he went, but you know what? It changed his life. He wrote an essay about the experience and submitted it with his law school application. He was accepted at Harvard."

A murmur rippled through the growing crowd.

"What's his name?" Logan asked.

"Ashok Mehta," the man answered. "Junior."

The murmur grew louder as the crowd recognized the man. He was the CEO of a large tech firm.

"I remember your son. He really threw himself into his work. Had an ear for language too, and, trust me, Wao is a difficult tongue. Not only did Ashok develop great people skills that allowed him to make a personal connection to the Indigenous community, he had passion. It burned bright and he made a difference. Sounds like it still does."

Logan turned to Dabo. "Do you remember Ashok?"

"Yes. Tarani gave him two names. First, *Gita*. It means dog. He was a little puppy." He made a whimpering noise. "Then he found courage in here." Dabo slapped his chest. "We gave him a new name. *Pogaeka*. Hawk. He flew high. Flew fast. Saw danger in the forest below and warned Tarani. Hawk looked out for us. Then. Now. Always."

The tech titan beamed as a couple of men slapped him on the back. "Hawk Mehta," one said. "Helluva name for a lawyer."

"Or a future CEO," the father said.

"What your son saw was how fragile life is in the rainforest, and what he was warning the Tarani about is how allowing oil drilling there would destroy it," Logan said. "Not only for Dabo and his people, but for all living things that call it home. We should all listen to Hawk Mehta."

"And your group, the one Hawk interned with, now you're trying to keep oil development out of there?" a woman asked.

"That's right. The extraction industry is barely regulated in the rainforest. The damage they cause is irreversible. Jim's company is poised to start drilling there, and Dabo and I've been trying to explain to him it doesn't make sense. Not financially, not ecologically, and certainly not from a human rights stand-point. Feels like he doesn't want to listen to us."

Buckle waved his hands. "Wait a sec, before you get out the tar and feathers, can I get a word in?" He gave an affable laugh. "What I told my old friend Logan the other day, and what I was trying to say tonight is, I do want to hear what they have to say. But at the right time and in the right place. All of us here tonight are big supporters of the arts community. It'd be a disservice to take the light off of them. The truth is, I've already scheduled a meeting with Dabo and Logan for tomorrow morning." He turned to Wheedling. "When's the appointment again?"

"Nine thirty," the corporate lawyer said without skipping a beat. "Your appointments secretary sent the invitation to Mr. Riggins." He cocked his head. "I suppose there could have been a technical hiccup on his end. Do you check your spam folder on a regular basis, Mr. Riggins?"

Logan smiled. "Consider the message delivered. Dabo and I are staying right here at the Grand. Your headquarters are next door, correct? We'll see you in the morning."

"Looking forward to it," Buckle said.

And with that he steered his wife away with Wheedling and Hunt in tow. Sarah hung back. She closed in on her ex-husband.

"Despite your many shortcomings, you always have been a good salesman. I see you prepped the Mehtas and other members of your Greek chorus. Nicely played, Logan."

"Coming from you, that's high praise," he said.

"Don't expect more." Sarah looked Mattie up and down. "Word of advice? Don't fall for Logan or his BS. Neither can be trusted."

She glanced at Jess, but her expression showed no recogni-tion at all. In a swish of green, she was gone.

Logan sighed. "Same ole Sarah. Hey, Jess, tomorrow morning, meet Dabo and me here for breakfast and we'll go over a game plan for the Buckle meeting. I need you there with us."

"Will do."

"Good. Now let's see how much booze and food our tickets bought us." He winked at Isabella. "Can't wait to see you and Dabo on the dance floor. Knowing what I know after having danced with the Tarani myself, you're in for a helluva an experience."

The five sat close to the stage. Servers matched the energy of the valets outside and full plates were placed quickly and empty ones whisked away. Wine glasses were constantly being topped off. Jess soon realized why. Jim Buckle mounted the stage and welcomed everybody, thanked them for their support, and then introduced an auctioneer who was on loan from Sotheby's.

With a mixture of an English accent and a late-night TV show host's snarky, bawdy sense of humor, the auctioneer soon had the attendees engaging in boisterous bidding wars for donated items that ranged from backstage opera passes, a dinner party at home prepared by a Michelin starred chef, signed lithographs by a notable Oakland artist, a Wild Things bedroom set personally designed by Sarah Newton, and a week's vacation at Buckle's Napa estate, which included the keys to his private cellar.

When the gavel fell on the last item, Buckle and Sarah took the stage together and applauded the audience. "Thank you for your generosity, friends," he said. "Now, the Foundation's Gala Committee set a pretty lofty goal for our annual event tonight. Five million dollars." He cringed. "Sarah? Did we even come close?"

She gave the audience a frown. "I'm afraid we didn't." People groaned. Then her face lit up. "We smashed it! Six point three million. A record."

Applause and cheers sent the crystal chandeliers swaying.

Buckle kissed Sarah on the cheek and they held hands and mimicked dancing. He gave her a final twirl and said, "Maestro, strike up the band!"

The pair left as a group featuring dueling guitars, a keyboard, and a rhythm and horn section took the stage. The vocalist covered top R&B, pop, and soul hits with a voice as sweet as it was powerful.

As the music played and people took to the dance floor, Jess went in search of the men's room. Walking between tables, he paused as he passed the one where Jim and Clare Buckle sat.

"My head is splitting," Clare said. "It's one of my migraines. I didn't bring my meds. I need to go home and lie down."

"Are you sure?" Buckle said.

"I'm sorry. I know it's your big night and hate to be a downer, but if I don't go, I'll end up vomiting. You know how it gets."

He patted her hand. "Of course. Let me call the front desk and have a valet bring the car around."

"No, no. You stay. If you leave, it'll signal the party's over. I've already dropped a pin for a Lyft. The driver's on her way."

"Are you sure?"

"Positive."

"If you insist. Give the girls a kiss goodnight for me. I'll be sure not to wake you when I get home."

Jess found the bathroom. When he returned to his table, Isabella and Mattie were talking.

"Where're Logan and Dabo?" he said.

Isabella shrugged and then looked up at the stage. "Oh, this should be interesting."

Logan was talking to the band members. Dabo, who was by his side, had taken off his shirt and sandals. His chest and arms were striped with red paint. When the singer finished a number, she handed the microphone to Logan.

"May I have your attention. Thank you. We have a very

special treat for you tonight, straight from the Caiman River in the Amazon. Watch, learn, and then join us as we dance a dance to celebrate life."

Logan took a pair of drumsticks from the drummer and began clacking them together. Dabo joined him with trills and chants. The drummer started keeping time by playing the conga. The bass player joined in by plucking a single chord. The horn player switched his saxophone for a flute. Dabo looked at Isabella and summoned her. She didn't hesitate for a second.

The music picked up and as the beat grew faster, the rhythm became hypnotic. Logan, Dabo, and Isabella hopped in place, drumming the stage with their feet. People still on the dance floor began swaying in place, some started to hop too. Dabo picked up the microphone stand and held it over his head like a spear. He crouched, he stalked, he lunged, he jabbed. Isabella began slinking and prowling like a jaguar. The band's singer started trilling as she shook her arms and hips.

More people crowded onto the dance floor. Jess looked over and saw Buckle signal Lyle Hunt. The security chief rushed to his side, listened for a second, and then hurried out of the room. The dancing kept going. The beat growing faster. The trilling and flute and bass grew louder. The drumming thundered.

Hunt came back. He was carrying the machete Dabo had given Buckle. It was still in the caiman-skin scabbard. Jess remembered overhearing Buckle instructing Wheedling to put it in his golf bag. It must've been in the trunk of his car.

Buckle yanked off his tuxedo jacket, pulled the machete from the scabbard, and got up on stage. His face was red as he began dancing next to Isabella, swinging the machete over his head while trying to trill. It was more like a drunken cheer at a football game, but it prompted the dancers on the floor to cheer back and begin chanting Buckle's name.

Jess said to Mattie, "Shall we?"

"You go. I want to get photos of this. Maybe even livestream it. This is free PR for Rainforest Now!"

His chair tipped over as he pushed away from the table and headed for the stage. As he reached the dance floor, a conga line was forming behind Buckle who continued to swing the machete. He led them snaking around the tables and through the ballroom. Jess joined Dabo and Isabella and was soon caught up in the magic of hundreds of people dancing and chanting as one.

7

Oakland missed out on the California lottery. Los Angeles got the film industry, San Diego landed the Pacific Fleet, high tech went to Silicon Valley, and San Francisco bottled up all the charm it could sell. Even Fresno and Long Beach grew bigger and richer. The only category Oakland led the state in was violent crime.

Jess knew that from firsthand experience as a member of Search and Rescue, but his adrenaline surged when he arrived at the Grand Hotel for breakfast with Logan and Dabo before their meeting with Jim Buckle. Four black and white patrol vehicles with their rooftop lightbars flashing were parked in front along with an unmarked sedan and a white paneled van.

A uniformed cop blocked the entrance. "Hotel's closed, sir. You'll have to come back later."

"What's going on?" Jess said.

"Police matter."

"Do you know when it'll reopen?"

"Nope."

"What about the restaurant, is it open?"

"Sir, are you a registered guest?"

Jess shook his head. "Meeting people for breakfast."

"Then you'll have to eat someplace else."

"But my friends are staying here. If something's going on, I need to know if they're okay."

"And I need you to keep moving. Now."

A rideshare pulled up and double-parked alongside the cop cars. Two men got out of the back seat while the driver ran around to open the trunk.

"Don't bother," Jess called to them while nodding at the cop blocking the door. "He's not letting anybody in."

"How come?" one of the men said.

The other passenger shrieked. "Run! There must be an active shooter."

He dashed into the street. A car slammed on its brakes and almost hit him. The other man started running too, tripped, and skidded on his hands and knees. The rideshare driver jumped back in his car and peeled out with the open trunk lid flapping.

The cop threw his hand up in front of Jess's face. "Freeze!" Then he spoke into his epaulet mike.

Minutes ticked and the front doors opened. A pocked-face man in a blazer the color of dirt stepped out. He was gripping a radio in his left hand and looked irritated. Nodding at the uniformed cop, he turned his gaze on Jess. Recognition added to his scowl.

"Parks, right? Work the lost kids and pets detail. What the hell? You trying to start a panic or something?"

Jess searched for a name. Ruiz. Something Ruiz. And then he found more in the memory bank. Detective Something Ruiz with Robbery-Homicide. Knowing that was like knowing his hold on a climb was crumbly rock.

"I have friends staying here. Who's been murdered?"

"Who said anything about anybody being dead?" Ruiz sent a hard look to the cop who backed up and waved his hands.

"Not me, Detective. Not a word."

Jess said, "Why else would you be here, Ruiz, unless you got busted down? And the van, that's the coroner's."

The detective's scowl grew. "The only reason I'm not going to have Lewis here write you up for yelling fire in a theater is 'cause what you did for Stone last year. Now beat it."

"As soon as I find out if my friends are all right, I'm gone."

"I don't got time for this shit." Ruiz sighed. "What are their names?"

Jess told him. The detective's pockmarks reddened. "Lewis, get your ass over here and hold him."

The cop grabbed Jess's arm and pinned it behind his back as Ruiz stepped away and started jabbering into his radio. He listened. "Yep. 'Kay, got it. Yep. On our way."

The detective jerked his head at the cop. "I'll take him. Don't let no one else in. Parks, you're with me."

He trooped Jess into the lobby. A man in a suit with a shiny gold nameplate pinned to it and a similarly attired woman stood behind the front desk with seasick faces. No guests were sitting on the leather couches and chairs. The door to the restaurant was closed. Another uniformed cop was standing by an open elevator. Ruiz waved Jess inside and stepped in behind him. He punched the button for the top floor.

"You going to tell me what's going on?" Jess said.

Ruiz slouched against the wall. "Housekeeping found a dead guy this morning. Not unusual, a guy in a hotel croaks, right? They get heart attacks. Too much stress making money or losing it. Or they take too many Viagras for the hooker the bellhop sends up."

He sucked a tooth. "Now and then, they book a fancy room and blow their brains out, not wanting the wife and kiddies to find them home in the study, the wall splattered with their blood and the desk covered with stacks of unpaid bills."

"But since you're homicide, it wasn't death by suicide, accident, or natural causes."

The scowl came back. "Stone's right. You are a pretty smart guy."

The elevator doors opened and there was Detective Tyrone Stone standing in the open doorway to a guest room. He was a big man with a shaved head and gray winning the race against black in his goatee. His dark blue suit looked snug around the chest. Jess knew that was a good thing, meaning Stone had put on weight following the hours he'd spent under the knife at Highland Hospital followed by two months on a vent in the ICU.

The detective kept his expression neutral, his eyes giving no sign that he knew Jess. "Ruiz tells me you came here to meet Logan Riggins and a little Indian. Uh, Dabo. No last name." He mispronounced it, saying, "Day-bo."

"I'm supposed to have breakfast with them," Jess said, trying to look past the big man to see into the room.

"How you know 'em?"

"They're not in there, are they?"

Stone raised his chin, swiveled his head as if the tie knotted beneath his jowls was too tight. "Let's me and you get this straight right here and now. Six months ago? Then was then. Now is now. I'm asking the questions, you're doing the answering."

"Logan and I go way back. I worked at his art gallery in Berkeley. That was before Wild Things changed and went big time."

"Did you quit or get fired?"

"Does it matter?"

"Only because if you quit, it wasn't too bright, was it? He wound up making millions. You going into the bed and plates business would've been a whole lot better paycheck-wise than searching and rescuing for free."

"No shit," Ruiz said. "Especially if they gave you the house discount. You wouldn't believe what my wife spends on decorating. Freakin' pillows on the couch change every month. Bathroom towels too. They're only towels, man. Who cares what freakin' color they are? Gonna be working overtime the rest of my life."

"Tell me more about Riggins and the little Indian," Stone said.

"If they're not the victims, then they got nothing to do with whoever is," Jess said. "What's going on?"

"There you go again, a question." The detective exhaled slowly. "Tell me, Riggins gone all this time and shows up out of the blue and calls you. How come?"

Jess didn't take a second to think about it. Right then wasn't the time to mention Blue Macaw. "Old time's sake. We used to be pretty tight. Rock climbing at Yosemite and the like."

"He tell you why he's traveling with the Indian, uh, Dabo?"

"They both live in Ecuador. They're trying to stop oil drilling there."

"Drilling's down in Ecuador, but they come to California?"

"The oil company that's likely to do it is from here."

"What company is that?"

"CaliCo Energy."

Ruiz suddenly had a coughing fit. Stone didn't blink.

"How many times you seen them, Riggins and Dabo?"

"Let's see, the day they arrived, the next, and again last night."

"Where last night?"

"Here at the hotel."

Ruiz coughed again.

"Where in the hotel?"

"Downstairs in the ballroom. At the gala for the Oakland Arts Foundation."

"Did you come upstairs?"

"No. I went to the gala. Went home."

"Anyone verify that?"

"The woman I came and left with."

"I'm gonna need her name. What about before then?"

"The first time, the three of us went to Richmond to attend a dedication ceremony CaliCo was putting on. Later that evening, Logan and I had dinner at Hannigan's."

"What did you eat?"

"Numbing chicken, sizzling rice."

"Madam Lau's special, huh? I can't eat there anymore. All that spice. On account of ..." He left it unsaid. "That it, didn't see them any other time 'cept for last night downstairs?"

"Not Logan, but Dabo, yeah. I met him the second day."

"To do what?"

"Show him around Oakland. He's never been here before. Never been to California or the States, for that matter."

"Being from the jungle and all."

"Right."

"You ever visited them in their rooms here at the hotel?"

"No."

"Not even when you took Dabo on a tour?"

"We met out front. Come on, Detective. Who's in there? What's this got to do with Logan and Dabo?"

A woman's voice from inside the room called Stone's name. He turned halfway to face her. She was dressed in a blue pantsuit and wore her braids pulled back. The latex gloves she wore made her hands look gray.

"Ready with the preliminary," she said.

Stone nodded. He turned back to Jess. "You want to know why I'm asking about your friends? Follow me."

Ruiz grabbed at Jess's shoulder. "Put your hands in your

pockets and keep them there. Don't touch nothing, don't step on nothing."

"How am I supposed to walk?"

"Don't be a wiseass."

The room was a suite. The area on the right had a sofa and two matching chairs surrounding a glass coffee table. The area on the left had sliding shutter doors that were open. The TV was on and turned to a Latin music channel. Salsa was playing through the speaker. The comforter and sheets on the king bed were turned down. A body was sprawled on the floor next to it. The carpet around it was no longer beige.

Jess looked down into the fixed stare of Jim Buckle's head that lay on his left shoulder. His neck had been cut in half. The rock crumbled in his hand and he was falling without a rope.

Stone didn't kneel next to the CaliCo CEO or poke or prod him. He barely gave him a glance. Three other people were in the room. They wore white Tyvek coveralls and gloves and booties. One was fingerprinting the bedside phone, door handles, and front of the dresser. Another was taking photographs. The third was crawling around on her hands and knees with a pair of forceps and a plastic bag.

"How long ago?" Stone said to the woman with the braids.

"I put it around eight, nine hours. I'll have TOD by close of business."

"Guess there's not much question about cause." Stone chinned at the nightstand.

The Tarani machete was inside a clear plastic evidence bag big enough to hold a sourdough baguette.

"We won't know if there were chemicals in his system or anything else involved until we get back to the shop, but, yes, I'd say it did the trick. The position of the head, the swing came right to left."

"Just the one swing?"

She nodded. "There are no other marks on him. Nothing defensive, either. If he'd put a hand up to block it, it'd be lying on the carpet. The way he geysered indicates he was standing when struck."

Detective Stone crouched down. He studied the red stain on the carpet. "You see what I see?"

The woman with the braids nodded. "We took plenty of pictures of that already. There's a couple more partials going toward the bathroom. They're smeared, but we'll cut squares out of the carpet and put them under the microscope to be sure."

"The killer went to the bathroom afterward?"

"Took a shower. And, yes, we collected the towel, soap, and are suctioning the drain for hair and blood samples to take back to the lab for DNA testing. It being a hotel, well, we'll see what we get."

Stone pulled a pen from his suit jacket pocket, held it above the dark blotch, and traced its outline in the air. Toes, ball, heel.

Ruiz whistled. "Perp tries to hack the vic's head off barefoot."

"You recognize the weapon?" Stone said to Jess.

"I've seen it a couple of times."

"When and where?"

"Dabo showed it to me before we went out to CaliCo. He gave the machete to Buckle as a goodwill gift when he asked him to spare his homeland from drilling. Buckle left with it. Lot of witnesses saw him take it. TV camera was recording it too. Then he had it at the gala last night. He was dancing with it. People were taking pictures."

Ruiz snorted. "Dancing with a machete, not his wife? What the—"

Jess said, "Logan and Dabo may be staying here, but so are hundreds of other guests. It's a big hotel."

"Uh-huh," Stone said. "But we get the call this morning and when we roll up everyone from the doorman to the front desk starts telling us about a run-in Riggins had with the deceased last night at the party downstairs."

"They also said Riggin's Indian pal don't wear shoes and socks," Ruiz said. "Only sandals. And he took them off at the gala last night when he was dancing. Took his shirt off too." He pointed at the bloodstain and footprints.

Stone raised his chin and rolled his head again. "You've been with Logan and Dabo plenty the past few days. At the Richmond thing, Hannigan's, joyriding in Oakland, last night. Now this morning you come calling on them. I got grounds to hold you as a material witness."

"Have you talked to any of Buckle's people yet?"

"What people?"

"I've only seen Buckle a couple of times, but they're always with him. His corporate counsel and chief of security. Pius Wheedling and Lyle Hunt. They always stick close to him. Buckle ordered Hunt to fetch the machete for him last night so he could dance with it."

"Lyle Hunt?" Stone turned to Ruiz. "That Lyle Hunt?"

"One and the same. He was always moonlighting, taking different jobs for the easy money, but when you were in the hospital, he caught another excessive force beef to go along with the others and resigned before they fired his ass. I guess he made moonlighting permanent."

"Hunt was OPD," Stone said to Jess. "Ten years on the job. Vice. Narcotics." He nodded at Ruiz. "We hear anything from him and the other fella, Pius Wheedling?"

"Not a word from them or his wife or anyone, but we'll be checking them all out."

"What about his cell? Anything on it?"

Ruiz shrugged. Stone looked at the woman with the braids. "Your team collect it?"

"Not yet. It could've slipped behind one of the chair cushions or bed. We haven't tossed the room until we're finished collecting hair and fibers and doing the fingerprints. Once we find it, I'll let you know."

Stone said to Ruiz, "Manager confirmed nobody saw Riggins and Dabo coming or going this morning. What do we got so far on whereabouts?"

"Zip. We checked their rooms. All the public spaces. Parking garage. Feds sent over their passport photos from when they cleared customs. Uniforms have it and are walking the streets looking for them."

Ruiz's radio burped. He put it to his ear. "'Kay. Got it. Yep. Will do." He lowered it. "That was LT. Says the word's out now. TV's on their way. They don't got the name of the vic yet, but you know reporters. LT already bumped it upstairs and now the mayor's in on it too. Turns out she knows him on account of who he is and being civic-minded and all. She's on her way over to his house to break it to the wife personally."

Stone's expression finally showed a hint of surprise. "He lives in Oakland, how come he's in a suite here at the hotel?"

"Piedmont. LT said he lives in Piedmont."

"Okay, Piedmont. He's got a wife and house only ten minutes away but was staying the night in a hotel room after a rubber chicken dinner. How come?"

"The hotel manager said CaliCo leases a few suites long term for out-of-town guests since the headquarters is right next door."

"But Buckle's not from out of town, is he?"

"Guess we'll need to ask the mayor about that," Ruiz said.

"Better we ask the wife," Stone said.

Ruiz looked down at Buckle's body. "The widow, you mean."

8

O akland PD didn't have to look too hard or too long for Logan Riggins. He turned himself in to the main police station on Seventh Avenue within two hours of the news breaking about Jim Buckle's murder. Logan was accompanied by an attorney and his alibi, Mattie Voss. He'd spent the night at her house. Against his lawyer's advice, he agreed to be questioned by Detectives Stone and Ruiz.

He called Jess right after they finished. "I need to make the most of this."

"Make the most of what, Buckle's death or Dabo's disappearance?"

"Both. And why I need your help more than ever. You know the old saying, can't let a good crisis go to waste. Oil company exec gets murdered, and the cops' first reaction is to try and pin it on an Indigenous person whose homeland is already under attack. This is a turning point for us, the leverage we need to get public opinion on our side."

"But what about Dabo? He's missing, probably on the run. The cops—"

"For starters, he didn't do it. I know him. I already have my lawyer working on his defense. I don't want to talk about it over the phone. Meet me at Mattie's and I'll explain." He gave Jess an address in Berkeley.

The tree-lined street was in the hills north of the university campus. Logan met Jess at the front door of a two-story brown shingle with a mug of coffee in one hand and his phone in the other. He motioned Jess in with his eyes as he kept on talking.

"Come on, Sarah. I'm only talking about a meeting. And, no, it can't wait. You know it can't."

Logan started pacing as he listened and then said, "You do understand you can't ignore this."

He led Jess into the kitchen as he listened some more and gestured at the fridge. "Help yourself," he mouthed.

Jess was neither thirsty nor hungry, but he opened the double doors anyway. The shelves were stocked with cartons of almond milk and glass bottles filled with organic juices that reflected every color of the rainbow. The vegetable drawers were packed. He closed the doors without taking anything.

Logan was waving his coffee mug. "Fine, Sarah. Have your people call my people."

He clicked off and tossed the phone on the kitchen counter. It spun a few times before coming to a rest.

"Now I remember why I left for South America in the first place. Seven years and she still acts like I'm the latest hemorrhagic fever."

"The police must have liked what they heard or you'd still be downtown," Jess said.

"Is that your way of asking if I killed Buckle?"

"Remember what you taught me on the rock? If you can take the most direct route, take it. If I was going to ask you, I would've."

"Point taken. Wasn't much I could tell them. Last time I saw Buckle was at the gala. Mattie and I left soon after you did."

"What about Dabo, did he leave then too?"

"A little earlier. He said he was tired of having to smile so much while getting his picture taken with strangers."

"You never saw him again that night, didn't go up to the room?"

Logan's eyes narrowed. "You sound like the cops who were grilling me, Stone and Ruiz."

"Difference is, they're asking because they're homicide detectives. For them, suspects are guilty until proven innocent. I'm asking because I'm your friend and want to save Dabo. If he's on the run, I need to find him before they do. It'd be better if he turns himself in with your lawyer at his side than getting chased and cornered on the streets. Finding him starts with creating a timeline with his last known whereabouts."

"Your search and rescue technique."

"Exactly."

"Stone and Ruiz, which one's in charge? While Ruiz did a lot of the talking, Stone sat back and watched and listened. Never took his eyes off me. I had the feeling he's running the show."

"He is. Stone has seniority. I should tell you, he's the cop I was with the day I got shot."

"The one whose life you saved? Won't he give you the benefit of the doubt if you tell him Dabo and I had nothing to do with this?"

"Not a chance. Stone's by the book."

"Did he at least thank you for what you did?"

"Not in words. I'm a reminder that he missed a step. That's hard for any cop to accept, and especially a cop like Stone."

"Meaning, you didn't."

"Meaning I got lucky. Back to Dabo and last night. As far as you know, he went to bed and that was it?"

"Wish I knew more. I'd turned in the rental car earlier that day and so when Mattie and I left we took hers."

"If Dabo went straight to his room, then he left sometime between then and when the cops went to search for him this morning. They're interviewing everyone. Even if no one saw him, there could be footage from security cameras. If they don't have it already, then they're getting a warrant or subpoena for it. Why I need to stay a step ahead of them."

"Then do whatever it takes. If you have to pay people to help you, don't worry about the cost."

"Are you going back to the Grand?"

"No, I'm staying here. I checked out right after I left the police station. There's more room here plus fewer eyes on me, cops and media included."

"Mattie seems pretty charmed by you."

"We have a lot common, like sharing the same goals when it comes to the environment and human rights. Mattie's not a rock climber, but she's not afraid to do whatever it takes to reach the top."

"Sounds a lot like Sarah and her quest to build a business empire."

Logan blew out air. "The difference is, Mattie likes people. She's committed to helping them, not using them. You want some coffee? How about a beer?"

"I'm good."

"Let's go outside. I don't like spending too much time indoors. Another reason I moved out of the Grand. The windows don't open."

The garden was planted with California natives. Clumps of orange poppies mixed with blue-blossomed ceanothuses and purple salvias. A canvas market umbrella shaded a wooden table and benches made from reclaimed bleachers. Jess sat while Logan paced.

"It was a mistake to bring Dabo here. I'll never forgive myself if something happens to him."

"More the reason I need to find him," Jess said. "You sure you don't have any idea where he might've gone?"

"None. I mean, where would he? He doesn't know anyone."

"What about when we drove around looking for Blue Macaw? Did he talk to you about that? Did he go out on his own afterward?"

"I don't know. He could've when I was at meetings. All he said was he'd talked to some Indigenous people when he was with you. A tribal member from California and a Peruvian at a bar."

"Benny Guerrero at Urban Rez and a Quechuan bartender at the Altiplano. We told them we were looking for his sister. Dabo told the bartender he was staying at the Grand and to reach out if he found out anything. Maybe he did. Maybe Dabo's at Blue Macaw's place right now. He might not even know Buckle's dead and the cops are hunting him."

"He'll find out soon enough. The cops have given his photo to the news and distributed wanted posters. He takes a step outside, he won't get a block before someone IDs him."

"I need to go back to the Altiplano and have a talk with that bartender. Also Benny at Urban Rez."

"What's that?"

"A Native American community resource center."

"Then you better get to it."

"What are you going to do?"

"I'm already doing it. It's why I called Sarah, as hard as it was."

"How can she help?"

"With money. I need to pay the lawyer a big retainer up front. Also, I need to set aside money for bail when they arrest Dabo. If they lock him up and he has to stay in jail waiting for a trial, he won't last a month. Dabo's a native of the rainforest. He's seen what happens to wildlife when they're put in cages."

"You have to borrow money from Sarah?"

"I told you, mine's tied up in the surety bond. She'll do it, but she'll exact more than a pound of flesh."

"Say I do find Dabo, what then?"

"Call me right away, but don't bring him here. I'll get hold of my lawyer and we'll work something out so that when we take him to the police station, he'll get processed and released right away. My lawyer will have members of his team camped out at City Hall to make sure nobody gets amnesia about human rights."

9

J ess returned to the Altiplano, but the bartender with the fedora didn't work on Sundays. He drove over to Fruitvale Avenue even though he figured Urban Rez was probably closed. It was. He called the main number and left a voice mail while standing in the hallway outside the locked door.

With a feeling of dread growing and no idea of what to do next, Jess did what he always did when he needed to clear his head. He went back to the boat shop and carried *Pursuit* down to the estuary. Before sliding into the cockpit, he reached down, cupped water with both hands, and splashed his face. It was a ritual his seafaring grandfather had taught him.

As the water ran down his chin, the old man's words echoed. "Taste and smell it before you shove off. All water's different, lad. If you ever get lost, you'll be able to find your way home."

Jess pushed away from the dock. His paddling muscles protested after the few days of inactivity, but in time he found his rhythm. As he stroked, all the events and people of the past few days swirled together like smoke trapped in a room trying to find a way out. Logan and Dabo. Pius Wheedling and Lyle Hunt.

Jim Buckle dead on the hotel room floor. Detectives Tyrone Stone and Ruiz.

He could hear Stone's deep voice questioning him, acting like they didn't have a past. But they did, and it was the same kind of bond Jess had with Logan. They'd faced death together and lived to see another day.

Lifting the paddle's blades out of the water, Jess let the kayak drift as he looked at the top of the East Bay Hills that back-dropped Oakland. It was up there at the entrance to Redwood Park where he and the detective had first met. The memory was as clear as the cloudless sky.

Stone was leaning against an unmarked sedan. When Jess approached, he said, "You the guy from Search and Rescue?"

"Yeah, Jess Parks. Sorry, they didn't give me your name when I got the call to meet someone here from OPD."

"And you look around a crowded parking lot and see a Black man in a suit and knew it had to be me."

"The holster bulge on your hip kind of gave it away."

Stone tugged the lapels of his jacket that was a little tight on him. "Married twenty years and the wife still knows the way to my heart. Spending the same number of years on the force chowing fast food on back-to-backs doesn't help either. Tyrone Stone, Robbery-Homicide. They tell you what I need?"

"Help looking for trails up here is all dispatch said. I'm guessing it has something to with the East Bay Strangler."

"That's a name the press came up with to help sell advertising. If it bleeds it leads." Stone studied him. "But, yeah, I could use a hand. Eyes, actually. Oakland born and raised, but can't say I've been here outside of Sunday picnics in the big meadow throwing the ball with my son when he was little. Now he pitches varsity. His heat, slider, and changeup is getting him looks from MLB scouts."

"From what I heard, the killer's victims have been found in

the other East Bay Hills parks. Roberts. Tilden. Joaquin Miller. Redwood wasn't mentioned."

"Those are the only ones we know about. There could be other victims and we haven't found their bodies yet or maybe victims who got away and were too scared to report it."

"How about any who did report it?"

"Only one. Her description was pretty vague and the sketch artist could only draw a John Doe. Male, thirties, strong, wiry, white. Victim said he stunk like an ashtray. She was a runner. He jumped out from behind a tree as she was passing, threw his arm around her neck, and forced her into the woods. As he was choking her, she fought back, got away, and made a run for it."

"Was that his MO at the other parks?"

"None of the other victims lived to tell, but why would he change it? He's a killer, not a rocket scientist. He's a dumb, twisted pervert with a tiny brain and a tiny dick. I'm gonna nail his ass."

Stone's anger came across cold and relentless, like the steady grind of the glaciers that carved Yosemite. His face gave no emotion away, but beneath the frozen expression, something was moving, scouring away, capable of turning granite into dust.

"All right, most of the hikers and runners here stick to the main loop trail along the ridge. I know because we've looked for lost kids up here plenty of times. But there're lots of other trails that fork off it, and that's not counting all the deer paths."

Stone looked past the parking lot at the forest. The trees were mostly pine and eucalyptus. The park's namesake redwoods were second- and third-growth, all the old growth having fallen to axes and saws to build San Francisco during the gold rush and new masts and yardarms for the schooners hauling bullion back around the Horn.

"He'd want something out of the way but close to the road so he could get in and out fast without being seen," the detective said. "He wants to catch them when they're finishing their workout and heading back to their cars. They're tired then. Put up less of a fight."

"I can think of a couple of trails that sound like what you're talking about."

"Lead the way."

Jess glanced at Stone's ox-blood Florsheim's. "Did you bring another pair with you? Boots, running shoes?"

"Don't worry about 'em."

They took the East Ridge trail from the parking lot. It was fairly level with a surface packed hard by countless running shoes, hiking boots, and dog paws. It ran along the face of the ridgeline, one hundred yards or so below the top.

"We walking even with Skyline?" Stone asked. He'd unbuttoned his suit jacket but hadn't loosened his tie.

"Parallel but lower," Jess said.

Stone had no trouble keeping up. Even so, beads of sweat appeared on his shaved head. "I recollect from driving here there're a few pullouts on Skyline. Places where you can stop for a view of the Bay or to move over and let a car pass."

"There're also spots on this side of the road that loop through the trees. Cyclists park their cars on them. It's off the pavement so they can take their bikes from the rack without getting hit. Skyline's a popular route. They can pedal from here to Berkeley and back."

"You park a vehicle in one of those, no one can see it from the road?"

"Not in some spots."

"Those pullouts, are there footpaths leading to and from?"

"None officially, but the deer have blazed some that people who aren't afraid of poison oak or don't know what it looks like use."

"Still, you wanted, you could walk down here from a vehicle parked up there."

"You could."

"Show me."

Jess led the big detective to a faint trail.

"That's no bigger than a rabbit's butt," Stone said.

"You want to hike it? It's probably a quarter mile straight up to Skyline. Deer don't switchback."

Stone took off his jacket and slung it over his shoulder. A semi-automatic with a walnut grip was stuck in a speed holster clipped to his belt. The trail was steep and slippery in spots where the sun hadn't had time to dry the dew in the shadows, but it only took them ten minutes to reach the pullout. The detective had to wipe sweat off his brow and loosen his tie, but his breathing was even.

"Well, look at that." He pointed to a black pickup parked on the edge of the pullout next to the trees. "One of those bicyclists you were talking about."

Jess went to check it out. He cupped his eyes and pressed his forehead against the driver's side window. "I don't think so."

"Why, because it doesn't have bike racks? Doesn't need 'em, it being a truck."

"Take a look."

Stone walked over and peered into the cab. He stepped back. "I read you. The man's a smoker. Doesn't exactly fit the picture of a health nut. Maybe he's taking Rover for a walk."

"If he is, Rover doesn't ride in the cab with him. No nose prints on the inside of the passenger window."

"I wouldn't let a dog in the family ride either. Muddy paw prints everywhere."

"Exactly. And there aren't any in the bed."

"I guess being an eagle eye is part of Search and Rescue, right?" Stone slipped a notebook and ballpoint pen from his pocket and jotted down the license plate number. "Chances are this is nothing, but I'll run it later. Let's go back to the main trail and you can show me one of the smaller trails. Something not too far from where this one meets up."

They retraced their steps down the steep, narrow deer trail and reached the intersection with the ridge trail. From there, they walked single file down another narrow path through the forest. It was dark beneath the canopy. After a couple of hundred yards, the trees gave way to thick clumps of chaparral. The brush was thick and the trail snaked through it. As they rounded a corner, a hiker coming the other way nearly plowed into them.

"Heads up," Jess said.

The man took his eyes off the trail. "Sorry. Didn't see you coming."

He was in his early thirties with dirty blond hair combed straight back. A daypack was slung over one shoulder and his untucked, unbuttoned, long-sleeved flannel shirt showed off a white T-shirt. He turned sideways and backed up against the bushes to let them pass. His eyes lingered on Stone's loosened tie and speed holster.

"You go all the way to the bottom?" Jess said.

"Yep."

"That's a workout. A lot of up and down, but worth it. Can be long depending on what loop you take. Where did you start?"

"Skyline. Took the Ridge Trail then cut down on the Toyon."

"You able to find a parking spot up there? Sure would save time rather than hiking all the way over from the main lot."

"Yep. Hey, gotta pick up the old lady from work." He started up the trail, disappearing around the corner.

"What was all that about?" Stone said.

Jess turned to face him. "Guy had smoker's fingers. I was trying to see if he belonged to the truck parked up top."

"Oh shit!" Stone said as a look of surprise crossed his face. He stumbled toward Jess.

A flash of white T-shirt caught Jess's eye at the same time a loud bang filled his ears. Blood was spurting out of Stone's mouth as he lurched against him. A second bang thundered and Jess fell on his back with the detective on top of him.

The T-shirt grew brighter as the man with the dirty blond hair stepped closer and fired two more rounds into Stone's back and was readying to pull the trigger again while aiming at Jess's face when his gun jammed. He tried clearing it, but then wheeled around and ran back up the trail.

Jess was trying to make sense of it all. His shoulder burned. The hard surface of the trail beneath him was turning into a feathery bed. He realized he'd been shot. He could hear a low, deep gurgle. It was coming from the big detective. Jess struggled to sit up. He lifted his knees toward his chin and rolled Stone off him. His face was ashy. Blood bubbled on his lips.

"Stone," Jess called to him. "Stone, wake up."

The detective's eyes jittered before finding Jess's. He tried to speak but couldn't get air. Jess didn't think, only reacted as his EMT training kicked in. Ignoring the pain in his shoulder, he plucked Stone's ballpoint pen out of his pocket, jettisoned the ink cartridge, and held the hollow plastic tube between his teeth. Then he ripped apart the detective's shirt, ran his fingers down his chest, counting ribs. Fishing out his Swiss Army knife, he jabbed him with the smallest blade, pressing with the heel of his hand so it would penetrate skin and cartilage. He inserted the pen.

It all took less than twenty seconds. He heard a sucking sound, then a bubbling wheeze as air hissed through the tube and the detective's lungs began to reinflate. Grabbing Stone's hands, he placed them on either side of the pen.

"Don't let go. Hold on tight while I call for help." He fumbled for his phone.

Stone spat up blood as he struggled for words. "Come back," he gasped.

"I'm not going anywhere."

Stone's eyeballs strained as he struggled for breath. "He, he'll come back." He wheezed. "My gun."

Jess pulled Stone's semi-automatic out of the speed holster, gripping it with one hand and trying to hold it steady as he trained it on the trail. It seemed to take too long. He heard the air hissing and spitting through the plastic pen tube stuck in Stone's chest, felt the fire burning in his shoulder. Buzzing filled his ears and bright lights flickered and flashed.

He sensed him before he saw the white T-shirt and the gun the killer was pointing. He could see the look of expectation on his face. It was like a kid's who'd just been handed a box wrapped in paper and tied with ribbon. Then his eyes filled with surprise as he realized the gift was not at all what he'd been hoping for.

Jess squeezed the trigger and kept squeezing it as red roses bloomed on the T-shirt.

10

———

A black SUV with tinted windows was idling in front of the boat shop's entrance when Jess came back from paddling. Lyle Hunt slid out from behind the wheel, but didn't kill the engine. He still wore the yellow-tinted glasses and tan hunting jacket.

"Mr. Wheedling would like a word," he said.

"What about?"

"You know what."

Hunt steered him around to the passenger side. The head lawyer for CaliCo sat stiffly looking at his phone. After a few moments, he put the phone on his lap and turned to face Jess. The window rolled down silently.

"The world is darker today than yesterday," he said. "A wife grieves. Two daughters grieve. A company's employees and board of directors grieve. A loving husband, father, friend, and brilliant business and civic leader has been taken from us. And for what?"

"I wouldn't know," Jess said.

"He wasn't asking you," Hunt snarled.

"Mr. Parks, we have been informed of your presence this

morning at the scene of the murder. We have also been made aware of your history with Detective Stone who is heading the investigation as well as your position with Alameda County Sheriff's Search and Rescue team. I am naturally supportive of local law enforcement's efforts to apprehend the fugitive and I am also supportive of the criminal court system's ability to deliver the appropriate justice."

His thin lips pursed. "However, as a close friend of Mr. Buckle, I know it would pain him grievously that his family and employees might be put through a long and tortuous public ordeal. Your association with Detective Stone, Mr. Riggins, and the fugitive gives you a unique vantage point. Your search and rescue training is an additional skill set. To that end, we would like to retain your services to assist in identifying the fugitive's whereabouts."

"Dabo didn't kill him," Jess said. "You both heard Buckle tell him last night he'd meet with him and Logan to discuss the debt-for-nature swap deal. Dabo knew it was the best chance his people had for keeping drilling out of their homeland."

"That will be for a jury to decide," Wheedling said.

"Sounds like you've already made up your mind."

"We are not asking you to apprehend Dabo, only locate him. Your information will be provided to the appropriate law enforcement agency. The City of Oakland operates under extreme financial challenges. The police department is woefully underfunded and understaffed. Not only would you be aiding them in carrying out their duties, you would also be aiding the public. The last thing the community needs is a killer on the loose."

"No thanks."

"We are prepared to offer you generous compensation for your time and skills."

"How generous?"

"A fifty-thousand-dollar retainer upon your acceptance and an additional fifty-thousand-dollar bonus for the successful completion of your assignment. Your expenses will also be reimbursed."

"And I'd be reporting directly to you?"

"Through Mr. Hunt."

"Can I think about it?"

"I need to have your decision immediately. Time is of the essence. For the Buckle family's sake and the public's."

"Okay, I thought about it. No thanks."

"Are you sure?"

"Positive."

"Why?"

"Because I don't trust you or him." Jess hooked a thumb at Hunt. "He doesn't strike me as someone who'd sit back once he had the information and let the cops do their job."

CaliCo's chief counsel rolled the window back up without another word and returned to looking at his phone.

Hunt jabbed his finger in Jess's chest. "I told him talking to you would be a waste of time. I worked Oakland streets longer than you've been breathing. I'll find the little Indian and he'll never see me coming."

Jess knocked his hand aside. "I wouldn't count on it. Think about where Dabo grew up, where he lives. Tarani have been able to survive in one of the most dangerous places on earth for thousands of years."

"We'll see about that. And guess what? Now that I know where you live, you'll never see me coming either."

Hunt got behind the wheel and drove away. Jess went upstairs and called Logan. When he didn't pick up, he left a message and sent a text as well. Then he opened his laptop and searched on Pius Wheedling and Lyle Hunt.

Most of Wheedling's online profile was confined to CaliCo's

website. He'd been with the company fifteen years, rising to the position of head of legal affairs. He was a member of the California Bar along with a couple of corporate legal societies. There was no mention of family or a residential address.

Hunt's web presence was devoted to posts chronicling his long history of police brutality. A list of citizen complaints and OPD disciplinary actions against him was also posted. Hunt wasn't on CaliCo's website, nor did he have any social media accounts in his name.

The sun was setting and the dwindling rays were turning the waters of the estuary gold then orange when Jess's phone rang.

"I got your voice mail," Benny Guerrero said. "I want you to know that Urban Rez is in Dabo's corner. They arrest him, tell him he doesn't need to settle for a public defender. We have volunteer lawyers ready to step up, lawyers steeped in protecting our people's rights."

"Thanks, but so you know, Dabo didn't do it."

"Of course he didn't, but they'll try to pin it on him anyway. Did you have any luck finding his sister?"

"Not yet. We went to the Altiplano, but even though the bartender is Quechuan, it didn't ease his suspicion that we were ICE."

"Don't say I didn't warn you. If you're still looking for Blue Macaw, I have something else you might try. She has to eat, right? And that means having a job. Immigrants, illegals, whatever, doesn't matter if they're mestizo or full-blooded Indigenous, from Mexico or Guatemala or Ecuador, about the only work they can get up here is manual labor. The men get gardening, construction, restaurant jobs. The women? Cleaning houses and hotel rooms."

"So?"

"I asked around. There's an outfit that specializes in hooking up South Americans with domestic work. It's called Casa Clean.

They do all the front-end stuff, customer contact, billing, and getting housecleaners to the job and paying them. She might be doing that to get by."

"Do you have an address or phone number?"

"That's the problem. Casa Clean is run by some old bruja. You know that word? It's witch in Spanish, but plenty of Natives use it too. Everything about Casa Clean is word of mouth. You either know about it or you don't. No office anywhere. Only a burner phone number that's always changing. Payment is strictly cash. I'll keep asking around to see if I can get a line on it."

"Thanks, Benny. Keep in touch."

"You see Dabo, tell him to keep the faith. He's got a lot of brothers and sisters here."

The freight elevator doors opened and Isabella entered as Jess was hanging up the phone.

"It's all over the news," she said. "I can't believe it."

"Don't. You're the third person in the past hour I've had to tell Dabo is innocent."

"Of course he is. I danced with him at the gala. Come on, let's go for a run. Some exercise will do you good."

"Already did it. Fresh home from a paddle."

"How did it hold up?"

"*Pursuit's* patch or my shoulder?"

"Both."

"Fine."

Isabella brushed the back of her fingers across his cheek. "Are you getting anywhere with your search for Blue Macaw?"

"Maybe." He told her about his call with Benny and Casa Clean.

"You can't find it online?"

"See for yourself." She watched as he clicked keys. "I don't know where else to look."

Isabella glanced around the loft. It made her raven curls take flight. "That's because you've never needed a housecleaner before. Your place is always spotless."

"Compared to yours, sure. All the costumes you leave thrown around, the floor a tangle of electrical cords. And when you have a class of kids over? Forget it."

"Making art is messy. If I put anything away, I might forget where. If I throw something out, it could be exactly what I need to finish a piece. And kids leaving stuff behind? It goes with being a kid."

Jess turned his attention back to the screen. "I can't find Casa Clean or Box Street. Something tells me Dabo got word about Blue Macaw and went to see her. He spent the night there and is now using it as a hideout." He rubbed his jaw. "Where are you, Dabo? Where are you, 365 Box?"

Isabella's head tilted. "Dabo and Blue Macaw are from Ecuador. Maybe Dabo's reading it backward."

"What backward?"

"The envelope. Remember I told you I lived in Rome when I was doing an internship with Futuro Danza? I had this three-story walkup in an ancient building. I always told people my address the wrong way because in Italy the number comes after the street name. My apartment building wasn't at 233 Via Attilio. It was Via Attilio 233. I bet Blue Macaw writes like Eudora Welty."

"The famous author?"

"That's right. The first time I read her was in high school. My teacher assigned us one of her short stories." Isabella's eyes and lips smiled. "Why I Live at the P.O."

Jess smacked the top of the chart table. "It's not a street, it's a post office box. Box 365. Blue Macaw wrote the return backward. You're a genius."

He started typing. "Now if only Eudora Welty could tell me which post office. There are thirteen in Oakland."

"But if she's here illegally, she probably didn't rent one at a post office. Too much identification required. She would've rented a box at one of those retail places."

"Like a no-tell motel. And probably one in the neighborhood where she's living, a neighborhood where an Indigenous woman from the rainforest can blend in."

Jess's sense of triumph quickly faded.

"What's wrong?" Isabella said.

"If we can figure it out, so can others."

"What others?"

"The two men with Buckle at the gala last night. Wheedling and Hunt have a connection inside the OPD who's feeding them information."

"How do you know that?"

"They knew I was at the scene this morning."

"You talked with them?"

"They were waiting for me when I came back from paddling. They tried to hire me to find Dabo."

"Do they know about Blue Macaw?"

"I didn't tell them, and I didn't tell the police either, but it's only a matter of time until someone does. Dabo's told everyone he's met he's looking for his sister."

"Then you'd better earn your nickname."

"How's that?"

"Be faster than them and find her. Make the sparks fly."

11

———

The next morning Jess started walking Foothill Boulevard near the Altiplano. Groups of day laborers crowded the street corners in hopes of being selected by drive-by contractors. No questions asked, no green cards needed, no taxes paid. Also, no recourse if they got stiffed after putting in a full day swinging a pick or wheelbarrowing concrete.

No questions were asked at the storefronts that rented mailboxes either. As long as the customer paid in cash, nobody cared what was sent or received. Packages that wouldn't fit in a rental box were stacked in a back room and recipients had to pay extra to collect them.

The first two places Jess checked were both so small they didn't even have enough rental boxes to warrant numbers past two hundred. The third place had gone out of business; its front windows were covered with sheets of plywood that had been sprayed with MS-13 graffiti. The fourth was a chain store that used a combination of letters and numbers for its boxes.

Back out on the street, Jess turned onto 23rd Avenue and tried another place that rented boxes. It was a convenience store painted the color of a dirty swimming pool and its shelves were stocked with canned food, packaged snacks, and beer and wine. There wasn't a fruit or veggie in sight. He did a quick count as he scanned the rows of mailboxes. Number 365 was on the second from the bottom row.

A woman sat behind the counter reading. He held up a stamped envelope he'd addressed to Mintaka, Box 365, Oakland.

"Excuse me. I found this on the sidewalk. Must've fallen out of the letter carrier's bag. It looks important. Can you check the name of the person renting Box 365 to see if this is the right place?"

The woman barely looked up from a paperback version of a popular telenovela. "Give it to me. I put it in."

"Maybe we should check the name on the box first. It could be for someone who rents one at another store. There are so many around here."

"Then go ask them." She kept reading the soap opera.

"I will once you check to make sure it doesn't belong here. It's the right thing to do, don't you agree?"

The woman put down the book. "What's the name?"

Jess held it up for her. "Mintaka. That's it. No second name."

She pulled a bound ledger from a drawer. "What number?"

"Three six five."

"*Tres seis cinco,*" she said as she opened the ledger. "*Tres seis cinco, tres seis cinco.*" She ran her finger along a line on a page. "No box here registered to Mintaka."

"You're sure?"

"No Mintaka nothing. It's rented by a business."

She picked up the book and held it close to her face as she resumed reading. The cover showed a woman in a low-cut dress clinched in a passionate embrace with a handsome man wearing a doctor's white coat.

"A soap." Jess said it out loud as he tried to grasp a connection slipping beyond his reach.

The woman looked up. "You want to buy soap? What kind, for washing dishes or yourself?"

A soap opera, Jess said to himself as his grip on the connection tightened. "The company that rents the mailbox, is it a housecleaning agency?"

She nodded. "Casa Clean."

"Do you have their phone number?"

She looked at the envelope still in Jess's hand. "You want house cleaned or mail letter?"

Jess figured the bruja who ran Casa Clean also kept a place nearby where she housed undocumented workers. She only let them receive mail at a rented box to keep the building's location hidden from authorities.

"Both," he said.

"You want cleaner, you give me your telephone number and a dollar. Next time they come for mail, I give your number and they call you."

"How often do they come to pick up mail?"

"Who knows? Once a day. Once a week."

He looked at the book's cover again. "I can't wait. I'm a doctor and my house is a mess and my new girlfriend is coming over for dinner. How about I give you twenty dollars and you tell me where they live? I can go right now and see if I can hire someone."

She huffed. "I don't know where. Only have the name. No address. No phone number."

"Fine. Here's my number." He wrote it down and handed it over.

"And a dollar," she said.

Jess paid her and left. He thought about staking out the store but quickly rejected it. It could be days before the bruja came to pick up the mail. Even so, he had no idea what she looked like. Nor was it likely she'd tell him where Blue Macaw lived even if he was able to identify her.

It was like being on the rock. He was stuck and needed help and so he reached out to the only person who could give him a hand. Jess pulled out his phone and dialed.

"Stone," the voice on the other end said.

"I didn't tell you something I should've."

"About the murder?"

"About Dabo."

"And how come you want to tell me now?"

"Because it may help us find him."

"Parks? There's no us. There's OPD and me, and there's you and your boats. We straight on that?"

"As an arrow. But you should know Pius Wheedling offered me a hundred grand to find Dabo. Said OPD wasn't up to the task."

"Bullshit."

"He was with Lyle Hunt. They knew I was at the Grand yesterday morning. Said someone on the inside at OPD told them."

"Who?"

"Didn't say, but Hunt used to be a cop, didn't he? You do the math."

"You take the job?"

"No."

"Hundred grand, why not?"

"Because despite Wheedling telling me all I had to do was find Dabo and he'd turn the location over to you, I read Hunt's record. I did the math."

The phone hummed with static. "Where are you at?"

"In the San Antonio. Foothill and 23rd."

Stone's exhale sounded louder than a front tire blowing out.

"Stay put. I'll be there in five. And Parks? Don't look like a mark or a narc and get yourself drive-by'd."

Five minutes later when the detective pulled alongside Jess's truck, he beckoned him to get in the front seat.

"Where's Ruiz?" Jess said.

"We're working this case from two directions."

"Is that code for you suspect he's the one leaking info to CaliCo?"

"Shut up and buckle up until I ask you a question."

"Where we going?"

"Trip down memory lane. Now, tell me what you know."

Jess gave it all up, about Blue Macaw, the letter, the mailbox, and Casa Clean.

"Blue Macaw, that's what the sister's name means?" Stone said. "What's Dabo's mean?"

"If it has an English translation, I don't know it. They don't use a last name because there are so few Tarani left. If one has the same name as another, they might say their father's name along with their own to distinguish themselves."

"They don't use junior? That's what my wife and I did when we named our son."

"Tyrone Junior?"

"But he goes by TJ. Let's get back on track here. You're saying you don't know if Dabo's at his sister's and you don't even have her address?"

"I don't even know if she's still in Oakland, but she was when she mailed the letter. Truth is, I don't know if she's even still alive, but Dabo's sure and that's good enough for me."

"How come he's so certain?"

"It's hard to explain."

"Try."

"He said ever since she disappeared, every time he took the boat back to the homelands, flocks of blue macaws would gather overhead when he was a few miles out and fly the rest of the way with him. They'd light in the trees and perch there the whole time, only leaving when he did."

Stone kept his eyes on the windshield, but his head was bobbing. "Not my place to question another man's faith or whatever. I'm gonna go along and believe the sister's alive too and here in Oakland and Dabo's holed up with her. That still doesn't get me where he's at and whether he's gonna stay put or make a run for the border."

They continued driving up 23rd Avenue crossing numbered streets, East 20th Street, 21st, 22nd. Most corners had a liquor store. Some of the buildings were boarded up. Junk cars and discarded furniture competed for parking spots.

"My old neighborhood, where I grew up, and then was my beat when I was uniform," Stone said. "The Twomps, the Roaring '20s, Murder Dubs. You ever heard of those names for it?"

"Oakland born and raised like you," Jess said.

"But you never lived over here, not during those days when crack was king and Oakland was a 3D horror show. Drive-bys, drug rip-offs, drug ODs. Crime and killings off the charts. Gangs shooting it out block by block. You're too young. I saw it though. First as a youngster and later as a cop."

Stone turned right onto East 27th Street. "They had this chart back then. All plotted on a piece of graph paper. Stock market, unemployment, interest rates, all the other leading economic indicators. On the same page they overlaid a chart of Oakland's murder rate. Was averaging close to a hundred and fifty homicides a year in the eighties and nineties. Whenever the money and jobs line went down, the murder line went up."

He stopped at an intersection. "Thing about the way they drew that chart? They made the economy line red, the murder line black. Black like those doing all the dying."

They reached Foothill Boulevard and turned onto it to finish completing the loop. Stone said, "Now I got a rich White man as a murder victim and everyone from the mayor to the police commissioner to the chief to the captain down to the LT wants it solved yesterday. So, tell me, Parks, why are you doing all the looking for Dabo and not the man who brought him here, Logan Riggins?"

"Logan's been gone a long time and I know Oakland better. Better at searching too. He's better at raising money in case Dabo needs it for bail and legal defense. That's what he's focusing on now."

The detective's gaze shifted back and forth on the street ahead, taking in everything, the cars cruising past, people loitering on the street, which stores were open and which ones were closed.

"What do you make of Riggins and his company?"

"Rainforest Now! is hardly a company. It's a nonprofit."

"I mean his personal company. The woman who alibied him."

"You mean Mattie Voss. I met her for the first time at the gala. She's a political campaign expert. Used to be chief of staff for a congresswoman."

"She's not a multimillionaire, like his ex?"

"No. You say you're getting it from all sides to solve this? The City. CaliCo. Does that also include Sarah Newton? There're a lot of campaign dollars that come with her."

"Elections don't mean shit to me. Catching killers does. You tell Riggins if he knows something more than what he told me when he had his juice lawyer with him, he better give me a call."

"I'll let him know."

A lowrider passed going in the opposite direction. The driver flashed the peace sign to Stone.

"That's an unmarked cop car," Jess said.

"Like I said, a regular eagle eye, aren't you?"

As they completed the loop and his truck was in sight, Jess said, "I told you what I know about Dabo and his sister. I've been straight up about Wheedling and Hunt and Logan and Mattie Voss too. How about answering something for me?"

"Like what?"

"Whose prints were on the machete other than Dabo's? His are since he made it and carried it from Ecuador."

"I'm not gonna tell you that. This is an ongoing murder investigation."

"Then I'll tell you. Jim Buckle's, Pius Wheedling's, and Lyle Hunt's. And that's for starters."

Stone tapped the brakes. "How did you know about Wheedling's and Hunt's?"

"Saw Wheedling take it when Buckle handed it to him when we were at the nature preserve dedication thing. Buckle told him to put it in his golf bag. Hunt's because Buckle told him to go fetch it so he could dance with it at the gala. I bet that wasn't the first time Hunt held it."

"What makes you say that?"

"Because of who Hunt is. He can't resist touching a weapon. It's like touching his—"

"Yeah, I got it." Stone checked the rearview mirror as if looking to see if he was holding up traffic. "You're right on all. Damn thing was passed around like a hookah at a party. Some other partials on it too. Looks like someone was trying to wipe those off. Haven't ID'd them yet."

"What about the carpet patches and shower drain swabs your team took? Results come in on those yet? Blood type, DNA."

"You know better than ask me that."

"Find Buckle's missing cell yet?"

"I told you what I'm gonna tell you. Now get out. You get a line on the sister, Min ... Min ..., on Blue Macaw, you call me."

"And you'll call me too. Right? Right, Stone?"

"Go on. Get out."

Jess said, "I'm assuming housekeeping discovered Buckle's body. What happened, she knocked on the door to clean the room, no one answered, and so she thought the guest had left and peeked in and found him?"

"I'll give you this one since a reporter's already got it and is gonna post it today. Someone called from Buckle's office to remind him he had that breakfast meeting with Riggins and Dabo. They got worried when he didn't pick up his cell or the room phone. Asked the front desk to go check on him."

"Who made the call, his secretary?"

"The corporate lawyer, Wheedling. He told us the secretary didn't know Buckle was staying the night at the hotel or anything about the appointment when we asked him why he called. Said Buckle had made the appointment on the fly at the gala and he knew about it because he was there."

"Did he also know Buckle didn't go home that night but went upstairs to a suite owned by CaliCo?"

"Yep. Said Buckle told him he'd had a bit to drink plus Mrs. Buckle had gone home with a headache and he didn't want to wake her or the kids. Said Buckle kept clothes in the suite and often stayed there when he had late-night meetings at the office and another one the following morning or had to catch an early flight."

"The TV in Buckle's room? I noticed it was turned to a Latin music channel. That isn't proof Dabo was in there. He speaks English as well as Spanish."

"Parks?"

"Yeah?"

"Goodbye. Adios."

12

Logan called Jess. "I need your help with Sarah. She won't listen to me."

"About what?"

"Everything. You need to convince her that I'm going to stop CaliCo from bidding on the leases in Ecuador and save Dabo too."

"What makes you think she'll listen to me?"

"Because she trusts you."

Jess laughed. "You do know she fired me from Wild Things and told me to stop climbing with you."

"Yeah, and I was plenty pissed off at the time, but Sarah explained why, that the business we were building could help lots of people, not just a few kids from the streets. She was right. We went on to make enough money to build youth outdoor activity centers all over the place and fund environmental causes too. Look at what I'm able to do for the Tarani."

Logan waited for Jess to say something. When he didn't, he said, "The point is, Sarah respects you for all your search and rescue work and saving lives. I need you to go talk to her about how you're looking for Dabo and Mintaka, how you have an inside track with Detective Stone. Sarah needs to know that putting money up for Dabo's bail and defense isn't a lost cause."

"Is that the only reason she's balking?"

"Fact is, it'll put her in an awkward spot. She has a long business history with Jim Buckle. Knows his wife too. People will call her a traitor."

"To what?"

"Her social circle. It's more important to her than doing the right thing."

"Fine, I'll go. But Logan?"

"What?"

"You know this is a dyno."

"It's why I'm asking you, Sparks. I've seen you make dynamic leaps and grab out-of-reach holds before. You'll stick it. I'm counting on it."

Jess drove across the Bay Bridge to Wild Things's headquarters in San Francisco. A receptionist escorted him to Sarah's office suite. She was at a standing desk talking on a speaker phone while doing arm curls with ten-pound dumbbells.

Until she'd met Logan, Sarah had never bouldered before, much less tackled big walls. He made it his personal mission to turn her into a rock star. He started teaching her at a gym equipped with climbing walls. From there, they built up to easy routes at Yosemite. A born competitor, her fears quickly turned into fierce determination. Sarah spent hours conditioning and strengthening. She was equally compulsive about what she ate, knowing that extra pounds for a climber were dead weight that she'd have to haul up a pitch.

"We didn't get a chance to talk at the gala," Sarah said as she moved away from her desk and offered him a cheek to peck. "I didn't even recognize you. You're all grown up. Is that woman you were with your girlfriend?"

It was an old jab, but he could still feel the sting. One afternoon, before she'd fired him, he was unpacking paintings in the backroom. Sarah came in and tripped over a box he'd left on the floor. She stumbled and grabbed hold of Jess to stop her fall, yanking his face into her breasts. Jess turned red and twisted away. Sarah laughed. "Oh my God, Sparks. Don't tell me you're still a virgin."

A couple of days later, Logan and Jess were at Indian Rock practicing short roping. Logan was standing at the top making a dead-lift pull with Jess tied to the other end when he said, "Sarah told me you made a pass at her."

"No way. It was an accident. She fell and—"

Logan stopped pulling, leaving him hanging. Jess looked up. He saw Logan's biceps bulging as hard as baseballs, the flexor muscles in his forearms writhing beneath his skin. Jess had spent enough time climbing to be able to sense a falling rock long before he saw it.

"You know I'd never do anything like that," Jess said.

"Like what?" Logan said.

"Whatever it is Sarah said or whatever it is you're thinking I did."

Logan resumed lifting and gave a final yank that hoisted Jess straight up until he was standing in front of him on the roof.

He grinned. "Sarah's right. You do turn bright red." The grin turned into a laugh. "Tell me I'm not the luckiest guy in the world to have a woman like her and a friend like you."

Now, in her office, Sarah said, "I only have a couple of minutes between meetings. What's so important that Logan sent you to come see me?"

"It's about Dabo," Jess said.

"The man who killed Jim."

"Suspected of. He's innocent."

"So Logan says. You too, I guess."

"If you met Dabo, you'd think the same. Logan wants me to tell you about him and the detective I've been working with."

Sarah tilted her head and gave an exaggerated look of surprise. "Excuse me, but did I miss something here? When did you join the Oakland Police Department, go through training, earn a degree in criminology?"

"I'm helping out in an unofficial capacity to find Dabo before he gets hurt. The detective leading the investigation and I have some history. We want to get him into custody before he gets hurt or anybody else does."

"Jess, Jess, Jess. Still one of the Lost Boys following Peter Pan. I had Logan all grown up and then he flew off to Neverland again. Second star to the right and straight on 'til morning."

"That's interesting," Jess said.

"Don't tell me you never read the book, saw the movie?"

"Jim Buckle said nearly the same thing about Logan when we saw him at the preserve dedication. Seems like you two are cut from the same cloth."

Anger flashed in Sarah's eyes. "How dare you speak ill of the dead. Jim was a friend of mine."

"And Logan was your husband."

She mimed rocking back on her heels. "Oh my. Little Jess finally grew a pair of balls." Her amusement quickly died. "If Logan sent you over here to try and talk me into giving him money, you're doing a piss-poor job of it."

"I told him it'd be a waste of time. He said he understood why you might balk at contributing to the defense since Buckle was your friend. By the way, how is Mrs. Buckle doing?"

"Devastated, I'm sure."

"You haven't seen her, spoken to her?"

Sarah glanced at her feet and then sighed. "Not that I need to explain myself to you or anyone, but I do run a global enterprise that spans every time zone. That tends to leave me little free time to send flowers."

"Even for a close friend who lost her husband?"

"Not that it's any of your business, but I serve on lots of boards with lots of people. Clare and I never had the time to become close. Now with what's happened, I regret that."

"I hope her loss hasn't brought on more migraines. My mother suffered from those. The only thing that helped were cold washcloths on her forehead and a pitch-dark room."

"What's that have to do with Clare?"

"She had a migraine. It's why she left the gala early."

"How do you know that?"

"I happened to be passing by when she told her husband she was leaving early and not to wake her when he got home."

"Whatever. Now, tell Logan if he really wants me to contribute to his friend's defense, he'd better show me something that convinces me it'll be a good investment."

"You know what else I remember from the gala? How after Mrs. Buckle left, you and her husband danced together."

"So what? He needed a dance partner. We're longtime friends."

"Does that mean friendly enough to go upstairs to one of his company's hotel rooms for a nightcap and—"

Her face twisted with rage. "How dare you! Get out before I have your skinny ass thrown out."

"Maybe that's the real reason you don't want to put up money for Dabo's defense."

Jess walked out before she could say another word, hoping she'd take the bait and write a big, fat check.

13

The steady clang of metal cargo containers, roar of trucks, and steely click-clack of train wheels greeted Jess after he exited the Bay Bridge and cut through the Port of Oakland. He passed by lines of giant container cranes that worked day and night tending to the nonstop flow of ships that steamed back and forth between Asia and the seventh-largest port in North America. Jess didn't know if the legend was true that the cranes were the inspiration for the Walker armored fighting vehicles in the *Star Wars* movies, but he could see the resemblance.

Hanging a right off Maritime Street, he pulled into the parking lot at a shoreline park ringing Oakland Middle Harbor. The lawns were brown from all the salt in the air and the trees bowed to the east because of the constant winds that blew through the Golden Gate. Seagulls perched on stanchions along the water's edge. A flock of Canada geese forsaking the call of the tundra had taken up year-round residence.

Jess walked to the Chappell Hayes Observation Tower that was erected to honor a community activist who'd devoted his life to protecting West Oakland's downtrodden neighborhoods. A shopping cart was parked beside a nearby picnic table. Carl was sitting on the bench, his little dog curled by his feet.

"I haven't seen you for a few days and was worried about you," Jess said.

"No need to worry about me and Kelp. We're fine. Been doing a lot, lot of thinking is all."

"I hope about moving into the Seafarers' House."

"Maybe thinking on it, but got to keep our eyes open so you don't get jumped again. And they won't let Kelp live there neither. Can't go nowheres without Kelp."

The little dog raised his head at hearing his name.

"How about if I give you a ride there and we ask if they'll make an exception?"

"Why would they do that?"

"Because Isabella did some poking around and found there's a law that guarantees people and their service dogs rights. That's what Kelp is. He's your service dog. The same as a person who's lost their sight needs a guide dog, you need Kelp."

"That's true. And he needs me."

"Let's give it a try, see what they say."

"We'll follow you with the cart."

"Beauty of driving a truck, I can put it in the back. Come on, you and Kelp hop up front."

They made the short drive to a building at the south end of the seaport. It was two stories high and painted nautical blue. Jess had called ahead after Isabella told him about service dogs and cleared the way with the house manager. Carl and Kelp were welcomed right in and shown where they could bunk, shower, and have meals.

Carl seemed lost at sea. "Now what do Kelp and me do?"

"You'll find a lot of friends living here. If you don't know them already from your days on ships, you'll see you have plenty in common. I'll come by from time to time to check on you and Kelp."

"What about Isabella?"

"She'll bring you pesto pasta."

"We'd like that, but we're not used to being inside. Around so many folks. Kelp and me, we don't think it's gonna work out."

"Try it for a week. If it doesn't feel right after that, you're always free to leave." Voices were coming from a room off the lobby. "Let's go see what's up."

Carl was carrying Kelp beneath his peacoat, the little dog's head sticking out. He followed Jess into the room. Several men were sitting around. A few were playing cards. Others were watching TV.

Jess said hello to a couple of men and introduced Carl. One of them knew him from when they served together as cargo tenders on the Matson Line.

Voices on the TV caught Jess's attention. A bright red chyron with "Breaking News" in white letters crawled across the screen. A reporter holding a microphone was standing in front of two police cars parked at angles to block a street. Jess recognized the intersection. He also recognized the name of the fugitive the reporter said had barricaded himself in a building. As the TV blared about SWAT being en route, Jess sprinted for the door.

His truck was never built for speed, but it banged through the potholes and over the railroad tracks without breaking a strut or shredding a tire as he kept it floored. He kept one hand on the wheel as he weaved between tractor-trailers hauling cargo containers and the other gripping his phone. He called Logan.

"Get hold of your lawyer and get him quick," he shouted as a truck driver gave him a blast of his air horn followed by a middle finger. "SWAT has Dabo in their sights. He's holed up in the Twomps."

"I'll call him from the car. I'm on my way," Logan said.

"Don't come. It'll be a war zone."

"Exactly, and Dabo's my responsibility."

Jess clicked off and shot up the onramp to I-880, which old-timers still called the Nimitz. He stayed on the shoulder and sped past the herd of commuters and big rigs, swinging off on the Embarcadero exit and gunning it up and over the 16th Street overpass. He tried an end-around on Foothill Boulevard so he could enter the street he'd recognized on the breaking newscast, but it was no use. OPD had it cordoned off on all sides. Three choppers were buzzing overhead. One belonged to Alameda County Sheriff's, the others to TV stations.

He parked and called Detective Stone's cell. It went straight to voice mail. Jess sent him a text saying he was there and could help talk Dabo out. His phone pinged. Stone responded with a curt message to meet him on the corner.

The detective waved Jess through the barricade and led him to a mobile command. A gray military-grade armored personnel carrier with SWAT painted on the side straddled the sidewalk. A man with hardened muscles and dressed in black was studying a map while barking orders through a headset. Jess recognized him from previous Search and Rescue missions. He was a SWAT team leader known for both his lack of humor and lack of remorse.

Jess looked across the street at a two-story duplex. The stucco walls were dirty pink. He asked Stone if they were positive Dabo was in there.

"We got a visual. He's in there, all right."

"Alone?"

"No. OPD gang unit told us that building's an MS-13 crib. Informant says a punk high up in the ranks bought it for his mama. She rents out rooms to illegals. Runs a housecleaning business."

"Casa Clean," Jess said. "You need to slow this down. Dabo's only a threat to himself. His sister's likely in there too."

"Out of my hands." Stone chinned at the SWAT team leader. "Shots fired."

"Anybody crazy enough to be shooting at cops has to be MS-13, not Dabo." Stone didn't say a word. "Come on, what's it going to hurt? Give me a bullhorn. Let me try talking him out."

"How much time we got?" Stone asked the SWAT leader.

"You know the rules, Detective. Gunfire stops the clock on talk. Snipers are in position. My go teams are waiting for me to give the word."

"What happened to bringing in crisis negotiators?" Jess said.

"Mara's don't have a lot of history on listening to reason," Stone said.

"But Dabo and Blue Macaw are innocents."

Stone sucked his molar and called out to the SWAT leader. "Man here knows the Indian on the inside. Says he's likely more a hostage than a shooter. His sister could be in there too. She's not the one who's wanted. Maybe he can talk them out. Spare us the blowback if noncoms get hurt or worse."

The SWAT leader's expression didn't change. "Not going to happen. Someone in there yanked off a full clip at our people. We don't want the street to get the wrong lesson plan here. We're going in and they're coming out. In cuffs or body bags, their choice."

"There's a whole lot of media here," Jess said to him. "Cameras in the sky, reporters on the ground, not to mention a hundred citizens livestreaming on their phones. Oakland is trending and thumbs aren't pointing up for OPD."

"Do I look like I give a shit?" the SWAT leader said. "We do it by our book, not theirs."

Jess said to Stone, "Logan Riggins is on his way. He's called his lawyer." When the detective's eyes glinted with fury, he held up his hands. "Don't shoot the messenger."

The SWAT leader was talking into his headset again. "Sit report? Copy. On my count. Flash bangs first. Red and blue teams go, green and yellow standby. Snipers, I don't care if it's Grandma pushing a broom. It even looks like a weapon, drop her ass." He took a breath. "Three, two, one. Go! Go! Go!"

Glass crashed, lights flashed, smoke curled, and then there were bangs. Lots of them. The two-story building appeared to inhale then exhale. Six cops rushed the ground floor unit's front door with a hand-held battering ram. The same thing was taking place at the rear door. The snipers stationed on the rooftops of the house across the street never fired a round although the pops of handguns going off inside were easily heard.

It was over in a minute. "They're bringing them out," the SWAT leader said.

"How many down?" Stone said.

"One of theirs." His tone said it all. The victim wouldn't be getting up again. Ever.

A commotion erupted at the barricades. Someone was yelling Jess's name. Logan was trying to push through a wall of cops. Mattie Voss was at his side. So was a man dressed in a charcoal gray suit and purple tie. He was waving a piece of paper like a ticketholder trying to get through the crush at a rock concert.

"It's Logan and his lawyer," Jess said.

Stone cursed. "Best thing you can do right here and now? Tell him to stay the hell out while SWAT does their thing. He gets inside the ropes, he's gonna get stepped on and it won't be by accident."

A phalanx of SWAT cops marched out of the pink duplex. Several women and two men walked between them. All had their hands zip-tied behind them. Dabo was in the middle. He had a dazed look in his eyes and snail trails of blood running from his nostrils and ears.

Logan was shouting to Mattie. "Are you getting all this? Zoom in. Tight. Tighter. On Dabo's face. Get the blood. Beautiful. I couldn't have hoped for better. This will win our case."

He started waving his arms at Dabo and yelling in Wao. The only word Jess recognized was Mintaka. Dabo didn't answer, but cast his eyes toward the sky. It was unclear whether he meant Blue Macaw had been killed and gone to the spirit world or had flown the coop.

14

———

The Oakland jail was officially named Glenn E. Dyer Detention Facility, but cops and crooks alike called it "Dire Straits." The building was the color of wet cement and the only architectural relief was the tinted, black-framed windows the width of gun slits. Its downtown location was no accident. It sent the message that Oakland didn't use prison overcrowding as a reason to be soft on crime.

They brought Dabo and the others through the basement and took them upstairs. The lobby was bustling with ambulance chasers and bail bond agents. Logan met Jess there and told him his lawyer would be glued to Dabo's side during questioning and booking.

"We're blasting tweets, posts, and emails," Logan said. "My goal is to have a thousand people down here demanding Dabo's release."

Jess gestured to the far end of the lobby. "I wouldn't count on the DA springing Dabo anytime soon."

Pius Wheedling was striding toward them with Lyle Hunt walking point. Three men and a woman dressed in pinstriped suits hurried to keep up.

"CaliCo's sparing no expense. Wheedling's hired white shoe lawyers," Logan said. "He probably has lobbyists meeting with the DA, police commissioner, and mayor right now reminding them about the size of the company's political campaign war chest."

Wheedling brought his entourage to a halt in front of Logan and Jess. "We can be thankful law enforcement prevailed tonight. Now it is our responsibility to make sure justice is served."

Jess ignored the CaliCo lawyer, keeping his attention fixed on Hunt. Though the disgraced cop turned security chief had to be unarmed to have been able to pass through the jail's metal detector, he acted as if he were packing a gun or two.

Logan smiled at Wheedling. "You're making this too easy." He raised his phone and snapped a video. One of the accompanying lawyers protested. Hunt tried to snatch it away. Logan tapped the screen and the sound of a text being sent whooshed.

Hunt made another grab for the phone. Logan seized his wrist ever faster and held the phone out to the side. "Smile, Lyle. You're streaming live."

Wheedling placed a hand on Hunt's shoulder and nodded at the four lawyers. They closed ranks and escorted them away.

Logan's lawyer crossed the lobby and asked him what he missed.

"Saying hello to opposing counsel. What happened upstairs? Can we bail Dabo out?"

The attorney had a young face but gray hair. "That will be a challenge. They are portraying him as a flight risk. Still, it is not out of the question, but I will not be able to secure a decision until preliminary and arraignment. He is here for at least seventy-two hours."

"When can I speak to him?"

"He is being booked now. As his attorney, I am the only one he can talk with."

"I have to see him right away. Make it happen."

"It is inappropriate as well as imprudent. They would never allow it."

"What about Dabo's sister, Blue Macaw?" Jess said.

"His sister?"

"The raid was on a flop house run by the owner of Casa Clean, right? I think Blue Macaw lived there and that's why Dabo was there. Was she arrested or killed by SWAT?"

"All occupants have been identified. There was no Indian girl from Ecuador listed as either deceased or having been arrested."

"We need to talk to Dabo right away," Jess said to Logan. "Once Wheedling finds out about Blue Macaw, he'll sick Hunt on her. She'll disappear like she did back in the rainforest."

Logan saw the loose rocks and overhangs as clearly as Jess did. If Blue Macaw could alibi Dabo, Hunt would make sure she stayed lost for good.

"Get us in to see Dabo. Make it happen," he ordered the lawyer.

"I will see what I can do." He headed back to the booking room.

"What do you think happened to her?" Logan said.

"She wouldn't've been able to hide from SWAT coming through the doors," Jess said. "Who knows, maybe she was out buying a quart of milk."

"Go find her before CaliCo and the cops do."

"It'd be better to talk to Dabo first. He's still our best lead for getting a line on her."

Logan's phone pinged with a text from the lawyer. He was making progress, but it would be another hour before he had a decision.

"Let's go outside and see if Mattie has been able to generate a crowd," Logan said.

They exited the front doors and halted on the top step. TV news vans had set up their dishes and lights at the bottom. Dozens of people holding their phones were milling about. As soon as they saw Logan, cameras started rolling.

Jess moved to the side. Logan posed with a resolute look and then began fielding questions. As he spoke, Mattie joined Jess.

"He's heroic," she said. "He's David fighting Goliath. All this coverage, all those videos and photos livestreaming, he's delivering his message around the world right now. Dabo and oil drilling and the mistreatment of the Tarani people will be the lead topics on podcasts and talk shows all week. Longer if I have anything to do with it."

"You really think so?"

"Absolutely. People need a Logan Riggins now more than ever. People need hope with all the negativity in politics, the environmental disasters taking place around the world, and forced migration due to climate change. People need a leader."

"That's Logan up here. As soon as he wins Dabo's release and blocks CaliCo, he'll be on the first plane back to the Amazon."

"Don't count on it. Once he wins this fight, he'll see there are a hundred more causes that need him. He'll want to fight for them too. It's in his blood now. It's in his soul."

Logan finished delivering his speech and answering questions. Mattie hugged him. "You're a natural."

"My lawyer texted. Jess and I need to go back inside. They're going to let us talk with Dabo."

"Great. I'll go back to Berkeley and keep the team sending out blasts and making calls. We have to keep the pressure up. A staffer from one of California's senators called from Washington.

She wants a briefing. We're already getting interest from major donors. I got a call back from CNN too."

The lawyer escorted Logan and Jess to an elevator that took them up two floors. They passed through another metal detector and signed release forms. Next, they were ushered into a room with a long metal counter separated from an identical counter by a thick wall of acrylic.

"Use the telephone to talk to Dabo when they bring him in," the lawyer said. "All conversations are recorded so be very careful of what you say. Do not ask him anything if the answer could be misconstrued or self-incriminating."

Fifteen minutes later, a door on the other side of the see-through partition opened and Dabo shuffled in. A uniformed guard with a black mustache was close behind. The Tarani was wearing rubber flip-flops and a baggy orange jumpsuit. The sleeves were supposed to be short so a prisoner couldn't conceal a shank, but they hung past Dabo's elbows. A chain linked the manacles fastened around his wrists to a leather waist belt. His ankles were similarly manacled and chained. The guard directed him to a chair, pointed at the telephone handset, and then stepped back and stood with his back against the wall.

Logan picked up the phone. "I'm sorry. I should never have brought you here. I'm going to get you out. I promise."

Resignation had taken up residence in Dabo's eyes. "I did not do what they say I did. I did not kill Mr. Buckle. They do not believe me."

"I believe you," Logan said, his voice rising as if he were talking on a long-distance call with a bad connection. "We all do."

Jess said to Logan, "Tell Dabo the police have the machete he gave Buckle. Tell him now that they've fingerprinted him, they'll match his prints on it. They'll take a DNA sample too. We need to know what time he left the hotel the night of the gala and what he's been doing since. Tell him we need to find Blue Macaw."

Logan covered the phone's mouthpiece. "I'm not going to say any of that. He's already scared enough as it."

"He should be. This jail is bad, but wait until they transfer him to Santa Rita County lockup. It makes this look five-star."

"Shh. The cops are recording this."

"They already know about her. Remember? I told Stone. But you know one thing the cops don't know? How to speak Wao. You think they'll be able to find a translator anytime soon?"

Logan grinned. "That's the Sparks I remember. Always finds the right trail no matter what."

He put the telephone back to his ear and started off speaking in Spanish without saying anything of consequence. Then he switched to Wao. When Dabo replied, he spoke very slowly. Logan nodded to show he understood.

When the guard made a move toward Dabo, Jess told Logan to hurry.

Logan asked Dabo another question. He looked puzzled and then answered.

The guard's black mustache didn't twitch when he reached for Dabo, snatched the phone away, and hoisted him by the back of his orange jumpsuit.

The acrylic was too thick to hear Dabo's words, but Jess could read his lips. "Save my sister."

The lawyer said, "Do not say a word until we are outside."

They exited the building and crossed the street. Logan relayed what Dabo had told him. The bartender at the Altiplano had left him a message at the hotel. Dabo called him, found out where Mintaka was living, and went there. The reunion was painful because Mintaka was ashamed of what happened to her in Ecuador and why she was living in Oakland. She wouldn't give him details and he didn't ask. All he said was no one blamed her, everyone would forgive her, and that he'd come to California to bring her home to see their dying mother.

They stayed up all night reminiscing about their childhood. In the morning, another woman living in the house run by the Casa Clean bruja turned on the television while she was making breakfast. The screen filled with a photograph of Jim Buckle and the reporter said he'd been murdered with a machete. Dabo's passport photo appeared on the screen.

Logan asked Dabo why he hadn't turned himself in since he had an alibi. He told him Mintaka begged him not to and said they both had to run. When Dabo asked her why, she said she could be accused of killing Buckle too. She'd cleaned his house. Logan asked Dabo where she was when the raid went down. He said she'd gone to look for a coyote to smuggle them into Mexico.

"Does Dabo know where Blue Macaw is now?" Jess asked.

The lawyer put up his hand. "I cannot hear this." He walked out of earshot and waited.

"He's sure she's already on her way home," Logan said.

"Why does he think that?"

"Because that was their plan. If they got separated or one of them was arrested, the other would keep going. He said she'd made the trip up here from the homelands and he believes she can make it back."

"That's crazy. Even if she took buses as far as Panama, she'd still have to walk across the Darien Gap."

"She won't have to do either. There's no warrant for her yet. Once she gets to the Tijuana airport, she's gone."

"But she must realize she's Dabo's alibi. She's all that's standing between him and San Quentin."

"She's frightened and on the run. We need to find her and explain they're both each other's alibis."

"Even if she makes it to Ecuador, we might never find her."

"Except Dabo knows exactly where she's going."

"He told you?"

"Yes, right after I told him about Lyle Hunt, that if he got her before you did, he'd kill her."

"Before I get her?"

Logan held up his palms, the twin scars showing like stigmata. "You need to do it because I have to stay here and work on Dabo's defense. Get him bailed out. Raise money to pay for the lawyer. Fend off Pius Wheedling and his team of sharks. You can fly to Ecuador, find Mintaka, and stash her in a hotel in Coca. She won't even need to come back to Oakland to testify. My lawyer will fly down and depose her there on a video conference call so the Oakland DA can witness it. What do you say, Sparks? It'll be like old times. You and me against the rock."

Jess stared at him long and hard before answering. "You know me, Logan. I'm always game to climb. But you remember what's important, don't you? It's not knowing how far it is to the top so that you bring enough rope to reach it. It's knowing how far it is to the bottom so that you play out just enough in case you fall."

15

———

Oakland had Piedmont surrounded. The town was akin to a tiny European city-state bordered on all sides by a big, unruly nation. The wealthy residents guarded their social positions as fiercely as their property values, and, at night, a police cruiser was parked at the entrance of every street that led into it.

The Buckles lived in a red-tile-roofed, white Spanish-style mansion on a quiet street shaded by magnolias and lined with verdant front yards and circular drives. The front door was made of carved dark wood with a hand-forged iron knob, knocker, and hinges. The sound of the doorbell mimicked a California mission's call to Mass.

A middle-aged woman wearing a mint-green blouse and matching pants answered when Jess rang it.

"Jess Parks to see Mrs. Buckle. I called earlier."

"Please wait." She shut the door in his face, returning a few minutes later. "Please follow me."

The woman led him across a foyer with a floor made of square terra-cotta tiles. She walked with a limp. They continued down a wide hallway to a family room dominated by a home theater system complete with three rows of plush theater-style seats facing an enormous screen.

"Please wait." She closed the door behind her.

Minutes later the door opened and Clare Buckle entered. "I've already told the other detectives all I know. I'm not sure what more I can add."

When Jess had called earlier, he'd told her he was helping out on the investigation and had a few questions. He didn't correct her when she assumed he was with OPD. Nor was he surprised that she didn't recognize him from the gala.

"First, let me say I'm sorry for your loss," he said.

Clare didn't acknowledge his condolences, but gripped a wad of tissue tighter.

"I'll be brief. The night your husband died, he was staying at the Grand—"

"I explained that already. We were attending the Oakland Arts Foundation gala that night. I went home early with a migraine. He didn't want to wake me when he came home later and so he stayed at the hotel in a suite his company keeps there. It wasn't unusual for him to do that. He often worked late and stayed there when he had a breakfast meeting the next day or was going out of town on business. The company jet is hangared at the Oakland airport."

Clare wrung the wad of tissue. Her grief seemed as heavy as the diamond wedding ring on her finger. "Please, I've gone over this so many times. It's quite burdensome."

"I realize that, but something new has come up that we need to look into."

"I was told the man who killed my husband has been apprehended. What more do you need?"

"The man in custody is only a suspect. He's an Indigenous person from Ecuador."

"So?"

"What hasn't been reported yet is that he has a sister. There's reason to believe she once worked for you."

Puzzlement overtook her grief. "I don't understand. Esme has been our housekeeper for years. She's from Mexico, not Ecuador."

"Perhaps this other woman worked here in another capacity. A nanny for your children. Extra staff. A substitute when your regular housekeeper was on vacation or out sick. Her name is Mintaka. That translates to blue macaw in her langauge."

"I don't know anybody by that name. She's never been in my home."

"Are you sure?"

She took a deep breath. "My husband bought me this house as a wedding gift. We've lived nowhere else and Esme has been with us the entire time. She lives here. We do employ a nanny for our two daughters, but she's Jamaican. I don't see how either can be related to an Indian girl from the Amazon."

"Perhaps I can ask Esme if she knew her."

"Very well."

She stepped into the hall. The woman in the mint-green uniform was waiting right outside. They spoke in hushed voices and then both came back into the room.

Clare said to Esme, "The police officer is asking about a girl from the Amazon named Mintaka. He believes she may have worked for us. I don't remember anybody by that name. Could she have taken your place on one of your days off when we were away too or maybe she was hired as extra staff at one of our dinner parties?"

"No," Esme said. "I do not know any girl that name. When I am not here, my cousin Delores takes my place. Always. No Mintaka. Never."

"Thank you, Esme." When the housecleaner had limped away, Clare said curtly, "Are we through?"

Jess pictured Dabo in jail. He had no reason to lie about Blue Macaw telling him she knew Jim Buckle, that she'd cleaned his house, that she was so frightened if the information came out, she was willing to risk going on the run.

He looked around the room and took in all the trappings of wealth. He thought about the Tarani homelands. Missing girls. Blue Macaw. Oil drilling. Jim Buckle. The Amazon was the largest tropical rainforest on earth. It was too big for coincidences.

There was no pendulum swing Jess could take to get around the question he needed to ask. It was take it head-on or climb back down.

"One more thing," he said. "A confidential informant said your husband found the girl in Ecuador and brought her to Oakland. Did he?"

The anger came off Clare in a hot wave. Jess braced for a slap across the face, but instead she went to the front row of the theater-style seats and sat down. She pushed buttons on a remote control built into the armrest. The large screen filled with Jim Buckle's grin.

"Hello there, Clare Bear," his voice boomed from the surround-sound speakers. "How's my little darling on our wedding anniversary? I made this to tell you how much I love you."

Jim's face dissolved into a pan of Paris shot from atop the Eiffel Tower. As the camera came about, it stopped to focus on the face of a figure standing at the edge of the observation tower. It was Clare. She was a little younger.

As music poured from the speakers, Clare said from the front row, "I was a new hire in CaliCo's marketing department. Jim took an interest in what we were doing. He became a frequent visitor to our floor. One day he asked me out to dinner. He picked me up in a limo and we went straight to the airport and boarded his jet. He didn't tell me the restaurant was in Paris. I couldn't believe it. He was like that. Always full of surprises."

The Paris shot was followed by other scenes. Jim and Clare on safari in Africa. Playing golf in Dubai. Luxury hotels in New York, Rome, and Tokyo. The next sequence was of their wedding. It was an outdoor affair at a Napa winery. She wore white silk and he a shiny tuxedo. The cake had five layers, the guests numbered in the hundreds.

"We honeymooned in Bali," Clare said as the video continued to roll and bell-like sounds from a gamelan filled the room while lithe women dressed in traditional costumes danced across the screen. "Our daughter Zoe was born the following year."

The next couple of minutes were like any young family's home movies. An infant held in her mother's arms. Baby's first steps. A proud father carrying his young daughter on his shoulders. Birthday parties. Pony rides. The arrival of a baby sister. More birthday parties. More pony rides.

Clare was breathing heavily as she watched. In the flickering light of the big screen, Jess could see tears shining on her face as silvery as dew trapped on a spiderweb. She didn't bother to dry them with the wadded tissue. "Jim was such a good father. A wonderful, wonderful husband."

The final scene was a continuation of the opening one. Buckle had a huge grin. "There you are, darling. You've given me the best years of my life. There's not an oil rig that can drill deeper than my love for you, a tanker big enough to hold what I feel for you in my heart. I love you, Clare Bear. Happy anniversary."

Jess slipped out of the room as the screen faded to black and Clare's sobs replaced the soundtrack. He didn't look back as he headed for the airport.

16

———

From the plane's window, Coca looked as if it were sliding into the muddy Napo River. Buildings crowded the banks and the raw jungle beyond revealed open wounds from logging and slash-and-burn agriculture.

Wet heat hit Jess when he stepped onto the tarmac. Right behind was a one-two punch of eye-watering fumes from crude oil and gasoline. A purple rain fell. The drops didn't splatter when they hit; they wiggled like Jell-O. Puddles shined with iridescence and the walk to the terminal left the soles of his boots sticky with tar. The place was primed to go up in a giant fireball if someone tossed a lit cigarette.

A battered taxi with a plastic Virgin Mary careening on the dash took him into town. The driver kept his hand pressed to the horn as he weaved between buses and trucks while swarms of motorbikes buzzed in all directions. Jess's sense of direction failed as they zigzagged through a maze of potholed streets lined with sagging buildings that seemed held up by their bright-colored paint jobs alone. Rows of rusting corrugated metal shacks leaned against each other.

The taxi dropped him off at the Hotel La Rosa. It wasn't

painted red or pink or any shade in between. The front door led into a cramped lobby that smelled of a backed-up toilet. A man wearing a damp undershirt snored in a swivel chair behind the front desk, a half-empty bottle of pisco within reach.

"*Pardonme. Quiero un cuarto,*" Jess said, relying on high school Spanish. "Do you have a room for me? I emailed for a reservation earlier."

The man woke with a snort.

"A room," Jess said again. "*Un cuarto?*"

"*Si, si. Cuantas noches?*"

"One night, possibly two."

The man wiped his face with the hem of his undershirt and took a swig of the sickly yellow liquid from the bottle. "*Su pasaporte por favor.*" Jess gave it to him. "*Ah, Norteamericano.* You work for oil company? How come you not stay at camp? It free, no?"

"I'm a tourist."

"*Ah, ecoturista.* Everyone go to jungle lodges now. They expensive, no? Charge you *mucho dinero* to look at birds. But birds fly free, so why pay to see, no?" He chuckled and then handed over a key. "I keep your passport. Give it back when you check out."

"Where's the nearest restaurant?"

"Around corner."

"What's good there?"

"The beer."

Jess ordered chicken and rice for dinner, but stopped chewing after he saw what looked to be fur on a drumstick. He drank a bottle of Club, silently toasting Dabo and Logan before calling it a night.

In the morning, he walked to a nearby plaza, the reason he'd chosen Hotel La Rosa. The square offered no shade, not even from the vines creeping from the sizeable cracks in the concrete.

A man selling ice cream cones and popsicles from a pushcart with a bell on it had a parrot perched on his shoulder. The back of his shirt was splattered with guano.

Jess checked the address on his phone with the buildings that fronted the plaza. He found the right number painted above a darkened hallway that served as the entrance to a structure made of unpainted cement blocks. There was a door on the left and one on the right where the hall ended. He knocked on the one to the left.

The door opened a few inches. A woman peered out. Her hair was unbrushed and a red mask of face paint ran from temple to temple.

"*Hola. Me llamo es Jess Parks. Soy amigo de Dabo y Logan Riggins.*"

She said something in Wao and then switched to Spanish. "*No lo conozco. No conozco esos hombres.*"

"I realize you don't know me, but Dabo used to live here. Logan's visited too. He gave me your address. Did you get his email saying I was coming?"

The door cracked open wider, revealing a man with a feathered headband. "Who are you?" He spoke English with an unmistakable New York accent.

"Jess Parks. I'm from the US. Oakland, California."

"Stop harassing us. We have rights. We will file another lawsuit."

He started to close the door, but Jess blocked it with his boot. He held out his phone and clicked on the video of Dabo and Isabella dancing at the gala. "Dabo's my friend. Maybe you heard that he's in trouble. I'm trying to help him."

"Anybody can download a video."

"Yes, but look at the last frame." Jess froze it. It was a selfie with the two dancers and Logan.

"What do you want?"

"Logan said you could help me get to Dabo's homeland."

"Why do you want to go there?"

Jess glanced over his shoulder to make sure no one else was listening. "To find his sister."

"What is her name?"

"Mintaka."

"Mintaka?"

"Yes, Mintaka. Blue Macaw."

"She is dead. She went missing years ago."

"Dabo found her. She's alive, but now she's missing again."

His nostrils flared. "What did she call her pet porcupine?"

"Apaika. Moon, because it always had milk around its mouth when she nursed it with a baby bottle after its mother was killed by hunters. But it wasn't a porcupine. Apaika was an anteater."

Skepticism turned into a nod. "Come in."

The room was as plain as the outside of the building except for colorful woven blankets that were neatly folded at the feet of several sleeping mats made from braided palmetto. The woman gestured for Jess to sit on one while she sat on another. The man retrieved wooden bowls and a kettle. He filled the bowls with tea and gave one to Jess and another to the woman before sitting down cross-legged.

"We got Logan's email. He said nothing about Dabo or Mintaka. He is careful. We all must be. Oil companies and their private armies have spies."

"Logan told me you're one of the reasons he got involved with protecting Waorani homelands, that he heard of your work and came to Coca to help."

"Yes, we have been working with an American environmental lawyer for years. He is from New York. Taught me English. Some law too. Logan came and paid him. Paid us. Paid rent. Bought our food. Logan does many things for all Waorani people, no matter their tribal group, no matter where in the

Amazon they live. He respects our ways. Loves our land. He is Waorani in spirit. A warrior."

"Dabo must have told you about his sister when he was looking for her, how you knew about her anteater."

"He always talked about her. He also talked to Mintaka in his head. That way he kept her close." He slurped some tea from the wooden bowl.

"She's been living in Oakland, but now she's on her way home."

"Why?"

Jess explained. "She fled out of fear, but she's Dabo's alibi. She can get him released from jail. I need to get to the Tarani homelands. That's where Dabo said she'll be."

"Which camp? All Waorani tribes have many camps. People move from one to another to hunt, to fish, to gather food. Food gets scarce at one, they move to the next."

"Like rotating crops," Jess said. "There's a priest who lives on the Caiman River, Father Banana. He taught Dabo and Blue Macaw. He'll know which camp. Logan said you could help me hire a boatman to take me."

"It is possible, but dangerous. Criminals, bandits, drug smugglers, wild animals, and very bad water on that journey. Even more dangerous are the *soldados privado*. Private soldiers. They work for the oil, mining, and logging companies."

He stared into his bowl of tea. "Hundreds of people trying to protect the Amazon are murdered every year. A third are Indigenous people." He put the bowl down and shoved it aside as if it were filled with poison. "The soldados privado are killers. They have no hearts. They show no mercy."

"That's why I need a skilled boatman to take me. He must know the way of the river, avoid trouble, and bring Blue Macaw and me back to Coca so the lawyer can take her testimony. He also needs to keep it a secret."

The man spoke rapidly in Wao. Jess recognized a single Spanish word: "Miguelito." The woman frowned when she repeated it.

"Is Miguelito a boatman?" Jess said.

"Yes, but he is only interested in money."

"Does he know the way?"

"He has been down the Caiman River many times. He has a woman there. She is Achuar not Tarani."

"Can he be trusted?"

"Only if he fears you. Do not tell him your reason for the journey. Do not say Dabo and Mintaka's names."

"How much will he charge?"

"Whatever he says, you say half and show only half that and say you will give him the rest when the trip is over."

"How do I find him?"

"I will tell him you are coming. He will be on the riverbank near the big bridge. His river canoe is named *Anguila Eléctrica*."

"Does that mean it has a motor?"

He nodded. "But the name means something else."

The woman spoke to him in Wao.

"What did she say?" Jess said.

"She asks if you have a gun or spear."

"Miguelito's that dangerous?"

"Not as much as the caimans are."

Jess returned to the hotel to retrieve his gear. A man in jungle fatigues was sitting on his bed smoking a cigarette while two similarly dressed men cradling rifles slouched against the wall. The pair quickly came to attention when Jess entered and aimed their weapons at him. There were no military insignias on their fatigues.

"Whoa!" Jess said and raised his hands. "Whoa!"

The man sitting on the bed watched indifferently. Finally, he exhaled smoke out of both nostrils. "Whoa? You think we are horses? You think this is a joke?"

"Sorry. You surprised me, is all. Are you sure you have the right room?"

"Why do you think I make a mistake? Because I live here? Because I speak English with an accent? Why do you think I make a mistake? Tell me. Please."

"Since I've done nothing wrong, I wonder why you're here."

"Are you certain you have not broken the law?"

"Positive. I flew to Quito from the States yesterday, went through immigration there, and transferred to a flight here. I got in last evening. Take a look at my passport. It's stamped with a visa."

Jess reached into the front pocket of his jeans before remembering the desk clerk had it. The two men with rifles charged and slammed him against the wall.

The man sitting on the bed took the cigarette out of his mouth and flicked it. A few sparks skittered across the tiled floor when it hit. He stood and ground the butt out with the toe of his black combat boot.

"What is your name?" he said.

"Jess Parks. And you? What's your name and rank?"

"Why do you care?"

"So I know what to call you. Are you with the Ecuadorian military or Coca police?"

"You ask a lot of questions."

"I think you should show me some identification."

"The only thing you need to know is I am the captain and I am the one who asks the questions. Why did you come to Coca?"

"I'm a tourist."

"I ask you again. Why are you here?"

"To look for wildlife in the rainforest."

"Yes? Where will you do that?"

"At one of the jungle lodges."

"Which one?"

"I haven't picked one yet."

"You do not have a reservation?"

"Not yet. I was going to try and find one that had a last-minute cancellation. You know, fly standby."

The captain lit another cigarette. He blew the smoke in Jess's face. "Standby?" He turned to one of the men and asked him in Spanish if he knew the word *standby*.

The man shook his head. The captain asked the other one and got the same response.

"They do not know that word. But I do."

He ordered the two men to take a step back as he moved closer to Jess. Then he slapped him hard across the face, backhanding his cheek as he followed through.

Jess staggered, but didn't raise his hands in defense.

"That is what *standby* means here. Now, enough of your lies. I ask you one more time. Why are you here?"

"Ecotourism. I want to look at birds."

The captain unholstered his sidearm and pressed the barrel against Jess's nose. "I ask you again. Why are you here?"

"To see the birds."

The captain's knee came up with surprising speed. Jess's stomach heaved and sirens went off as he tried to clasp his crotch. He started to fall to the ground, but the two men grabbed his arms and held him up.

The captain rocked back and forth in his combat boots. He blew smoke in Jess's face again.

"Final time. Why did you come to Coca?"

"To save the rainforest. To stop oil drilling."

"Finally, the truth." The captain clamped the cigarette between his teeth and reached into the breast pocket of his jungle fatigues. He pulled out Jess's passport. "Of course, I already knew that. I know all about you. Do you think I am stupid?"

He stuck the passport back in his pocket and extracted a folded piece of paper. He unfolded it and held it up. It was a printout of Dabo's passport photo.

"I know all about *el salvaje*. The savage. I know all about his sister. Where is she hiding?"

"I don't know."

"You are lying."

"I'm not."

The captain dropped the photo. Jess watched it flutter to the ground.

"The savages are criminals. Terrorists. Communists. If you help them, then you are a criminal too. The punishment is severe."

He slugged Jess in the solar plexus and followed with a kidney punch.

Jess couldn't cry out or say anything. He was too busy wheezing for air and swallowing blood.

"Where is Dabo's sister, Mintaka?" the captain said.

All Jess could do was tell the truth. "I wish I knew."

He closed his eyes, waiting for the blows that were sure to follow.

17

———

Jess puked when he came to. That did little to slow the spinning. He was lying on a hard, wet floor. He touched the wetness and brought his finger to his lips. It was only vomit, not blood.

He pulled himself to a sitting position. His muscles ached. His nerve endings twitched. His arms and legs were stiff. The last time he felt so beat up was on a climb in the Pinnacles. A ledge collapsed and he fell thirty feet. The scabs took weeks to heal, the sprained ankle and cracked ribs longer.

A broken beam of light shined above him. He crawled toward it and struggled to stand. Finally on his feet, he crossed his arms tightly against his stomach to keep from puking again.

The light was coming through a small barred window that had been cut eye-level in a metal door. He peered out and saw what looked to be a hallway lined with similar doors. A jail, he thought, and then remembered coming to when the cigarette-smoking captain's two men were dragging him out of Hotel Las Rosas. They shoved him into a jeep with no military markings and drove to a walled compound. The gates had no signs. No

Ecuadorian flag was flying and no uniformed sentries guarded the entrance.

They frogmarched him into a sweltering room and sat him on a metal folding chair. Bright spotlights were aimed at his face. He could sense other people standing behind him, but the ropes that bound him to the chair prevented him from turning around. The captain sauntered in and resumed interrogating him.

"Where is Mintaka? Who helped her escape? How do you know she returned to Ecuador? What do you know about Señor Buckle's murder? What evidence do the Oakland police have?"

Each question was punctuated with a slap, each answer with a punch. The captain kicked the legs of the folding metal chair and sent Jess tumbling onto the cement floor if he didn't like the answer.

Now, looking out the barred window in his cell, he could hear voices coming from down the hallway. They were speaking English. One sounded like the captain. He'd heard the other voice before, but struggled to picture the speaker.

His head cleared enough to remember what happened during the interrogation. The captain kept insisting on the truth and Jess kept insisting he was telling it, that he was trying to prove Dabo innocent, that if he didn't believe him, then give him a lie detector test.

The captain's smile revealed tobacco-stained teeth. "If you insist."

He ordered Jess to be untied and his boots and socks removed. They stood him up, pushed his feet into a bucket of dirty water, and forced him to grab a metal bar hanging from a chain in front of him to keep from falling down.

It wasn't out of politeness. It was attached to a truck battery with jumper cables.

Jess slumped back down on the cell's wet floor. He drew his

knees up to his chin and thought of home. He could see dawn breaking on the Oakland Estuary. He could see himself paddling *Pursuit* past Jack London Square, past the cargo ships and rows of cranes at the marine terminals, and under the Golden Gate Bridge. He could see the swirling, foamy waters of the Potato Patch that guarded the entrance to San Francisco Bay, the tops of the swells of the Pacific on the other side, and the outline of the Farallon Islands thirty miles beyond.

He could see his kayak blades dipping and sweeping and rising. Over and over again. And then he was there, in the lee of the largest island. His presence spooked the cormorants and gulls nesting in the crags of the wind-carved, wave-slapped sea stack. They took wing and circled over him.

He pulled his paddle up and drifted. He thought of his parents who'd drowned when their sailboat capsized there. He thought of his grandfather who'd taken over raising him, whose ashes resided in the coffee can wedged between his legs.

Balancing his paddle on *Pursuit's* deck, he picked up the humble urn and poured the contents over the side. The ashes met the water, but didn't immediately sink. They turned into a long, undulating cloud that glowed against the blue-green of the water. It dipped and swirled just below the surface as if flying. He reached over the side, cupped water, and splashed his face, making sure to get it in his nose and mouth. As his grandfather's spirit swam deeper to join those of his parents, a feeling of peace came over him. "I'm not lost," he said. "I'm home."

Jess said it again in the cell. "I'm not lost. Wherever I am, wherever I go, I'm home. I carry it with me. I carry them. I'm not lost."

The cell door swung open and a boot kicked his shin. A bright light flashed and he tried to shield his eyes. Gruff voices barked at him while hands that smelled of old fish and onions yanked him upright and dragged him down the hall. His tormentors came to a stop and forced him to stand. His head spun and he fought to focus, vowing to himself he'd do everything he could to fight off the coming blows.

The captain came into view. He was sitting at a desk, smoking a cigarette, and flicking the ashes into a green metal ammo box that overflowed with butts. Jess recognized his passport next to the ammo box. The captain pushed it toward him.

"You can go now."

Jess didn't know whether it was a trick or not. A dull pain burned in his groin, his cheeks stung, and his nerve endings still felt like he'd stuck a wet finger into a light socket. He wanted to ask the captain why the sudden change of heart, what did he say to convince him to let him go, and if the American's voice he'd heard was Lyle Hunt's, and whether CaliCo's security chief had stayed in the shadows during the interrogation or was the one who connected the jumper cables to the truck battery.

He said none of those things. Instead, he pointed to his bare feet. "What about my boots? Are they free to leave too?"

18

―――――

The desk clerk at Hotel La Rosa was slouching in his swivel chair and working on a fresh bottle of pisco. He sat up with surprise when Jess staggered in.

"You're back!"

"Why wouldn't I be?"

"They ... they ... You don't stay here last night or night before, no?"

"And you did nothing to try and stop the men who took me?"

"Soldados privado," he said, as if that explained everything. "You're lucky. Your amigos bought your release, no?"

"What makes you think that?"

"If they hadn't, you'd still be there, no?"

"Did you see them? My *amigos*."

"Maybe." He held out his palm.

"Was one wearing glasses with yellow lenses?"

He snatched his hand back. "I make mistake. Saw nothing. I swear it."

It was all the confirmation Jess needed. Lyle Hunt had been there. When the captain couldn't beat Blue Macaw's whereabouts out of him, Hunt figured it was best to cut Jess loose and follow him. It'd be more fun that way too.

"I'm checking out. I already have my passport. But you know that already since you gave it to the captain."

"But you owe me for three nights?"

"Take it up with the captain."

Jess's room had been ransacked. His clothes were scattered, the bed overturned, and the dresser drawers pulled out. He hobbled into the bathroom. There was blood in his piss. When he looked in the mirror, bruised cheeks and raccoon eyes stared back.

He packed his gear and went down to the river with little confidence Miguelito would've waited. As he searched for *Anguila Eléctrica*, he didn't ask any of the other boatmen to take him. Lyle Hunt had plenty of breadcrumbs to follow as it was.

The captain's beating and the beating of the tropical sun were taking their toll as he walked carefully to keep from slipping on the muddy banks and sliding into the big brown river. He was about to give up when he saw an orange hull tied up at the water's edge.

"*Pursuit!*"

He quickened his pace, not even trying to make sense of how his kayak could've magically appeared four thousand miles from home.

Only it wasn't a kayak. It was an eighteen-foot wooden river canoe with the words *Anguila Eléctrica* painted on the side. The bow was painted with dark eyes and cloudy pupils poised over fat red lips pulled back to expose jagged rows of pointy teeth.

A man was curled up on a thwart beneath a tattered canvas canopy. Beams of sunlight poured through the Swiss cheese-like holes.

Jess called to him. "Miguelito." No response. He tried again. Still nothing. "Miguelito!" he shouted.

"Aiee!" The boatman jumped to his feet and drew a knife from his belt.

"Miguelito?" Jess said, realizing why the diminutive *ito* had been added to his name. The boatman was barely five feet tall.

"Who wants to know?"

"I'm the American."

"You're late. You owe me for the days I waited. Even if we don't go, you pay. Time is money."

"I'll pay for those days and the ones ahead, but only the going rate. Half now and half when the trip's completed."

"Show me the money."

"Show me you can pilot a boat."

"Gringos. I took some to a jungle lodge once. They vomited in my beautiful *Anguila Eléctrica* the whole way there and didn't even give me a tip."

"I'll tip you twenty percent, but only if you can get me to where I need to go in record time."

"Then why are you wasting time talking? We go now. *Ahorita!*"

With that, he pulled the starter cord to the outboard. The propellor was attached to the motor by a four-foot-long extension. The blades whirred and the water churned as Jess threw his gear on board.

In seconds they were pulled into the main current of the muddy Napo River and began the journey into the deepest part of Ecuador's Amazon.

Miguelito cooed to his boat while he steered. "My sweet, my beautiful, my powerful *Anguila Eléctrica.*"

"What does her name mean?"

"Electric eel." He explained that the river was filled with the nearly blind and lungless creatures. They reached six feet long and packed the equivalent of six hundred volts, enough to kill a man.

After his encounter with the truck battery, Jess had no desire to go swimming no matter how hot the sun broiled.

The Napo was flat and wide, but swift. It rose and fell as much as twenty feet in a week depending on how much snow melted in the Andes to the west. The overflows from the seasonal flooding spread three miles across and turned vast stretches of the rainforest into shallow lakes the color of tea.

Miguelito and Jess weren't the only ones traveling on the river. Flotillas of river canoes and flat-bottom boats hauling passengers and everything from stalks of green bananas to monkeys tethered in wooden cages traveled in both directions. Indigenous people too poor to buy outboard motors paddled dugouts carved from tree trunks. Steamers whose decks were crowded with passengers and cattle alike sputtered downriver for the Amazon River that would take them into Peru and then Brazil and all the way to the Atlantic Ocean.

As the *Anguila Eléctrica* rounded a bend, a helicopter flew overhead. The chopper was green but had no military markings on it, not even an Ecuadorian flag. It dipped low as it passed, climbed, banked, and headed back until it was hovering directly overhead, its twirling blades pushing the water into a frothy pattern like a giant white carnation.

Miguelito raised his hand and gave a friendly wave while Jess, who was sitting amidship beneath the canvas canopy, ducked and studied his feet. After a couple of minutes, the chopper continued following the river.

Jess asked if there was a military outpost nearby.

"They're not regular army," Miguelito said. "They're *sicarios*. Hitmen. Mercenaries. If they're not paid by the oil drillers, then they are by loggers or drug smugglers." He spat. "They do what they want, kill who they want."

"Doesn't the real army ever go after them?"

"How? The jungle's too big and the sicarios have bigger guns also."

"There's no military outpost out here?"

"At the border with Peru. But the border's like the river. Always changing sides. Someone's always shooting at someone there."

Hours later they came to a clearing on the riverbank. Palapas were perched on stilts near the river's edge. Miguelito guided the canoe toward the thatched huts. He shut off the engine and the *Anguila* glided to shore, its toothy bow sliding up onto the slick bank. A passel of kids came running out. He threw them a line and they fought over who got the honor of tying the boat off.

Miguelito rubbed his stomach, which stuck out like a soccer ball had been stuffed beneath his T-shirt. "Hungry?"

They climbed the slippery bank to the largest palapa. A shirtless man wearing nappy black polyester pants cut off below the knees stood in the doorway. Miguelito brushed past him without a word and entered. It was a single room with a rough plank floor and a crude wooden table in the middle. Sleeping mats lined the floor against the wall. A smoke-blackened fifty-five-gallon oil drum that had been cut lengthwise and fashioned into a stove stood in the corner. Its stovepipe was made out of topless and bottomless tin cans soldered together. A woman wearing a flower print skirt and nursing a naked baby stood next to it.

Miguelito boosted himself onto a homemade stool. He waved at the stool across from him. "Sit."

When Jess did, a furry creature scampered over his feet. It skittered across the floor and ducked behind a cardboard box. Miguelito hopped off his stool and waddled over. He reached behind and hoisted a guinea pig by the scruff of its neck.

"You like them?" he said.

"Never had one—"

Before Jess could add "as a pet," Miguelito snapped the guinea pig's neck. He tossed the lifeless rodent to the woman. She held it over a metal bowl and slit it from anus to mouth, making circular cuts around the neck and legs as if tracing a collar. With one swift yank she turned the guinea pig inside out, stripping off its fur in a single piece. She wrapped the tiny carcass in a banana leaf and placed it on top of the embers smoldering inside the oil drum.

"You will like *cuy asado*," the boatman said.

After lunch, Miguelito stretched out on a palmetto mat for a siesta. Jess went outside, scattering a gaggle of scrawny hens that were scratching around for bugs. A red rooster with a lizard pinched between his beak strutted by. Two pigs grunted in a pen made of sharpened sticks. Plantains, yams, and manioc grew in a small garden.

Several acres of land that had been slashed and burned spread behind the compound. Green stalks of sugar cane sprouted among the blackened stumps. Jess picked up a handful of dirt and rubbed it between his fingers. It was only a few acres, but there were millions of others exactly like it. The Amazon was dying a death of a thousand cuts.

They pushed on after Miguelito's siesta and spent the night at another family riverside encampment. They were served fish, not guinea pig, for dinner. The second day on the river started much like the first. The sun beat down. The air grew hot and sticky. The river began a long, slow series of S turns.

They came around a bend and the Napo was transformed into the River Styx. Smoke, flames, and grinding noise had turned the rainforest into a burning hell. Oil drilling derricks crowded the riverbank, shuddering and banging as their rotating bits screamed and whined. A thick, black pall of smoke from their diesel engines hung in the air. Pipes snaked between the rigs as oil sprayed from joint after leaky joint. Open pits swirled with brown goo the consistency of chocolate pudding. The toxic smell from drilling wastes burned eyes and throats alike.

"Aiee!" Miguelito cried as clots of crude oil bumped up against the river canoe's bow. "Look what these turds are doing to my poor beautiful *Anguila.*"

A couple of Quonset huts stood in a large clearing in the middle of the drilling derricks. Chain-link fencing topped by concertina wire surrounded them. A green helicopter with no insignias was parked on a nearby landing pad. Jess figured it must be the one that had flown over them earlier. Guards dressed in jungle fatigues and carrying automatic weapons patrolled the fence line. As the river canoed passed them, Miguelito smiled, waved, and muttered, "May a poisonous snake bite you in the ass."

At the end of the row of derricks, a pair of yellow bulldozers chewed into a wall of vegetation. The sound of chainsaws drowned the call of birds. One enormous tree after another toppled like dominoes.

Two miles past the drill site the river split in two. Miguelito steered toward the smaller fork.

"The Caiman. Keep your hands in the boat." He laughed nervously.

The river narrowed and in some stretches the rainforest pushed in on both sides and the tree canopy formed a tunnel. Ringed kingfishers springboarded off low-hanging branches and plunged into the river, snapping up fish with razor-like bills. Colorful tropical birds turned bushes into feathered orchids. Orioles peered from long basket nests that drooped inches above the water. Flocks of screeching parrots drowned out the burble of the river only to be drowned out by the haunting howls of horned screamers.

Miguelito had his hands full steering the *Anguila.* Though

the river was running high, the dark water was awash with bubbling cauldrons and vicious whirlpools stirred by submerged snags. Hundred-foot-long ceiba trees uprooted by floods or felled by loggers waved their branches from the river's bottom. The ghostly wooden fingers snatched at the prop, wrenching the *Anguila* violently, swinging the boat broadside. Water flooded over the gunwale.

Miguelito swore as he fought the tiller, trying to bring the craft around as it started to swamp. Jess grabbed a rusty paint can used as a bail bucket and went to work while throwing his weight on the upriver side to keep them from capsizing. The boatman finally got the bow pointed downriver again. He chinned at Jess's boots and cheered. Dozens of shiny fish flopped beside them.

"Look! The *Anguila*, my beauty, my love. She catches us dinner."

They kept chugging down the river late into the afternoon. The sun slid into the horizon, emblazoning the sky as scarlet as any macaw that winged overhead. When the sunset melted into indigo, Miguelito switched on an automobile headlight wired to a car battery.

"Keep a lookout. We don't want to sink now."

The light shone onto the shallower waters along the riverbank. Pairs of unblinking yellow eyes gleamed back.

Miguelito's laugh turned high-pitched. "Hello, you big ugly lizards."

"Aren't we going to make camp?" Jess said.

"And sleep with them? Not me." He gave the motor a goose. "We're close to the mission now."

"Father Banana's?"

"Yes. There's a palapa on stilts where we can string our hammocks. Caimans don't climb ladders."

They continued motoring through the dark. The mosquitoes

sounded louder than the *Anguila's* outboard. Jess started thinking about Dabo and how many times he'd made the same trip. He wondered if Logan's lawyer had succeeded in getting him bailed out. He knew Detective Stone would still be looking for leads, nailing down the ones he did have, testing both facts and theories as they came up. He tried to imagine what Blue Macaw looked like, and, if he succeeded in finding her, what he could say that would convince her to return with him to Coca.

A large thump followed by a sharp curse returned him to the moment. Miguelito cursed.

"What's wrong?" Jess said.

"We hit something. The prop isn't turning. The shaft broke."

"Steer us toward shore. We'll have to tie off and deal with it in the morning."

Jess grabbed the car headlight and aimed it at the riverbank. Miguelito pushed the tiller, trying to follow the beam. The bow wouldn't stay on course without the churning prop. The current quickly pushed the boat broadside.

"Aiee! We're going to drown."

Jess set the headlight down, grabbed the bowline, and dove. The water was ink black and warm as soup. He didn't stay under for long, but got his head up and began kicking for shore. The pockets of his shirt and jeans soon ballooned with silt. He wrapped the rope around his wrist and kept swimming.

The *Anguila* trailing behind jerked from side to side, tightening and then loosening the bowline, making the rope burn across his shoulders as he clawed for shore. Something brushed up against him, but he couldn't tell if it was a tree trunk, electric eel, or giant catfish. All he knew was it couldn't have been a caiman. If it was, he'd already be dead.

Jess finally reached the bank, grabbed a handful of tree roots poking out of the slippery mud, and pulled himself out. He crashed through the understory and ran the line around a tree trunk. It pulled taut and twanged. He braced one foot against the tree and began hauling the rope hand over hand. It was heavier than any climbing partner he'd ever hoisted, but he brought the boat to shore.

Miguelito scrambled out, cursed, and kicked the *Anguila's* hull. "*Puta!* You ungrateful whore."

The headlight revealed an impenetrable wall of trees. "Looks like we're stuck for the night," Jess said. "Should we sleep in the boat or climb a tree?"

Miguelito howled. "Only if you're a monkey."

He rummaged around, found something, and then switched off the car headlight. The tropical night wrapped them in black velvet.

Miguelito slapped metal. A weak beam turned on. He slapped the flashlight again. The beam shone in Jess's eyes.

"Sorry," the boatman said as he brushed past him. A case of beer was tucked under his arm.

"Where are you going?"

"You want to go to Father Banana's mission? Start walking. It's not far."

Jess followed the flashlight. It stopped at a tangled wall of plants and creepers. "How are we going to get through that?"

Miguelito laughed as he plunged straight into it. "Sometimes it pays to be small."

19

———

They reached the mission sometime after midnight and strung their hammocks inside an empty palapa. Miguelito promptly chugged three beers and passed out, his snores adding to the drone of cicadas and a million other insects that made the rainforest the noisiest place on earth. Jess spent a restless night, and it didn't have anything to do with the inability to straighten his back in the hammock. Every time he drifted off, he started having the same dream: a chopper piloted by the captain was bearing down on him with Lyle Hunt firing a .50 caliber machine gun from the open bay.

He gave up trying to sleep as his thoughts returned to Oakland. Logan wouldn't be the only one playing the court of public opinion game. Pius Wheedling would've paraded Clare Buckle and her two daughters in front of the cameras for all to see. The grieving widow, the heartbroken children—a gruesome family tragedy that would fuel the public's fear for their own safety. The threat of vigilante justice against Dabo would be high, in or out of jail, should he make bail.

That made the responsibility of finding Blue Macaw weigh even heavier. The success of locating her in the vastness of the

Amazon was far from guaranteed. She would be on the move, traveling with the Tarani from one seasonal camp to the next. Even if he found the right one, what could he say to make her trust him and go back upriver to Coca? Why would the tribe even allow a cowori to take her away?

The only thing for certain, it was a race against time to find her before Hunt and his private army of mercenaries did. Jess was on foot. They had a helicopter. They might have planes and drones fitted with cameras and thermal imaging devices like the ones Search and Rescue used to locate lost people and hidden bodies. They might even have access to government satellites. Anything was possible with an oil company footing the bill.

A screaming piha sounded reveille as soon as dawn broke. Jess swung out of the hammock and followed a path that led across a clearing to a semicircle of palapas. From behind them came a thumping sound. A skinny man with a yellow face was dribbling a basketball on a patch of dirt. He wore baggy shorts and a sleeveless tank top. A wooden crucifix hung on a leather cord looped around his neck. The priest aimed and fired at a bottomless rattan basket that had been nailed to the trunk of a palm tree. The rattan rustled when the ball dropped through.

"That's what I call a real basket," Jess said.

The missionary turned, smiled, and stuck out his hand. It was yellow too. "I'm Father Bernardo, but everyone calls me Father Banana."

"Jess Parks. Sorry, we didn't ask if it'd be OK to hang our hammocks last night. We didn't want to wake anyone. Our boat broke down upriver and we had to hike for it. The boatman is still asleep."

"No one needs to ask permission to stay here. We are a mission. We're not in the business of turning people away."

"Well, thanks again."

"You sound American."

"I am."

"Would you like breakfast? We have chicken eggs and coffee. A real American breakfast for a real American."

They walked over to a table set beneath a canopy made of palm fronds. A wood-burning stove made of hardened mud stood nearby. An Indigenous woman wearing a cotton shift with red embroidery was stirring a smoke-blackened pot. She clutched a young child to her hip. Two more kids hid behind her, sneaking peeks at Jess.

"Do you want milk with your coffee?" Father Banana asked.

"Black's fine."

"I read everyone in America drinks their coffee with milk. Foamed milk. Almond milk. Oat milk. Soy milk. Flavored milk. So many milks. We only have powdered here in the Amazon. Most of the country's dairies are in the Andes." He paused. "Is it true there are nearly two hundred Starbucks in New York City?"

"Wouldn't surprise me."

Father Banana glanced at the woman and smiled. She brought over coffee and then went back to the wood stove and cracked eggs in a cast-iron skillet.

Jess asked how long he'd lived at the mission.

"Twenty years. Twenty-one." He moved his lips as if counting. "No, twenty-two years. Yes, come Easter."

"Do you ever leave?"

"Leave?"

"Go to Coca or Quito for a conference or vacation. Go home to visit."

"This is home."

The eggs snapped and sizzled as they fried. Smoke curling from the stove escaped through the canopy's fronds. Geckos clinging to the palm trunks chirped.

"It hasn't always been that way," Father Banana said. "When I first arrived from attending seminary in Guayaquil, I didn't think I'd last a month. Now I can't remember living anywhere else."

"Time flies when you're busy saving souls."

"I leave that to God. I'm too busy saving lives. Lack of faith isn't the cause of the Tarani's problems. Their damnation comes from the cowori."

"Outsiders," Jess said. "Dabo taught me that word."

"Dabo?"

"Yes."

"You know Dabo? You saw him in Coca?"

"No, in Oakland, California, where I'm from. He was there with Logan Riggins who's an old friend."

"Both are friends of mine too." His head started bobbing. "Oakland, you say? The Golden State Warriors. So many NBA championships. Steph Curry, small in stature but giant of game. I've always dreamed of going to the Coliseum and seeing him play."

"The Warriors only play exhibition games there now. They moved to San Francisco. The Oakland Raiders football team has left too. Again. This time they moved to Las Vegas. The A's baseball team is right behind."

"That's a shame. Sports is like religion. Both require faith and commitment. Both teach the importance of embracing humility. When a team abandons a community, the people lose a way to bond in victory and defeat."

"I'm getting the impression you didn't receive an email or phone call from Logan about me coming here?"

"There is no telephone service here and our computer is broken. We haven't had Internet for months. Mail comes very infrequently. Would Logan have told me why you've come all this way and why Dabo is with him in Oakland?"

The woman finished frying the eggs. She slid them onto

plates and placed them in front of Jess and Father Banana and added a ladleful of black beans.

Jess waited until she left. "He probably wouldn't have out of concern someone might be listening to the call or reading your email."

"Who would do that and why?"

"Because of why I'm here. Dabo's in trouble. A man was murdered. The police think Dabo did it and arrested him."

"He couldn't do such a thing. Dabo is a man of compassion."

"He's innocent, all right. Logan and I are positive of it. I'm here to help prove it."

"What help is here?"

"Dabo's sister, Mintaka. Blue Macaw. She's been living in Oakland. He was with her the night of the murder. After he was arrested, he told us she fled and was going home to the Tarani homelands."

"And is that why you're here? To find her and take her back to the US?"

"Find her, yes, because she's Dabo's alibi and can prove his innocence. But not to take her back to Oakland, only to Coca. Logan will send his attorney there to get her statement. He'll have Ecuadorian lawyers with him and arrange to have her testify on a video conference call with the authorities in Oakland so they can ask her questions."

"And the lawyer couldn't do that here?"

"Like you said, there's no telephone service." Jess held up his phone. "See, no bars, no signal. Logan said he got satellite Internet where he lives on the Napo River, but that's closer to Coca. From what Dabo told me, the Tarani homelands don't even have electricity."

The priest stayed quiet.

"I need your help, Father. I need to know where the Tarani

are this time of year and which camp Blue Macaw is likely to be at."

"What makes you think I know?"

"Because you've lived here twenty-two years. It's your home. The Tarani are your friends, your family, your flock."

The priest glanced at the woman who'd resumed stirring the pot of beans. Without saying a word to her, she nodded and gathered the children and disappeared into one of the palapas.

Father Banana clasped his hands, bowed, and started praying. Howler monkeys bellowed in the distance. A toucan perching on a nearby branch started croaking. It sounded like a frog. Minutes passed. Jess's impatience grew. He took a deep breath.

"The man who was murdered was the head of CaliCo Oil, the company that's poised to win the right to drill on Tarani homelands. You know what that will do. Cowori will come and Tarani will die."

The priest didn't stop praying.

"Dabo isn't the only one in danger. Blue Macaw is too. While she lived in Oakland, she'd worked as a housecleaner at the victim's home. It's the reason she fled when the police arrested Dabo. She feared they'd think she was guilty and arrest her too. Now the oil company has sent a man down here to find her. He didn't come to get her testimony or arrest her. He came to kill her. And he'll kill anyone who gets in his way."

Father Banana unclasped his hands, picked up a long-bladed knife, and pulled a papaya from a basket set on the table.

"People come to the rainforest and pretend to be one thing when they are really another." He sliced the orange fruit into pieces. "They say they're birdwatchers, but they're really looking for oil. They say they're scientists studying the trees, but they're really road builders mapping the forest. They say they're doctors come to help the Indigenous, but they're really from pharmaceutical companies conducting drug trials on people without their permission."

Father Banana pointed the blade at Jess. Sweet, thick juice dripped from it and splashed the table. "How do I know you're not the man you speak of?"

Jess showed the dance video from the gala again, freezing it on the selfie.

"Dabo told me about you, Father. How he and Blue Macaw lived here for a while. How she was faster than him at everything you taught them—quicker to learn Spanish and English. She was faster than Dabo at running and climbing trees too, at everything but paddling a dugout because she would always stop to look at birds. Dabo said that after she disappeared, every time he came back home, flocks of blue macaws would gather overhead as he neared and flew the rest of the way with him."

"It's true," Father Banana said. "They do the same for me when I visit in my dugout. The blue macaws are a gift from God, telling me Mintaka is still alive. And when I received her first letter, I knew the birds had been right and God was truly benevolent."

"The first letter? Do you mean the one she wrote to her mother and Dabo?"

Father Banana started to speak, but then quickly picked up a slice of papaya and ate it, wiping the juice off his yellowed chin with the back of his hand.

"I need to know if you believe in God. Do you go to church?"

Jess looked beyond the clearing where pink and purple bromeliads festooned the green walls of thick vegetation. A hummingbird with a throat that blazed like fire sucked nectar from a pitcher plant. Spider monkeys squealed and squeaked among a canopy of trees dancing with sunlight.

"I can't think of a holier place than right here. The way the light shines, the colors sparkle, it's more beautiful than any stained glass window in any church I've ever been in. So many different forms of life? They can't be here by accident, can they? Seeing it, being here, I get the same feeling I do when I'm rock climbing. When I reach the top and look down, all around, and up, see the beauty, feel the light, I can't imagine there's a more sacred place. I can't imagine being any closer to the Divine than in that moment."

Father Banana took the cross hanging from his neck and kissed it. "It's the same for me. The rainforest is my temple, not some grand cathedral made of stone and gold paid for by poor people."

He sighed. "Mintaka's story is hers to tell. She told me little by little in the letters she wrote me as she searched for understanding and forgiveness. And then she told me all of it in the sanctity of the mission's confessional two days ago." He pointed toward a tree that towered above all others. "There, beside that ancient shihuahuaco. It's sacred to Indigenous tribes throughout the Amazon, including the Tarani."

Father Banana sighed again. "Forgive me for not being forthcoming that I already knew about Mintaka and Dabo and Oakland."

"But you had to be sure about me."

"Yes, because Mintaka is in more danger than you know because of what happened to her here years ago."

"The Amazon's too big for coincidences," Jess said.

"What?" Father Banana said.

"Something I've been telling myself. Jim Buckle, the head of CaliCo Oil, the man who was murdered, he had something to do with Blue Macaw's disappearance, how she wound up in Oakland, didn't he?"

The priest frowned and bowed his head again. "Mintaka came to me as a penitent, to confess her transgressions, to receive mercy and divine forgiveness, to partake in the holy sacrament of healing. I cannot and will not reveal what took place between her and God. It's not my right."

"I understand, but can you help me find her, help me save her?"

"I can and will. But let me ask you this, do you know who killed Jim Buckle?"

"I wish I did. It could be any number of people. It could've even been a stranger, a robber or someone who got the wrong room in the hotel and was there to kill someone else. A very competent homicide detective is working on it, but Oakland's a big city and I'm afraid that with a suspect already in jail, his bosses will redirect toward solving new crimes."

"Then we must hurry and get you to Mintaka."

Two hours later, Father Banana and Jess stood on the bank of the Caiman River. The *Anguila Eléctrica* rested onshore with its stern hoisted by a rope looped over a tree limb.

"Look at the shaft," Miguelito moaned. "It's broken. My poor beautiful *Anguila*."

Jess asked if he could fix it.

The stubby boatman jutted his chin. "I can fix anything, but for this, I need a welding torch."

"The oil drillers will have one at their camp on the Napo River," Father Banana said.

"That'll take too long," Jess said. He was anxious to get going. Father Banana had told him the seasonal Tarani encampment where Blue Macaw had gone was another twenty miles downriver. "Don't you have a boat with a motor we could use?"

"Only a dugout. For longer trips, I go by river canoe. They're like buses. They pass by from time to time. I put up a flag when I need one to stop."

Jess turned to Miguelito. "Can you paddle the *Anguila* back upriver to the oil camp?"

He slapped his chest. "I'm a *riberno*, a river rat. No current can beat me."

"How long will it take to get there, fix it, and come back?"

"With one of us paddling and one poling, two and a half days. One day there, one day to fix, and a half to come back."

"Could you get there on your own?"

"You don't want to go?"

"There's something else I need to do. I'll pay you fifty percent more on what we agreed upon."

He shook his head. "Triple."

"Double."

"Deal."

"One other thing."

"What?"

"You can't tell anybody about me or where you're going when you've fixed the boat. Don't let them follow you back here."

Miguelito crossed his arms. "Tell me what you're up to. Don't lie. I don't want to be part of a crime."

"I'm not a criminal, nor is Father Banana. But it's better for you if you don't know."

"I changed my mind. I won't do it."

"I'll make the tip forty percent."

"Sixty."

"Fifty."

"Deal."

Jess helped Miguelito lower the stern and they pushed the orange river canoe with the electric eel painted on the bow back into the Caiman. The little boatman climbed aboard and stuck close to the bank as he propelled himself upriver with a long pole.

Father Banana showed Jess his dugout. "The river becomes

confused in about a mile as if it doesn't know which way to go. It forks and then forks and forks again. That makes navigation difficult, but easier for the Tarani to stay hidden. This time of year, always take the fork to the left. They'll see you before you see them."

He tied a strip of yellow cloth around Jess's left bicep.

"Is that to remind me always to take the left fork?"

"No, it is for the Tarani to know you are my friend so they will not kill you." He smiled. "Twenty miles is a long way to paddle this dugout if you're not used to it."

"If it can float, I can boat."

The priest made the sign of the cross. "Then go, but go with God. Tell Mintaka he sends his love."

"Before I shove off, I must warn you the men looking for Blue Macaw are hired killers. They have a helicopter. Probably a plane and river boats too. I'm sure they've heard of you by now. They will come here to find out what you know. They won't ask politely."

"It won't be the first time I've dealt with such men. God protects me."

"These men are different."

"And sometimes God protects me by telling me to go deep into the forest before such men arrive and wait until they grow tired of being stung by insects and bitten by snakes and leave."

They shook hands and Jess slid into the priest's dugout. It proved much more tippy than *Pursuit*, but within a few minutes he found the right balance to keep it on an even course without swamping. The mission disappeared behind him as he rounded a bend.

Jess lost track of time as he paddled. He tried to picture what Blue Macaw looked like, but Isabella's face kept coming to mind. It had been doing that a lot lately, ever since he was shot in Redwood Park. She was so many things, so many contradictions.

Artistic, practical, enigmatic, generous, oversharing, independent, funny, infuriating.

He hadn't known what to think of her the first time they met. She'd answered his rental ad and was thirty minutes late to the appointment. As they rode the freight elevator up to the second floor, she peppered him with questions about how many electrical outlets it had. Were they 120 or 220 volts? Were there extra slots in the main panel in case she needed to add more circuit breakers? Were utilities included in the rent? Did he have a problem with loud music?

"What are you going to use the space for?" he asked her.

"To live in and make art," she said.

"Don't you only need paint and brushes to do that?"

It was the first time he saw her eyes and lips smile at the same time. When they reached the second floor and he slid open the wooden picket safety gate, she stepped out, glissaded across the loft, twirled around, and moonwalked back.

"It's perfect. How do you feel about children?"

"Living here? Never thought about it. Why, how many kids do you have?"

"It varies."

"I don't follow."

Isabella laughed. "I teach dance. Mostly in the schools, but I also found that some children can express themselves better when they dance outside of it. You know, all the peer pressure to conform and the bullying that goes with it."

"Kids here, huh?"

"You do like children, don't you?"

"Sure, I mean—"

"Good. I'll take it."

"But you didn't even look at the electrical."

That was the second time he saw eyes and lips smile together.

The sun was arcing lower when the Caiman River narrowed and entered a gorge. The river had eaten away the forest, exposing a forty-foot cliff. The clay wall was ablaze with emerald-green parrots, scarlet macaws, and white-eyed conures. The seedeaters were pecking at the mineral lick to aid their digestion.

Gusts began rippling across the water, but not from a breeze. Jess looked up. A blue macaw flapped its wings right over him. A second joined, and then a third. The sky turned even bluer from the growing flock.

Blue Macaw was close.

20

A s Jess passed through the gorge, two dugouts suddenly appeared behind him. Each held two men with the same haircuts and tattoos as Dabo. One paddled, the other stood in the bow holding a spear.

Jess spotted a notch in the riverbank and steered toward it. A pole made from a tree trunk had been pounded into the mud close to shore. He pulled alongside it and tied off with a length of liana. The two dugouts held back, but one man gestured with his spear at a muddy slick that looked as if it was used by river otters. Jess waded toward it and scrambled up.

A faint trail led to a small clearing no larger than a suburban backyard. No one was there, at least no one he could see. Smoke curled from a firepit. Four palapas had been erected near it and palmetto sleeping mats were piled nearby. Hammocks strung between trees were empty. All was quiet. Even the blue macaws that had landed in the canopy stopped squawking.

Jess went to the firepit. A dozen pairs of unblinking eyes stared at him from behind the green veil of the jungle as the spears, blowguns, and arrows aimed at his chest remained unwavering. He looked up at the mintakas in the trees and held his breath as he waited for their namesake to appear.

When he lowered his gaze, she was standing in front of him. He hadn't heard her footsteps, her heartbeat, her breath. Though Jess had never seen Blue Macaw before, he knew it was her. She had Dabo's eyes and his thick hair, although hers was not bowl-cut; it hung below her shoulders in an indigo cascade. Small blue feathers served as earrings and a red band of face paint with a black outline accented her expression that was equal parts determination and defiance.

She yanked the strip of yellow cloth from his arm. "Who gave you this?"

"Father Banana. He's both our friend."

"What do you want?"

"To save Dabo. I'm Jess Parks. Maybe he told you about me."

"What do you know about my brother?"

"That he'd do anything to keep you safe and I believe you'd do the same for him. Dabo's in the Oakland jail and he'll never get out alive if you and I don't help him."

Others had followed her out of the jungle. An old man wearing only a leather codpiece fastened with a cord around his waist pointed a spear at Jess. It was a sharpened tree limb and didn't have a stone tip, much less a metal one. His eyes were rheumy and his face as textured as a walnut shell. Dark wooden plugs adorned his earlobes.

Another man held a machete like the one Jess had last seen in an evidence bag next to Jim Buckle's corpse. He wore a pair of old Reeboks without laces. A teenager holding a bow with an arrow strung stood next to him. His tattered T-shirt had the faded silhouette of palm trees with the words Miami Beach printed on the front.

Worry replaced Blue Macaw's fierceness. "You saw Dabo in jail, spoke to him?"

"I did. They're charging him with Jim Buckle's murder. The evidence is stacked against him."

"He didn't do it."

"Of course he didn't. Dabo stayed with you that night and not at the Grand Hotel where Buckle was killed. He told Logan Riggins and me he'd found you. You need to tell that to Dabo's lawyer. You're his alibi."

"I can't go back to Oakland."

"You don't have to. The lawyer will meet you in Coca and take your testimony. I'll go with you. A boatman is coming with a motorized canoe in a couple of days to take us."

"I won't go. I'll never leave Tarani homelands again. Never."

"It'll only be for a few days. Logan has hired a very good lawyer for Dabo. He'll have Ecuadorian lawyers alongside him to make sure your rights are safeguarded. I'll be there too to protect you. So will the people Dabo was working with in Coca. They'll put out the word that you need help. You'll be surrounded by Waorani."

Her shoulders slumped. The flash in her eyes dimmed. "You don't understand. You can't."

"I stayed at the mission last night. Father Banana told me about the letters you wrote him, about hearing your confession beside the shihuahuaco tree. He wouldn't tell me what happened to you, but I believe Jim Buckle was responsible for whatever it was."

Blue Macaw shuddered and Jess reached out to reassure her, but the old man lunged forward and pushed the sharpened tip of his spear against his throat. Surprised by the old man's speed, Jess stepped backward. The spear's tip followed. Blue Macaw gently took hold of the old man's wrist, but he wouldn't let up. He kept pushing the spear, speaking Wao rapidly, his leaking eyes locked on Jess.

Blue Macaw told him that Jess knew Dabo and could be

trusted. The old man finally relented and stalked off. The man wearing the laceless Reeboks and the teenager in the Miami Beach T-shirt followed close behind.

"He's very quick for someone his age," Jess said.

"Don't think unkindly of him. He's our jaguar shaman. Tarani believe we descended from the mating of a jaguar and harpy eagle."

She tilted her head as she spoke. The sun made her long black hair shine. "He's seen too many of our people disappear. Those who didn't die from cowori diseases or were taken and killed by cowori have fled deep into the forest and live alone. Because you're cowori, you represent death. Tarani believe when we die, we must walk a trail to the spirit world. A giant anaconda —*obe* in our language—lies in wait. Those who can't escape obe will never dwell in the spirit world."

"More cowori are coming. CaliCo has sent a man to find you, to stop you from testifying. He's being helped by hired killers."

"You told them about me, led them here?"

"They knew about you before I left Oakland. I've been careful since I left Coca and don't believe they followed me to this camp, but they know about the Tarani homelands and are hunting for you. They have aircraft and special equipment. If they find you, they won't only kill you, they'll kill the shaman and everyone in your tribe. They'll stop at nothing so their bosses can drill for oil here."

"I told you. I can't go back. You don't understand." Blue Macaw walked into the forest.

Jess didn't follow. He sat with his back against a tree and waited. Eventually the Tarani started to ignore him. The shaman, Reebok shoes, and Miami Beach T-shirt squatted nearby and kept a watch on him. Occasionally, the shaman would point his spear at him and chant.

As the day wore on and the heat of the tropics settled down

on the clearing with the weight of a hot, wet blanket, the women and children overcame their fear and trickled back to seek the shade of the palapas. By early evening, a couple of the braver kids had also taken to squatting near Jess and observing him. Whenever he stood to stretch his legs or scratch himself, they imitated him and giggled. As the sky turned dark, Jess unrolled his hammock and strung it between two trees. He wrapped himself in a mosquito net and tried to sleep.

The next morning, he walked down to the river to check on Father Banana's dugout. It was still tied to the post. He picked up stones and skipped them as he thought of next steps. Laughter erupted behind him. Someone threw a stone. It skipped all the way across the river and reached the far bank.

Jess turned around to see who threw it. Miami Beach T-shirt was standing with a bunch of younger kids. He threw another. It skipped across easily. Jess signaled he was impressed by flexing his bicep and miming throwing.

"You have a heckuva an arm. You could make varsity like Detective Stone's son did."

The teen came down to the river's edge and said something in Wao. Jess understood he was challenging him to a contest.

"Bring it on, but, first, what's your name? I'm Jess." He patted his chest. "Jess. My name is Jess. What's yours?" He pointed at him. "Your name?" He patted his chest again. "Jess." He pointed at him. "You?"

The teen finally nodded to show he understood. "Moipa." He patted his chest. "Moipa."

"Glad to meet you, Moipa."

Jess skipped a stone. It didn't make it across. The kids watching laughed. Moipa threw. His made it easily. The kids cheered. They threw a few more times. Jess got closer, but still failed to reach the other side. Moipa pointed to himself, demonstrated how he gripped the stone and positioned his body so his shoulder was lower. He handed him the stone. Jess tried the new grip, dipped his shoulder, and threw. When it hit the far bank, the kids cheered. Moipa beamed.

They trooped back to the clearing. Blue Macaw had joined the women mashing plantains and peeling fruit. Jess didn't approach her, but returned to where he'd strung his hammock and sat on a nearby log.

Monkeys chattered. Parrots squawked. Insects droned. But then a louder drone filled the air, frightening the animals, birds, and insects into silence. The people in the clearing ran into the forest and hid beneath the canopy. Jess recognized the sound of an airplane passing overhead. It was following the river. He wondered if it was a search plane equipped with thermal imaging devices, and, if so, hoped the trees provided enough cover to shield the Tarani.

When day turned to dusk, people returned to the clearing and gathered around the firepit. Moipa walked up from the river, holding his bow in one hand and a large fish with an arrow sticking out of it in the other. The women wrapped it in wet banana leaves and placed it on a bed of coals. When the meal was ready, the shaman left his perch and chanted over it. He refused a wooden bowl of food when offered, but went back to his spot and resumed his watch.

Blue Macaw put a piece of fish in a bowl, spooned some mashed plantains next to it, and picked a pair of bananas from a stalk. She brought the food to Jess.

"Here. Eat."

"Only if you join me." He patted a seat next to him on the log.

She hesitated before sitting.

"It's beautiful here," he said.

"It is, but it must seem awfully slow to you."

"That's part of its beauty. The rainforest has a rhythm all its own the same as the Oakland Estuary does where I paddle my kayak every day. I like it there. I like it here."

Blue Macaw grew quiet.

Jess said, "How old were you when you started living at Father Banana's mission?"

"The first time? Four years old. Influenza struck. Nearly all of us got sick. Many people died, including my father, a little brother, and a baby sister. I got very sick too. The elders used to tell stories about a cowori shaman who threw balls into baskets and sang songs to a tree. They said he had powerful magic. Our mother could not take care of me, and so she told Dabo to take me there. We were living in a camp much farther away than this one. It took us a week to make our way through the forest. Dabo carried me on his back."

"He saved your life."

"I know."

Jess motioned at the people eating around the firepit. "Which one is your mother?"

Blue Macaw pointed to a palapa. "She's very weak with cancer. She'll walk the trail to the spirit world soon."

"She must be happy you're here."

"She is, but if what you say is true, then no one will be happy with me if I bring death down upon them."

"What about other family members? Brothers, sisters, cousins, are they sitting by the fire?"

"Tarani are all family. It's the same for the other Waorani tribal groups. There are so few of us left." Blue Macaw pointed to a young woman with two children. "That is Dabo's wife, Nimu, and their son and daughter."

Jess picked a piece of fish out of the bowl. Cooking it in the banana leaves had kept it moist. It was delicious and made him realize how long it'd been since he last ate.

"When did you go back to the mission again?"

"I was thirteen. Dabo had been living there for a year or so. When he'd come home, he'd tell us what he learned and how I should come back with him because I liked learning too."

"What were your favorite subjects?"

"Reading. All the books were written in Spanish and English. I like learning different languages because it is like knowing the languages of the animals in the forest. The birds talk one way, the insects another, the jaguar still another. All are saying similar things and, when they say it at the same time, it's like a song. I live in this tree. I live in that hole in the ground. I fly here. I slither there. I eat bugs. I sip nectar. I eat everything. I'm looking for a mate. I want to have children. I already have children. Don't kill me. Don't kill them. The rainforest is our home. Don't destroy it."

"So, you speak macaw, jaguar, monkey, and anteater in addition to Wao, Spanish, and English."

"All Tarani know what the animals are saying. Animals are like us. They have spirits too. We live with them. We share the forest with them. In our language, forest is *ome*. We use the same word for world. Ome is our whole world. It sustains us and protects us."

"But you left the mission. You didn't because you wanted to, did you?"

Blue Macaw inhaled sharply. "It's hard for me to talk about."

"Then don't."

"No, I need to. Father Banana told me it is better if I don't hold it inside anymore because it was like the cancer eating my mother. He said what happened wasn't my fault. He said that I deserved to be forgiven, but I must forgive myself first."

She took a deep breath again. "I'd been going back and forth to the mission for a couple of years. One day I took a dugout upstream to look for star clouds."

"In the sky?"

"No, in the forest. They're a kind of orchid. Very rare and very beautiful. Once you smell one you never forget. It's like the first moment after a new rain. Butterflies and hummingbirds gather among them. While I was upstream it started to storm. The river flooded and pushed my dugout into the limbs of a fallen ceiba. It capsized and I had to hang on to the branches. I was sure I was going to drown."

Blue Macaw squared her shoulders. "I was preparing to walk the trail to the spirit world, planning on how I could get past obe, when a large boat with a loud motor came by. It wasn't a river canoe, but a cowori's boat. The people saw me. They stopped and pulled me onto it."

"Jim Buckle. He must've been out with an exploratory team testing for oil reserves."

She looked down at her toes. "He told the others to give me a blanket and food. He asked me where I was from, but I couldn't answer, my teeth were chattering so hard. I was very weak, very frightened. It was growing dark and so he ordered the boat to turn around and head back upriver. When we finally pulled to shore, they carried me to a metal building and brought me dry clothes and lots of food."

Blue Macaw took one of the bananas and started to peel it. "I was exhausted and fell asleep. The next morning when I woke up he was sitting beside the bed. He was holding my hand and stroking my hair. He was trying to speak to me in Spanish, but he didn't know many of the words. I told him I spoke English. I asked him where he was from. He told me America. I asked him how far upriver that was. He laughed. He described a beautiful city and said if I wanted to see it, he'd take me and then bring me right back home."

"You couldn't have known how far away it was."

"I know, but he was offering me a gift and it would be wrong to refuse it."

She told him how Buckle flew her to Oakland on his private jet. They bypassed immigration and he whisked her to a high-rise apartment overlooking Lake Merritt. When she cried and said she wanted to go home, he told her he'd take her back as soon as he could, but had work to do first. He told her not to worry and showered her with gifts. He also told her never to open the door. It had a keypad lock on the inside and he didn't give her the combination.

"The next day he brought me a pretty box with a big red ribbon." Blue Macaw said it so softly Jess had to strain to hear. "It was a dress, the most beautiful I'd ever seen. It was as white as a star cloud orchid and made from fabric smoother than Apaika's nose. I could hardly breathe when I saw it."

She clenched her hands, her eyes fixed on the ground. "He asked me to put it on. Right then, right in front of him. I was shy. I said I didn't want to, but he insisted. Not wanting to be ungrateful, I turned around and slipped off my clothes and put on the beautiful dress. When I turned back around, he said I was very beautiful. He called me the sexiest little girl he'd ever seen."

Her shoulders trembled. Tears roll down her cheeks. "He'd been sitting in a big chair watching me, but then got up and turned me around and around until I grew dizzy. He put his arms around me and pulled me close. He ran his hands up and down my back and then grabbed my bottom. His breath—it sounded like he wasn't getting any air. He was holding me so tight, I couldn't move. When I tried to push away, he squeezed me even tighter. He started pulling at the dress, pulling it up over my hips. When I tried to push it back down, he called me a little savage. He said it over and over."

The words choked in her throat and she shuddered.

"He tore off my underwear. When I cried, he covered my mouth with his. He pushed me to the ground and ... His face turned so red, his sweat showered me. I didn't have the strength to make him stop. All I could do was think about how beautiful the dress was, how I hoped he wouldn't rip it."

She started crying. After a while, she shook her head as if shaking off a bad dream.

"I told myself we were married. I told myself that was what husbands did on their wedding night. I said it to myself every time he came to the apartment and did it again. 'We're married. I'm his wife.'"

Blue Macaw tossed the banana on the ground without taking a bite. "I was so stupid, so young. Everything was so new. It was so different than anything I could've imagined growing up in the rainforest. I truly believed he loved me. I prayed every day that I'd have his baby. That would prove we were married."

"But something changed. What happened?"

"Since I couldn't leave the apartment, I watched a lot of television. My English got even better. One night on the news there was a story about a big party. It showed all the fancy people there. The room was decorated. The women wore beautiful dresses. And then there was Jim Buckle. He had his arm around a woman who was wearing a dress more beautiful than the one he'd given me. He told the reporter he was the happiest man in the world because he and his wife were expecting another baby."

She clenched her fists. "The next time he came to the apartment, I told him what I'd seen. I called him names and said I'd tell his wife, tell everyone. He slapped me, called me a dirty little Indian whore. He tore off my clothes, my underwear. I tried to fight back, but he was too strong. He kept calling me a dirty savage and was choking me while he raped me. When he left, I knew he'd never let me tell anyone the truth. He was going to do to me what happened to all the other Tarani girls who disappear back home. I ran out of the apartment. I ran for my life."

"How did you get the door open?"

"I started pounding on it with a frying pan and screamed for help. A neighbor called the apartment manager who opened it. I told him I was Mr. Buckle's niece and got locked in and forgot the code. He said he'd have to give him a call. We got in the elevator to go to his office, but as soon as we reached the lobby, I ran."

Jess asked her where she went.

"I just ran until I ended up on a street where all the store signs were in Spanish. I was tired and so I sat down at a bus stop and cried. A woman waiting there started talking to me. When she learned I was from Ecuador, she offered to help, to give me a place to live, a job."

"The bruja from El Salvador. Casa Clean. Did you think you could save enough money and go back to Ecuador?"

"Go back to what? After what I'd done, I couldn't go back and face Father Banana and Dabo or my mother and the jaguar shaman. No, I worked. I learned to forget."

"Dabo said one of the reasons you fled the night of the raid was because the police would find out you'd worked at Buckle's house as a maid."

The indigo cascade of hair rose up and down her back as she nodded. "If I'd known it was his house, I'd never have gone. I would've quit Casa Clean. But when the bruja took us there, it was only another rich cowori's mansion. The regular maid was there. An older Mexican woman. I remember her because she walked with a limp."

"Esme," Jess said. "That's her name."

"How do you know?"

"I went there before I came here. Esme said she'd never met you, that they never used temporary housecleaners."

"You said the oil company knew about me before you left Oakland. It's because you told them."

"I did tell a detective after Buckle was murdered and the

cops were searching for your brother. I didn't want Dabo to get killed when they found him. Someone in the police department told CaliCo."

"The detective."

"No, not him, but I have an idea who." He put the empty bowl down. "How did you find out it was Jim Buckle's house?"

"I was dusting a bedroom and knocked a photograph off the nightstand. When I picked it up, I shrieked. It was Jim Buckle and the woman I'd seen on TV, his wife. I was holding it when she came in to see why I'd screamed. She looked at me, looked at the photograph and told me to put it back and to leave the room immediately, to get out of the house and never come back."

"Clare Buckle. Somehow she knew about her husband and you."

"A wife always knows."

"I have to ask you this because if you come to Coca with me and talk to Dabo's lawyer, he'll ask you himself. If he doesn't, the Oakland authorities on the video conference call will."

"What is it?"

"After Dabo found you that evening, did you go to the Grand Hotel to look for Jim Buckle?"

Blue Macaw stood and walked into the forest without saying another word.

The feeling that someone was watching him woke Jess the next morning.

Blue Macaw stepped out of a halo of golden sunlight. "I've made my decision. I'll go to Coca and tell the lawyer Dabo was with me that night."

"Thank you. As soon as the boatman gets here, we'll leave."

"But I need the jaguar shaman's blessing first."

"How do you get that?"

"You'll see." She stepped backward and the brightening light swallowed her.

Jess went to check on Father Banana's dugout tied to the pole. Hoping he'd see Miguelito grinning from the stern of the *Anguila Eléctrica*, he batted away the what-could-go-wrongs one after another. The current had been too strong for Miguelito to paddle upriver. The oil workers wouldn't lend him a welding torch to fix the busted propellor shaft. Lyle Hunt and the captain were at the camp, realized he was Jess's boatman, and tortured him. The plane that flew by captured images of the Tarani and pinpointed their location.

A capybara swimming across the river caught his eye. The

planet's largest rodent resembled a hundred-pound version of the guinea pig he'd had for lunch. It was nearing the shore when the water around it erupted. The animal grunted pitifully and then rose from the river, clenched in the jaws of a black caiman. The killing was over as quick as it had begun. The reptile submerged with its prize and all that marked the spot was a red air bubble floating on the surface. Soon it popped and disappeared too.

When Jess returned to his hammock, Blue Macaw was sitting in it, swinging back and forth. He asked her if she'd spoken to the shaman.

"I told him I had to leave and he must take everyone far away from here. There are other camps they can go to that are deeper in the forest and won't be so easily spotted from the river or the air."

"Will he do it?"

"I hope so. He's old. His world has changed so much."

"Yours too. Oakland is a long way from all this."

Blue Macaw kept swinging. "I told my mother what happened to me, why I'd been gone all this time. I begged her for forgiveness. You know what she said? It was her that needed to beg for mine because she hadn't found me after I was taken. But how could've she? The only world she's ever known is the forest and river."

The rain started falling. It fell long into the afternoon, drumming on the leaves of the canopy and splashing down on the clearing in big dollops. Jess used a palm frond as an umbrella, but it only helped a little.

Moipa came over. He was carrying his bow and made signs asking if Jess wanted to go hunting.

"Lead the way," he said and tossed the soggy palm frond aside.

They walked quickly and quietly as they followed a faint

trail that wound through the understory and between tree trunks as big around as cars. Birds called to one another. A family of capuchin monkeys that were named for an order of monks who wore brown robes with large hoods scampered among the branches. Lianas hung from limbs. Jess saw them as climbing ropes and recalled Logan telling him how he'd once clambered to the top of a tree that gave him a magical view of another world.

The trail led to a lake. The rain stopped as Moipa and Jess reached the shore. The water reflected the passing storm clouds. Hoof prints leading in and out of the lake showed in the mud. Moipa pointed to them and said, "*Titae.*"

"*Titae?*" Jess said, trying to mimic the pronunciation. "What is that?" He shrugged to show he didn't understand.

Moipa hunched his back and used his arm to mimic a trunk. Then he cupped his mouth and made wheezing hiccup noises and squeals. Finally, he drew a figure next to the prints.

"A tapir," Jess said. "*Titae* is Wao for tapir. You're hunting for a tapir." He mimed shooting an arrow at the drawing.

Moipa shook his head fiercely. He pointed to the drawing. "Titae." Then he pointed to himself. "Tarani." Next, he did it the other way around, calling himself a titae and the drawing a Tarani.

"I get it. Tarani and titae are equals. You don't hunt and eat your own kind."

Moipa nodded and they resumed walking.

Jess spotted a bird the size of a sparrow that was flitting among a bush festooned with long, tubular pink flowers. Its back feathers were sapphire and the wings the color of a turquoise ring. The beak was long and curved and the tips upturned. The bird used them to scissor the stem of a flower and steal its nectar from a hole it pierced at the base.

When it drank its fill, the sapphire and turquoise flowerpiercer flew to a nearby branch. Downy heads bobbed above the edge of a nest and the mother bird leaned in and fed her chicks by regurgitating into their open beaks. With the feeding over, she perched next to the nest. Jess edged toward it to get a closer look. It was too close. The mother bird issued a high-pitched whistle and flew straight at him, making him duck. Moipa laughed.

They walked around the edge of the lake looking for more tracks. Moipa pointed out other animals and gave their names. *Kogikoo* was a sloth, *gata* a woolly monkey, *kowatai* a wild turkey. He stopped, crouched, and traced the print of a peccary's cloven hoof. Jess flashed on Detective Stone doing the same with the bloody footprints leading away from Jim Buckle's corpse. The murder was starting to feel farther and farther away.

They resumed circling the lake and wound back where they'd started. Moipa motioned for Jess to stay put. He walked toward a rotting tree trunk fifty yards away, carved a circle in it with his knife, and then came back. He strung an arrow, aimed, and fired. He hit it dead center. Then he handed him the bow and another arrow.

Jess strung the arrow and pulled back. The bow wasn't as flexible as he thought it would be and he had to pull even harder. His hands were shaking from the effort as he sighted and let go. The string stung the inside of his wrist as it snapped back. The arrow wobbled as it flew and landed fifteen yards short.

Moipa didn't laugh like he had when the flowerpiercer went after him. He handed Jess another arrow and stood beside him, holding an imaginary bow and pulling back the string. He inhaled and exhaled and inhaled again and held his breath. With his hands and head perfectly still, he pretended to let go.

It took Jess three more tries before he shot an arrow that hit the circle on the tree trunk. It wasn't a bullseye, but Moipa acted like it was. He trilled his approval.

They returned to camp. The jaguar shaman and Reebok intercepted them and began talking to Moipa. The teen pointed his bow in the direction of the lake. The shaman shook his spear and the three started walking. Jess realized they were going after the peccary whose prints they'd seen. He waited for Moipa to beckon him to join them, but he didn't.

An hour later, the trio returned, the shaman leading the way. Moipa and Reebok were holding the ends of the old man's spear. A fifty-pound peccary was skewered on it. Men, women, and children crowded around and trilled. Jess trilled his congratulations too.

Blue Macaw joined him. "The shaman is going to hold a yagé ceremony tonight because I'm going away."

"That's good. He gave you his blessing. As soon as we finish meeting with the lawyer in Coca, I'll bring you straight back myself." Jess motioned at the wild pig. "Is that for the feast tonight?"

"Yes, but a yagé ceremony is more than a celebration. Yagé is one of the shaman's medicines. It gives him powerful visions. He wants to look into the future to see what dangers might lie in wait on my journey so he can warn me."

"What's yagé made from?"

"A vine. It's also known as ayahuasca."

She explained that the powerful hallucinogen took users on a journey some called the medicine wheel. It had different paths. One was the eagle path, where the meaning of life was revealed. Another was the dragon path that took them to a union with the Divine. On the serpent's path, they shed their past. The jaguar path was the most dangerous of all. It's where they faced death and either lived or died.

"You didn't answer when I asked if you went to the hotel the night Buckle died," Jess said. "The lawyer is sure to ask and we need to be prepared."

"We can talk about that after the ceremony or on the way to Coca. We'll have plenty of time."

"But—"

She shushed him by holding her finger against his lips. "Tonight is going to be very special. Have patience."

The rain started to fall again in silvery sheets that made the huge leaves of the philodendrons shudder and the gathering puddles quiver.

The wild pig was roasted on a spit over the firepit. Dabo's wife, Nimu, and other women mashed cassavas and peeled fruit. Manioc beer was brewing in a log that had been hollowed and laid on its side. When the peccary was cooked, Reebok and Moipa removed it from the spit and placed on a platter made of woven banana leaves. The people gathered around in a semi-circle and began singing.

Blue Macaw joined them. She wore a traditional skirt made of dried palm leaves and was bare-breasted like the other women. A fresh mask of red with black outlining had been painted on her face and her lips were dark purple as if kissed with acai berry juice. Her hair was tied in a braid with a star cloud orchid in it. The blue feathers in her earlobes shined brighter than ever.

As the people sang, the jaguar shaman appeared. He started chanting as he stood over the pig and raised a machete. The flames reflected in the sharpened blade. He brought it down in a flashing arc and cleaved the roasted pig in two. The women and children let out a cheer. The shaman disappeared again while the meat was being sliced.

Blue Macaw handed Jess a wooden gourd filled with chicha. He took a gulp and then another.

"I told you tonight was going to be special," she said and clutched his arm.

He could smell the star cloud orchid in her hair, smell the recent rain. "How so?"

"You'll see when you embark on the medicine wheel."

A hand gripped his other arm. It took him a few moments to realize it was Moipa's, not hers. She let go as another hand clasped him. It was Reebok's.

"Go with them," Blue Macaw said. "Don't be frightened. Trust them. They are your brothers on the journey."

Moipa and Reebok shepherded him to an enclosed palapa. The only light inside came from a fire in the center of the room. The jaguar shaman was sitting cross-legged on the other side of the flames. They let go of Jess's arms and motioned for him to sit down. Then they sat on either side so that the four men faced the fire.

The red glow gave the old man's face an eerie hue. He had a jaguar pelt draped over his shoulders and wore a headdress woven with yellow, blue, red, and green feathers. Perched on the crown was the head of a harpy eagle. The shaman held a rattle in one hand and a diamond-shaped god's eye made out of bright woven flower stems in the other. A low moan escaped his lips and he opened his eyes. They were no longer rheumy, but bright black orbs floating on a sea of red.

The shaman handed Reebok a long tube of hollowed wood. He took it, raised it, and pointed it in the four directions. Then he put the top end to his lips and tilted it back. His Adam's apple bobbed. When he finished drinking, he handed back the tube, opened his mouth, and showed his tongue to the shaman.

The old man grunted his approval. He refilled the wooden tube and handed it to Moipa. The teen raised it, pointed it to the four directions, and put it to his lips and drank. He opened his mouth, showed his tongue, and handed it back.

The shaman refilled it and passed it to Jess who took it but hesitated. The old man glared and shook the rattle and waved the god's eye at him. Reebok grunted to Moipa. The teen's expression darkened as if he were being blamed for the cowori's affront. He raised his finger and mimed pointing and drinking.

"How bad can it be?" Jess muttered. He pointed it to the four points of a compass, raised it to his lips and poured the contents into his mouth.

The broth was foul and burned his throat. He struggled not to spit it out. Moipa grinned and pointed to Jess's mouth to show his tongue to the shaman.

Jess did. He was a little buzzed from the chicha, but otherwise felt fine. Not knowing what to expect, he checked on the others.

The jaguar shaman had closed his eyes and was rocking back and forth. Reebok started shivering and then shaking. His eyes rolled back. Moipa slumped forward, his chin resting on his chest. A long string of green drool hung from his lips and created a wet spot on his T-shirt. He started muttering incoherently, groaned, and started to pitch headfirst into the flames.

Jess grabbed his arm to pull him back. The teenager's skin felt cold and scaly. He wrenched his hand away as Moipa threw back his head and glared at him with glowing yellow eyes. His nose and mouth were a caiman's snout and his teeth were long and jagged. He snapped them as he lunged.

Rearing backward to stay out of reach, Jess howled as he broke into a feverish sweat. Wave after withering wave of nausea swept over him and bile came roaring up his throat and shot out in a writhing, green snake of vomit. Lightning flashed and thunder boomed. Someone was crying. Someone was moaning. Someone was yelling.

"It's not real," Jess groaned. "It's not real."

He curled into a ball and squeezed himself to keep his guts from spilling out. The lights kept shooting on and off, so he closed his eyes, and the bright flickering soon took the shape of fractured images like the kind Isabella used in her performance pieces.

A silhouetted boat sailing in front of a setting sun. A sneaker wave cresting and breaking over the boat's mast. A man and a woman trying to reach for each other's outstretched hands as they plummeted to the bottom. A young boy standing next to an old man refinishing the teak deck of a schooner and polishing oxidized brass fixtures to make them shine again. A teenager inching his way up a sheer wall of steel gray granite. A young man standing atop a spire and shaking his fist at the sky. A grown man lying on his back and squeezing a trigger at another man's chest and watching roses bloom.

The red continued to grow until it filled Jess's vision. He blinked and saw it spread across a beige hotel carpet, splash against his feet. A voice was speaking. It came from a head lying by itself in the growing stain. He could not make out the words and so he crouched to listen.

"I can't understand you," Jess said. "What are you saying?"

He put his ear to its lips and felt the hot breath of the head's words and then the sting of its teeth as it sunk them into his ear. He jerked up and felt the weight of the head. He batted it to knock it loose.

"Let go!" he screamed. "Let go!"

The shaman's eyes were open and staring, but he didn't speak. Reebok appeared unconscious. Tears were streaming down Moipa's face. Jess bolted out of the palapa, hurtled over the women and children sleeping around the fire, and ran into the forest.

Creepers and lianas grabbed at his feet, trying to trip him at every step. Wet branches slapped his face and stung his eyes. Shards of bright, neon colors burst all around. A million unseen creatures buzzed, cried, and howled. Above them rose voices. Logan Riggins saying he'd do whatever it took to bring CaliCo down. Detective Stone telling him he was being played. Lyle Hunt threatening to hurt Isabella if he didn't back off. Clare Buckle lying about not knowing Blue Macaw. Sarah Newton raging at him for suggesting she was having an affair with Jim Buckle. The only voice he couldn't hear was Dabo's.

A roar drowned them all. It grew louder as Jess ran. He sped up, but the roar grew closer. His breath came in painful gasps. His heart pounded so hard he could see it pressing against his shirt to get out. He threw on the brakes and wheeled around and came face-to-face with a jet-black jaguar.

The sleek and powerful feline padded toward him, her claws silent on the soft rainforest floor. A sliver of moonlight poked through the canopy, broken only by the tip of her long black tail flicking back and forth. Jess backed against the buttress of a tree. The jaguar drew closer. He stared into her yellow eyes and remembered that taking the jaguar path on the medicine wheel meant facing death.

"The jaguar mother," Jess said, recalling what Dabo had said at the gala. "*Menye baada.*"

He didn't blink. Not even when she pounced, sailing through the air in one swift, graceful movement, pinning him against the tree with the full weight of her body. Her breath bathed his face, the beat of her heart thumped against his chest. He smelled the first moment after a new rain.

"You don't fear death?" she said.

"No," he said.

"Is that because you took a man's life?"

"How do you know about that?"

"Because I can see inside your soul."

"I don't fear it because I've faced it, like I'm facing you right now."

"You think I'm death?"

"If you're not, what are you?"

"Life," she purred, her lips acai berry purple, her flicking black tail a long indigo braid. "I told you the journey would be special. Are you ready?"

"For anything."

He put a hand on her shoulder and together they ran, racing through the forest, sending ocelots, margays, and smaller nocturnal predators scurrying to stay out of their way. Boas and anacondas tightened their coils around tree limbs to keep from being knocked loose. Monkeys cowered and sloths shook off their torpor to climb higher.

They reached the lake and leaped in without hesitation. He hugged her neck to hold on as they swam. Reaching the other side, they entered the mouth of a stream and ran up it by leaping from rock to rock. At the end was a silvery waterfall and Jess and the jaguar didn't let go of each other as the cascade beat down on them while the moonlight danced and the stars sparkled.

When it was over, and the night sounds of the rainforest resumed their symphony, Jess felt more alive than ever.

22

The early morning sky was pink with streaks of red. They faded into orange and then yellow and finally blue. Jess watched the sunrise from the crown of a shihuahuaco tree fifteen stories above the forest floor. While he couldn't recall having climbed it, he remembered everything about his journey with the jaguar.

As aerial rivers of scarlet, blue, and green macaws streaked above, he looked out on a sea of treetops that spread as far as he could see. Braided by rivers and dotted by archipelagos of lakes and meadows, it teemed with millions of species of fish, plants, insects, and animals.

Logan was right. It was magical, otherworldly. It was Eden.

His stomach muscles were still sore from the ayahuasca, and a deafening *thwap-thwap-thwap* filled his head. It sounded as if gigantic wings were flapping inside his skull. Recalling the other paths of the medicine wheel, he decided it must be the dragon coming to take him to meet the Divine.

A swirling gust washed over him. Jess breathed in deep, expecting to inhale the intoxicating scent of flowers, but got a choking whiff of fuel instead. He looked up. The green underbelly of a helicopter hovered overhead, its rotor blades egg-beating.

"No," he shouted, realizing it wasn't another hallucination.

Jess grabbed hold of lianas and rappelled down the trunk. Ten feet above the ground he let go, rolled when he hit, and sprang to his feet. He raced back to camp, running faster than when the jaguar was chasing him, running with even more wild abandon than when they ran together.

He broke into the clearing as the chopper finished its initial pass. The wash from its rotors blew palm fronds off the roofs of the palapas and embers from the firepit. They ignited one of the huts. Nimu and her son and daughter ran out. They froze as the whirling beast banked and came back.

"Keep going," Jess yelled as he sprinted toward them.

The helicopter attacked with the angry buzz and sting of a giant hornet, its prop wash plowing up chunks of earth and spitting them out. Jess reached Nimu and the kids, threw his arm around them, and charged for the safety of the jungle. Clods of dirt kicked up by the *chuck-chuck-chuck* of .50 caliber machine gun rounds firing from the open bay peppered the back of his legs as he shielded Dabo's family.

Several more yards to the trees remained when a big clod sent him sprawling. As he went down he shoved Nimu toward the understory. The impact of hitting the ground sent a jolt through him stronger than the captain's truck battery. The green gunship rose steeply as it neared the tree line and cleared the crowns with only inches to spare. It banked and came back around for another pass. A couple of Tarani dashed out of a palapa. The machine gunner didn't miss. Their bodies were torn to shreds.

Jess reached Nimu and the kids. "Mintaka. Where is she? Where's Blue Macaw?"

Dabo's wife was dazed. He repeated himself. She pointed toward the palapas.

"I'll get her. Take the kids and run. Go deep in the forest. Don't look back. Run and hide."

The helicopter hovered over the clearing, the machine gunner sweeping it as he searched for fresh targets. Jess ran in a crouch and reached the nearest palapa. Its roof had been torn apart by bullets. Blue Macaw sat inside cradling an emaciated woman. A thick splinter of palm frond stuck out of the old woman's thigh. Blood oozed around it.

"My mother needs help," she said.

"We can't pull it out. It could've hit an artery and is plugging the hole."

The *thwap-thwap-thwapping* of the chopper grew louder. The chopper was landing.

"We have to get out of here," he said. "We have to go. Now!"

Blue Macaw didn't budge. "I left her once. I won't leave her again."

"You won't be any good to her if you stay. This isn't the army trying to arrest anyone. These are mercenaries. Killers. Sicarios. They'll be on the ground in seconds."

"We'll fight them."

"They have guns. They'll kill everyone."

She set her jaw. Her lips still showed traces of acai berry. "I won't leave her to die. I won't leave any of my family. I'll fight with every breath I have. I am Tarani!"

Shouts came from outside. The jaguar shaman, Reebok, and Moipa stood shoulder to shoulder. The old man's face was streaked with red and black paint and he still wore the headdress with the harpy eagle on it. He jabbed his spear at the gunship hovering above the clearing. Reebok was painted too. He brandished a machete. Moipa held his bow with an arrow pulled all the way back. The pilot banked so the machine gunner could aim right at them.

The shaman chanted and hurled his spear at the green metal beast. It spiraled sixty feet, struck the fuselage, and bounced off. Moipa let his arrow fly at the same time. It shot straight and true, right into the open bay of the chopper, burying its point into the machine gunner's chest. He slumped forward, pulling the trigger as he did. The barrel of the deadly .50 caliber belched flames.

The ground around the three exploded as the high-powered slugs slammed into the dirt and stitched a zigzag line. The pilot yanked the stick and the helicopter leaped away.

The slugs missed the shaman and Moipa, but not Reebok. He was knocked to the ground, blood pouring from multiple wounds. Moipa stared at his body. The shaman gave him a glance and then retrieved his spear.

"Go!" Jess yelled at them. "Get out of here. The chopper's going to land. The killers inside will come for us."

When Moipa didn't move, he grabbed his shoulders and shook him. It snapped him out of it and they took Reebok by the arms and dragged his body into the forest. The shaman trilled and people hiding in the palapas scurried out and dashed for cover.

Jess returned to Blue Macaw. "Let's get your mother out of here." He tore off a strip of cloth and tied a tourniquet around her leg. "We'll head for the river and hide until dark and then take my dugout and paddle back to the mission. Father Banana has medical supplies. He'll be able to help her."

"But I need to stay and fight."

"You stay, you'll die."

He picked up Blue Macaw's mother, surprised by how light she was. Her lips tightened in pain, but she didn't cry out. They hurried out of the palapa and crossed the clearing. Instead of taking the regular trail down to the river, they cut through the understory to keep from being seen.

They ended up a little downriver from the notch where the dugouts were tied. Jess placed the old woman on the ground.

"She's bleeding too much," Blue Macaw said. "She won't live to see dark."

"Wait here. I'll get a dugout and drift down and pick you up."

He kept to the understory as he made his way upriver. When he neared the dugouts, he poked his head out to check for gunmen. As soon as he did, two jumped out from behind the trees and pinned his arms before he could run and dive into the river. It was the pair from Coca.

"Ah, Señor Parks. We meet again."

Jess smelled the cigarette before he saw him. The captain was right behind the two gunmen. Twin trails of smoke curled from his nostrils. He held a semi-automatic at his side. He barked an order and another gunman appeared behind him, dragging a trussed-up Miguelito. The boatman's face was badly beaten. One eye was swollen shut and his nose clearly broken.

"Aiee! I piss on sicarios. I didn't say shit to them. They found the camp with special cameras." One of the gunmen kicked him. "I piss on your mother's grave." That earned him a gun butt to the back.

The captain barked again. The gunman dropped Miguelito and dashed downriver. He returned with Blue Macaw.

The captain grabbed her by the arm and wrenched her close. "What do we have here? A murderer's sister. A terrorist and her gang of savages."

She tried to struggle free, but he squeezed harder. She spat at him. He slapped her.

Jess lunged, but the two men pinning him held fast. "How much are the oil companies paying you?" he said.

"What?" the captain said.

"How much are they paying you to sell out the Tarani?"

"We're not paying him a goddamn dime," Lyle Hunt said as he stepped out of the understory. "He's only doing his job. Plus he enjoys shooting game, like I do."

CaliCo's security chief was wearing his tan hunting jacket with cartridge holders above the pockets. Brass gleamed from each one. He cradled a large-caliber rifle fitted with a high-powered scope. The mirthless eyes behind the yellow lenses didn't blink.

"You won't get away with it, Hunt. The whole world will know. Logan Riggins will tell everyone."

"Tell them what? That a tribe of stupid savages went extinct all on their own? That a dumbshit tourist took the wrong trail and got lost forever?"

"Was she alone?" the captain said to the gunman.

"There's an old woman back there with a stick in her leg."

"What are you waiting for?"

"You want me to bring her here?"

"You know the mission. Do your job. After that, get the other men guarding the helicopter and go round up any savages you can find. Complete the mission."

He marched off. A rifle shot soon echoed.

"That was my mother!" Blue Macaw cried.

"Yes," the captain said with a sneer. "*Was.*"

"Murderer! Assassin! This is Tarani land."

The captain twisted her arm. He turned to Hunt. "Do you see what we have to deal with down here? They're no better than animals. Wild animals."

Jess tried to break free again, but got smacked in the back with a rifle butt for his efforts.

"Murderer?" the captain said, his face inches from Blue

Macaw's. "And what do you call your brother? What about him?"

"Dabo is innocent."

He took a drag of his cigarette and blew the smoke into her face. "You're filthy. You stink. All you savages do."

Blue Macaw spat at him again. He slapped her again.

Miguelito cried out. "Aiee! Let me up and I'll show you how hard I can slap your ugly face."

Gunfire erupted from the direction of the clearing where the helicopter had landed. The forest couldn't block the screams and cries.

Hunt smirked. "Like I said, the little grass shackers went extinct all on their own."

Blue Macaw trilled.

"Shut her up before she bursts my eardrums," he said.

The captain started to raise his pistol.

"Wait, a million dollars!" Jess shouted. "Yeah, a million bucks US. It's Logan Riggins's money. He has it buried at his place on the Napo River. I know where it is. I'll take you. Just let the Tarani go and it's all yours."

Hunt's thin lips pulled back in a wolfish leer. "You don't get it, do you, Parks? No one walks. No one talks. The girl. You. The boatman. Everyone. It's the big adios, amigo."

Everything started to move in slow motion. The captain resumed raising his pistol. Blue Macaw was looking at Jess, her shiny black braid flicking, the star cloud orchid blooming white, her acai-berry-kissed lips opening wide. She trilled. She trilled loudly.

Then everything sped up again. It was as if all the points of a compass that Jess had pointed the ayahuasca to suddenly came rushing back toward the center and crashed into each other. Other trills answered hers. An arrow struck the captain's shoulder. He dropped the pistol. The jaguar shaman rushed in, plunging his spear into the captain's neck so hard it jumped out the back like a jack-in-the-box. He hoisted him off the ground. Blue Macaw lunged at Lyle Hunt before he could shoulder his big gun and shoved him off the edge of the bank and into the river where a back eddy pulled him from shore.

Jess dropped to the ground between the two surprised gunmen, scissor-kicking one's legs out from under him while pulling the other one down. As he wrestled with him, Moipa ran over, his bow slung over his shoulder, a pair of laceless Reebok's on his feet, his dead friend's machete flashing in his hand. The blade came down. The gunman's head came off.

Jess rolled toward the other man. He'd dropped his rifle when he fell, but yanked a sidearm from his holster and was aiming it. The machete flashed again and the hand holding the pistol hit the ground. The gunman shrieked as he watched blood spurt from his severed wrist and then he toppled over.

Lyle Hunt thrashed in the river. A torpedo-shaped shadow zeroed in on him. "Help!" he screamed. "Help!"

"Aiee! You big, beautiful lizard. Eat him," Miguelito said with a laugh.

"You win, Parks," Hunt shouted as he struggled to keep the weight of his cartridge-ladened jacket from pulling him under. "Shoot him and everybody walks. I swear."

Jess picked up a rifle and took aim. The black caiman raised his head out of the water. His eyes were yellow, his mouth open wide, his white teeth long and sharp. He was very big. That meant he was very old. That meant he was very tough. That meant he'd figured out how to live through droughts and floods, how to avoid poachers, how to keep from being run over by motorized boats and poisoned by oil.

"What are you waiting for?" Hunt cried as he dog-paddled. "Shoot him!"

Jess kept looking down the barrel. He saw the man struggling in the water, his arms flailing, his legs kicking, the shooter's glasses pushed down on his chin. He saw the black caiman swimming fast, closing in. Who was the fittest? Who was the strongest? Who deserved to survive?

He lowered the rifle. It was an easy choice. It was the law of the jungle.

23

———

The shaman swung his spear and flung the captain into the river. Jess and Moipa pitched the bodies of the two gunmen after him. More caimans joined the feeding frenzy. Blood bobbing with body parts quickly stained the water.

"No cowori," Moipa said and kicked off the laceless shoes. The caimans snapped at them when they hit the water. He ripped off the tattered Miami Beach T-shirt and sent it swimming too.

"We must find Nimu and the others," Blue Macaw said.

"And fast, before the rest of the killers realize what's happened here and get the chopper airborne again," Jess said.

He untied Miguelito. "Can you walk?"

"If I can't, I'll crawl."

Jess handed him a rifle. "Use it as a crutch."

"Until I use it as a gun."

The shaman was already on the move. Moipa was right behind. Jess picked up the other rifle along with the captain's semi-automatic. They reached Blue Macaw's mother. The young woman knelt beside her body and chanted, wishing her safe passage past obe so she could enter the spirit world.

When they reached the outskirts of the camp, they stayed hidden in the trees. Jess counted heads. The pilot was still behind the stick of the chopper. The engine was on, but the main and tail rotors weren't spinning. Two gunmen stood guard. No Tarani were visible.

"Ask the shaman if he knows how many cowori there are besides those three," he said to Blue Macaw.

The conversation was brief. The shaman made jabbing motions with his spear. Moipa held up fingers.

"Maybe three more," she said. "They chased women and children into the rainforest. Other warriors lay in wait for them with blowguns, spears, and arrows."

"What do you think?" Jess asked Miguelito.

"If they didn't get lost, they got speared."

An unseen jaguar roared.

Miguelito grinned. "Or eaten."

Hunt's words echoed. *No one walks, no one talks.* Jess shouldered the rifle. "We can't let the chopper take off."

"I spit on helicopters," Miguelito said and started firing.

Jess aimed at the tail rotor and squeezed the trigger. The two gunmen standing guard quickly hit the dirt and shot back. The pilot flipped switches and started the rotors spinning.

As the gun battle continued, a round hit the chopper and triggered a spark. It ignited the fuel tanks and, boom! A fireball nearly as high as a shihuahuaco tree shot into the sky and hundreds of birds of every shape, size, and color took flight.

The concussion from the explosion rolled across the clearing. Jess ducked. When he looked back up, he saw Blue Macaw running across the clearing. She had Moipa's bow in her hand with an arrow drawn. One gunman was still alive. As he turned his rifle on her, she let the arrow fly. It didn't miss.

Jess scrambled after her, sweeping his gun as he ran. He needn't have bothered. It was all over.

The shaman and Moipa joined them. Miguelito did too. Blue Macaw trilled. Soon, trills answered back from the forest and the survivors of the onslaught emerged. Jess saw Nimu and her two children. The shaman raised his spear over his head and began chanting. The others joined in and then all fell silent as they went about the business of collecting their dead and carrying them into the forest.

Blue Macaw turned to Jess. "My people need me here, but my brother needs me there."

"You can't go to Coca now. It's too dangerous. When the helicopter doesn't return, they'll send another. Lead the Tarani deep into the forest, someplace where they can't find you."

"What about Dabo?"

"Don't worry about him. Logan and I'll keep fighting to free him. I'll catch the real killer. I promise."

"I never answered when you asked me if I went to the Grand Hotel that night."

"I know you didn't. How could've you known Buckle was spending the night there? Dabo wouldn't've known that either. He left the hotel before the gala was over. I only asked because I didn't want you to be surprised when the lawyer questioned you on a video conference."

"But I need to explain why I didn't answer. It's because I realized I might also be asked if I'd ever thought about killing him. The truth is, I had. Lots of times."

She looked up at the sky and then back at Jess, her eyes finding his. "After I cleaned his house and knew where he lived, I used to go there at night and stand outside and imagine myself sneaking inside when the lights turned off. Going to the kitchen and getting a knife. Tiptoeing to his bedroom. Standing over him. Waking him up so he would know it was me when I plunged the knife into his heart. I hated him that much."

"But you didn't."

"It wasn't until Dabo found me and told me he and Logan were going to meet Jim Buckle in the morning that I realized my hatred was his power over me. I decided to go to the meeting with them and tell him he no longer had that power, but I had power over him. I could tell his wife, tell the world what he did to me. I would use it against him if he didn't go along with the plan to save our homelands."

"And it probably would've worked, but someone killed him first."

Blue Macaw nodded. "You said the rainforest is too big for coincidences. What about Oakland?"

Jess felt the ground shift as if he were on a big wall and the ledge he was standing on started to crumble.

"It's the same," he said.

The shaman and Moipa joined them. The old man spoke rapidly while tapping Jess on the chest with the tip of his spear.

Blue Macaw translated. "He said he knows you looked in the eye of the jaguar mother last night and didn't flinch. You didn't flinch here either when death was near. He says you are Tarani in your heart because you love the forest—ome—and believe like we do there is no distinction between the physical and spiritual worlds."

Jess bowed to the shaman. "I'm honored."

Moipa started speaking too and, again, Blue Macaw translated. "He said next time he sees you, he'll take you hunting and you can kill the peccary. But you can't use a gun. You must use his bow and arrow."

Jess put his hand on Moipa's shoulder. "And when I hit it with your arrow, it will be because you taught me how. Until then, brother."

The shaman and Moipa walked into the forest. Blue Macaw took the feathers from her ears and pressed them into Jess's palm.

"So you will always remember us."

"I could never forget you."

"Save Dabo, and when he's free, tell him to come home."

"How will he find you?"

"I'll be waiting for him where we set Apaika free. He knows the place. If he has forgotten the exact spot, tell him the blue macaws will show him the way."

She slung the bow over her shoulder and disappeared into the forest without looking back. Jess felt the feathers in his palm and, if not for them, would've wondered if the whole morning had been another ayahuasca hallucination.

"Hurry, we must go," Miguelito said. "Scavengers will smell the bodies. We don't want to be part of their feast."

They returned to the river where the dugouts were tied to the post.

"If we paddle hard, we can reach Father Banana's by night-fall," Jess said. "We can put up the signal and catch a river canoe to take us the rest of the way to Coca."

"No, you can't go back there. Not to Coca ever. The river has ears. News will travel about what happened here before you get there. Other sicarios will be waiting for you. You must go down-river and cross the border into Peru. Go to Iquitos. It has an airport."

"It won't be safe for you to go back to Coca either."

Miguelito snorted. "I can go anywhere I want. I'm a riberno. I will always survive."

Jess dug into his pockets and pulled out a wad of cash. He handed it to the boatman who counted it.

"You said you'd give me a fifty percent tip for taking you here and back to Coca."

"True, but you didn't take me back."

"But this is sixty percent. Here, I give you twenty percent back."

"No, you keep it all."

"You drive a hard bargain. I give you back ten percent."

"You give me back zero percent. That's the deal. Take it or leave it."

"Deal!" Miguelito grinned. "Now I give you some advice for free. When you go downriver, think like a riberno. Be a river rat. Look for timber smugglers when you get close to the border. They float big rafts of logs into Iquitos at night. Pull your dugout next to them. Pretend to be a log and you won't get caught. When they near the docks, go to shore and go home."

They shook hands, got into their dugouts, and paddled in opposite directions. Each stroke took Jess closer to Oakland and farther from the Tarani, from Blue Macaw, and from the jaguar who showed him how to look within himself and find the wildness that dwelled there as surely as his heart.

24

———

The freight elevator rumbled and Isabella hit the stop button so it wouldn't bypass the second floor. She slid open the wooden picket safety gate, took one look inside, and winced.

"What did you do, fall out of a tree?"

"Something like that," Jess said.

"This whole time you've been gone and not so much as a word. You had me worried. You worried a lot of people. Logan Riggins stopped by a couple of times looking for you. So did Detective Stone. They wouldn't tell me anything. There's been lots of news about Dabo, but nothing about you."

"Has he been arraigned?"

"They had a preliminary hearing and the judge denied bail. Logan said it didn't matter, that he had a big surprise that would prove him innocent and get him released." Floorboards creaked. The elevator groaned. Jess stayed mum. "You couldn't find Blue Macaw?"

"I did, but it's safer if she stays lost."

"Why?"

"Because a lot of things happened in Ecuador."

"What sort of things?"

Jess shook his head.

"Oh," she said.

They stared at each other. Jess said, "I'm beat. I need sleep. A lot of it." He reached for the button.

She grabbed his hand. "Sleep here. That way if anybody comes looking for you, I can tell them you're still not back."

"I'm not sure that's a good idea."

"But I am. Come on, I'll run you a bath."

Isabella's tub was in the back corner of her loft. She didn't switch on a light, but burned candles. Jess stripped off his clothes and eased into the water. It was achingly hot. He closed his eyes, letting the heat go to work loosening the muscles in his back and shoulders that were still knotted from days of paddling the dugout down the Caiman River and onto the mighty Amazon and into Iquitos.

The water level rose. Isabella slid in facing him. Her hair was tied back and she held out a tumbler. "Drink this."

"What is it?"

"Grappa."

He took a sip, wishing it was ayahuasca so he had the power to be able to see into the future and know what dangers lay in store for Blue Macaw and the Tarani. He wanted to be able to warn them, help them. Though he was thousands of miles from the rainforest, he still felt connected to it, to her, the shaman, Moipa, all of them.

Isabella slipped her legs on either side of his. He swallowed some of the brandy and watched the shadows from the candles flicker across her skin.

"We don't need to talk about it if you don't want to," she said.

"I know," he said.

She put her hands on his shoulders and inched closer until their noses were touching. He set the tumbler down and slid his hands behind her back. They clung to each other until the candles melted and the tub water cooled. He kissed her throat and pulled her even closer and then stood while lifting her with him. She wrapped her legs around his hips and he carried her to the bed.

Standing over it, he hesitated. It wasn't that he didn't want to, nor was it from guilt of having had a hand in Lyle Hunt's death and those of the captain and the other mercenaries. But he did feel remorse for having left Blue Macaw and the Tarani on their own.

Isabella squeezed tighter. "It's okay. Whatever happened there happened. All that matters now is you're back. You're safe. Let it go."

"I can't," he said.

"Why not?" she said.

"Because I left them there. The Tarani."

"To lead their lives like they've always led them."

"That's just it. They can't anymore. The world won't let them."

"Then help them so they can. Do whatever it takes and don't stop doing it."

"Okay," he said.

"Okay," she said.

"Tomorrow," he said.

"Good," she said.

And he let go, just for a little while, and they fell onto the bed and into each other.

Jess had no idea what time it was when he finally woke. It took him a few minutes to get his bearings, that he was back in Oakland, back in the building with the boat shop on the ground level and his loft on the top and Isabella's between them. She was sitting across the room at her desk, her back turned to him while she edited a video streaming across a flat screen.

"What time is it?" he said.

"Three o'clock in the afternoon."

"I've never slept so long in my life."

"You had a little help." She smiled. "You had a lot of help."

He got up and placed his hands on her shoulders and rubbed his face in her hair.

"Welcome back," she said.

He made coffee and looked out the front windows at the estuary and the boats in their slips and the silhouette of cranes at the marine terminals. A ferry was coming in from San Francisco. They were all images he'd grown up with. They were familiar, reaffirming.

Isabella asked him what he was going to do next.

"Call Logan. Let him know what happened."

"Will you tell Detective Stone?"

"Some, but not all. I can't put him in that kind of position."

"You couldn't let Buckle's murder drop even if you wanted to, could you?"

"I don't want to drop it."

"Good, because I don't want you to either. Dabo's depending on you. Blue Macaw too."

"I need to find Logan."

"So, go find him, but now that you're back, all safe and sound, promise you'll try and keep it that way."

Jess got dressed and drove to Mosswood Park. Metal chain nets rattled, basketballs thumped against backboards, and sneakers squeaked on asphalt. Tyrone Stone was playing shirts, and if any of the opponents half his age playing skins thought the gray in his goatee meant they could jam him or drive past him, they quickly got schooled. He was wearing long black nylon warm-ups and a gray Police Athletic League T-shirt. It was yoked with sweat. He was an outside shooter who wasn't afraid to take it inside through a gauntlet of flying elbows and slamming palms.

"Hey, old man, you're holdin' on to the ball like it's your walker," one of the younger skins taunted as Stone dribbled around center court waiting for a fellow shirt to get clear. "Give it up before you give yourself a heart attack."

Stone didn't respond. He didn't look at him either. The closer the heckler got, the slower the big cop bounced the ball. Finally, when the young player ran out of patience and made a grab for it, Stone juked left, spun right, and shouldered his way past, leaving the defender flailing his arms to stay upright as the detective slammed home the winning dunk.

The shirts laughed and high-fived.

"That's what we love 'bout you, Stone," a teammate said. "You don't leave nothin' behind but old sweat and young fools."

The detective went to a scarred wooden bench and pulled a towel out of a gym bag. He wiped the sweat off his face before draping the towel around his neck. He was slipping on an OPD windbreaker when Jess approached.

"You're standing there like no one's gonna notice you," Stone said. "The only other White dudes ever come around here are busters thinking they're Nikola Jokic."

"Good to see you too," Jess said. "Anything new with the case?"

Stone zipped his windbreaker and closed the gym bag. He put a foot on the bench and retied his shoelaces, chinning at the fading bruises on Jess's face. "Who gave you the beatdown?"

"You don't want to know."

"And where was the giving done?"

"Here, there, and nowhere."

"In other words, doing something someplace you don't want to talk about in a place you can't say you were at."

"It's best that way."

"Uh-huh. Well, not that I'm gonna say anything that you can't read about it, but it's a regular episode of *Law & Order* now. Ruiz and I had our half hour. We're in the background while the lawyers and judges take the prime time."

"Speaking of Ruiz, I think he's the one who was feeding inside info to CaliCo."

Stone loosened the towel around his neck as if it had been tied as tightly as a necktie. "Don't come here and tell me how to keep my house in order. You hear what I'm saying?"

"Yeah."

"My house? It's all back in order. And that means everyone living in it. Understood?"

"Perfectly. I heard they denied Dabo bail."

"What do you expect? He's a flight risk. He already rabbited once. No way a judge is gonna OR him. And even if they did set a million-dollar bail, who'd bond him? He skips, there's not a bounty hunter in Oakland dumb enough or desperate enough to go down to the jungle and try and find him. Or his sister, Blue Macaw." He paused as he studied Jess's face. "Is there?"

When he didn't reply, Stone said, "Yeah, that's what I thought."

He finished tying his shoes and then moved in so close Jess could see the veins working in his temples. "I don't know what happened down there. I don't know if I want to know. But the way I figure it, you standing here and me not hearing anything from Logan Riggins about his big surprise that's gonna free Dabo, means you didn't find the little sister."

Jess still didn't say anything.

"She's never gonna be found, is she?" Stone sucked his molar. "Seems like there's a whole lotta disappearing that goes on in the jungle."

"What do you mean?"

"Whatever you want it to. Head of security for a local oil company goes down there on a business trip and doesn't come back. Government down there doesn't know where he went or what happened to him. Homeland Security up here? They send an alert to the local cops where the man calls home in case he shows up so they can sign off and not have to worry that he was kidnapped and being held for ransom by some no-count guerillas."

"You lost me there."

He shifted the gym bag. "What's Riggins gonna say when you tell him Dabo's alibi has gone the way of the dodo?"

"Knowing Logan, he won't skip a beat."

"And what about you? What are you gonna do about it?"

"Whatever it takes to catch whoever killed Jim Buckle."

"Even if it turns out to be Dabo?"

"You heard me. Whoever."

"And if it's Logan Riggins?"

"It won't be. He's got an alibi."

"Maybe yes. Maybe no."

"What's that supposed to mean?"

"Means I'm still looking into it."

They walked to his unmarked sedan. He popped the trunk and threw in his gym bag. It landed next to a long metal box that was padlocked and bolted to the floor.

"What's with the mobile weapons locker?" Jess said.

"SOP."

"I'm guessing MS-13 was none too happy about the take-down in the Twomps."

Stone shut the trunk. "I'll be seeing you around."

Jess drove to Berkeley. The living room in Mattie Voss's house had been turned into a command center. All the couches and easy chairs had been pushed to the sides and a square of long folding tables jammed with laptops, scanners, and coffee cups occupied the center. A dozen young people sat tapping on keyboards while talking through their earbuds.

"Hello, my name is Jennifer and I'm calling on behalf of Rainforest Now!" a woman said when her screen showed she'd reached a live connection. "Tonight a man's life hangs in the balance and only you can help save him. In doing so, you'll also be helping save his home in the rainforest and all the creatures that live there. Let me tell you about Dabo and the oil company trying to destroy the Amazon."

Jess spotted Logan. He was pacing in the kitchen talking on his phone. "Come on, Sarah. I thought we saw eye to eye on this. Why are you doing this now?" When he saw Jess, surprise and then anger flashed across his face. "I got to go."

He clicked off. "What the hell are you doing back here? You were supposed to stay in Coca with Mintaka. My lawyer is on standby waiting to jet down there."

"Outside," Jess said.

Logan followed him to the garden. "What happened?"

"Lyle Hunt and a private army of cutthroats caught up to us. It was a bloodbath. On both sides."

"Was Mintaka killed?"

"I'm saying Blue Macaw is not going to Coca. She's not going to testify. She has a bigger reason than ever to stay lost now."

Logan burrowed his chin into his breastbone. He went completely still. It was as if he'd stopped breathing. After a minute, his chest heaved.

"All right, Dabo doesn't have an alibi, but we can still reach the summit. I'll step up what we're doing here."

"The room in there with all the callers, that's your idea of an alternate route?"

"We need as much popular support as we can get."

"Are you raising money for Dabo's defense or to cover your bond for the debt-for-nature swap?"

Logan stiffened. "I'm going to pretend I didn't hear that and you didn't mean it. Come on, don't go soft on me now. Media doesn't come cheap and neither do lawyers. Our phone banks are only pulling in ten-, twenty-dollar donations per supporter. We need to reach out to as many people as we can."

"How much money are you talking about?"

"Two million, at least. Maybe three."

"That's a lot of phone calls. That's a lot of lawyers."

"The phone banks are only one tactic. We're going after foundations and celebrities too. Mattie's putting together a fundraiser at the Fox Theater that will tap right into the A list. It should net us a million easy."

"We need to tell Dabo about Blue Macaw and his wife and kids. I hear they're still holding him at Dire Straits. We can go see him tomorrow morning during visitation."

Logan shook his head. "Time is our greatest enemy now. We need to divide and conquer. It doesn't take two to tell him. You go."

"We're talking about our friend. He might give up hope and start thinking he'd be better off tying a sheet around his neck and trying to evade the giant anaconda as he walks to the spirit world. He knows you. Trusts you. You can give him hope."

"So can you. Get a grip. Don't lose sight of the summit now."

"Fine. So long as you don't lose sight of Dabo."

"Never. And Sparks? Now that he doesn't have an alibi, you need to find the real killer and find him fast."

25

The jailer marched Dabo into the visitor's room. His orange jumpsuit looked baggier, his face gaunter, his eyes hollower.

Jess picked up the telephone handset on his side of the acrylic barrier. "I'm sorry, my friend, but I have sad news. Your mother died."

The bowl haircut dipped. When he looked back up, tears glistened. "She was sick. Now she is home with the ancient ones."

"She saw your sister before she died. I'm sure it helped ease her pain."

"You found Mintaka? That is good. Did she speak to the lawyer in Coca?"

"She couldn't go there. It wasn't safe."

"Why not?"

Jess remembered the lawyer's advice about the conversations on prison telephones being recorded. "Cowori," he said.

Dabo mulled that over. "Did she go later?"

"No. She is with Nimu and your children. The shaman and others too. They are hiding because the cowori made it unsafe.

They will see you where Apaika was set free. The blue macaws will show you the way."

"But I will need to leave here."

"And you will. You must keep hope and faith alive. Logan has been busy mounting your defense. He's raising money to pay the lawyer and building public support for you. A lot of people are on your side."

"I will try, but it is difficult. Too many men in cells and not enough beds. I sleep on the floor. I cannot go outside and feel the air, smell the trees, hear the birds. Without them, I will never be free."

"We're doing everything we can to get you out."

"Yes, but whoever killed Buckle will do everything they can to keep me here so they can be free."

"I'm going to promise you what I promised Blue Macaw. I'll find the killer. You have my word."

Dabo stared through the acrylic wall. "What about the cowori who made it unsafe for Mintaka and Nimu and my children?"

"You'll have to ask the caiman."

Dabo placed his palm flat against the see-through barrier. "Thank you, my friend."

Jess put his palm against his. "*De nada.* It was nothing."

As he crossed the lobby, he spotted Stone leaving through the front door. He followed the detective outside.

When they were on the street, Stone turned around. "You visited Dabo?"

"It's time to compare notes."

"What did he tell you?"

"Quid pro quo, right?"

Stone cocked a brow. "You got something, you best give it up right here and now. I don't got to give you shit in return."

Jess glanced at all the storefront lawyers, bail bond agents, and reporters trolling for clients and gossip.

"Buckle kidnapped Blue Macaw in Ecuador when she was a young teen. He flew her here on his private jet and locked her in an apartment on Lake Merritt. He didn't bother declaring her when he came through customs and he sure as hell didn't waste time before he started raping her."

Stone shot up his hand like he was stopping traffic. His eyes darted at the crowd of lowlifes to see if they'd heard him. "Let's go."

He led Jess into the jail's parking garage and unlocked his unmarked sedan. Stone didn't say a word as he fired the ignition and squealed the tires leaving. He crossed the city and turned up Snake Boulevard when they reached the foot of the East Bay Hills.

Stone kept his foot on the gas as they headed up the steep, winding road, taking every curve too fast. He turned right when they reached Skyline and followed the ridgeline south. They passed the entrance to Redwood Park. Stone didn't even glance at it even though six months earlier he'd been life-flighted from the parking lot with three soft-nosed rounds in him and a less than one-in-a-hundred chance of surviving.

A half mile past the entrance, he pulled into a turnout and parked the sedan with its windshield facing the view of Oakland and San Francisco across the Bay.

"You been busier than an Eagle Scout, I see that now. You tell me, I tell you. What else have you got?"

Jess told him about how Blue Macaw finally escaped from the apartment at Lake Merritt. How she went to work for Casa Clean and how she ended up cleaning Buckle's house in Piedmont.

Stone was nodding as Jess finished. "Did she go to the Grand Hotel the night he died?"

"No. She didn't know Buckle was spending the night there in a suite upstairs."

"Maybe her brother told her."

"How would've he known? He left the gala soon after Logan and I did."

"Somebody went up to that room. It had a whole lot of traffic going in and out considering the condition of the occupant."

"How do you know that?"

"Prints on the carpet. Lab had a time puzzling them all out, putting a timeline to each set. There were three sets. Two were shoeprints. We figure one of those for the housekeeper who called it in. The other one? Unknown."

"That leaves the third, the barefoot one."

"The killer's. We're still working on that."

"Maybe one set of the shoeprints was the killer's after taking a shower and getting dressed."

Stone didn't say anything.

Beyond the sedan's windshield, a pair of turkey vultures were riding the thermals wafting up the face of the East Bay Hills. The wind made the surrounding eucalyptus trees rattle. Jess rolled down the window and breathed in their tart and oily smell. A blue jay scolded him from a nearby limb.

"What did you find out about the call made to Buckle's secretary that prompted her to call the hotel's front desk to send up housekeeping to check on him?" Jess said. "She said no one could reach him on direct dial or his cell. Sounds like someone was trying to goose a discovery."

"It was Pius Wheedling. Appears checking up on Buckle and keeping him on schedule is part of his job description."

"Among other things."

Stone twisted in his seat. "Wheedling's phone call wasn't the only one that caught our eye. Someone called Logan Riggins's room from a house phone in the lobby right around the time we figure the murder was going down."

"That doesn't fit. Logan left with Mattie Voss. She vouched for him. And then there's the time-stamped valet receipt for her car."

"That's right. Still, someone called his room after that."

"Who?"

The big cop shrugged. "Don't know exactly. Most hotels don't even bother putting phones in rooms anymore because everyone uses their cell. Grand's old-fashioned that way. Not only does every room have a phone, guests can set it up with their own personal voice mail. Logan had. His voice was still on it when we checked, but whoever was calling him didn't leave a message."

"Maybe somebody misdialed."

"Not a chance. The phones in the lobby only connect to the hotel operator. She's got to put the call through to the room. A caller can't ask to be connected to a room number. They got to know the guest's name. Privacy and all."

"The operator didn't write down the caller's name?"

"No. See, the operator's not even in the hotel. Call goes to the hotel chain's switchboard somewhere back east. And when I say back east, I mean India. They handle hundreds of calls an hour from hotels all over the world."

"If the caller was using a lobby phone, it could be on the security camera video. I'm assuming you've already gone through it to pinpoint when Dabo left the hotel that night and for any other traffic on Buckle's floor."

"Privacy laws again. There isn't any video. Class action lawsuit against another hotel chain put the freeze on a lot of others using video security. You know, who wants to stay in a hotel where your face may end up on tape. Maybe who you checked in with wasn't your spouse and it gets used as evidence against you in the divorce. Only cameras the Grand uses are out in the parking garage making sure no one's breaking into cars."

"Maybe whoever was working the front desk or a bellboy or a housecleaner saw someone on the house phone."

"We canvassed everybody. Nothing. It was busier than MacArthur BART station at rush hour. You know, with the gala going on."

"Sounds to me that whoever was calling Logan's room hadn't gotten the word he'd moved on," Jess said.

"Yeah," Stone said. "Moved on by moving in with his new girlfriend."

26

The CaliCo Oil refinery was lit up like a house at Christmas. Strings of white lights outlined the cracking units and blending plants while a blue flame flared from the top of the main stack. Even speeding by with the windows up, Jess could smell the stench of rotten eggs.

He wondered if it was true that right before you die, your life flashes before your eyes and your senses remember all that you saw, heard, tasted, and smelled. Did Buckle have the tang of crude oil in his nostrils when the machete came down? Did Lyle Hunt see the reflection of his shooting glasses in the unblinking eyes of the caiman? Most of all, Jess wondered if Pius Wheedling was wondering the same thing about Hunt and what he planned to do about it.

He crossed the Richmond–San Rafael Bridge and entered Marin County. A dog-leg south on Highway 101 took him to Sausalito. Oakland was only twelve miles across the Bay as the brown pelican flew, but it might as well have been a million. Where the Oakland Estuary was jammed with hulking marine terminals and gigantic cranes offloading container ships, Sausalito's postcard-pretty little harbor berthed sleek sailboats, luxury yachts and custom-built houseboats. Boutiques and trendy cafes lined the waterfront. Even the artist studios were upscale and upbeat. Homes with water views started north of $10 million dollars.

Sarah Newton's glass and steel contemporary was no exception. She opened the front door herself and led Jess into a living room that had floor-to-ceiling windows and a sweeping view of Alcatraz and San Francisco beyond.

"Why did you ask me to come over?" Jess said.

"I wanted to apologize for being rude when you visited my office," she said. "Forgive me?"

"Sure."

Sarah smiled and gestured at a beige leather couch. They took seats. She plucked a bottle of chardonnay from a silver ice bucket and filled two glasses. Her upper arms looked as if she could still hold her own on a pitch. Jess flashed on the time a cocky rock jock who'd joined Logan, Sarah, and him for an assault on Nutcracker complained that she'd slow them down. Sarah promptly challenged him to a side-by-side pull-up contest on a tree limb. The rock jock made it to twenty before he let go. Sarah kept at it until she hit fifty.

"You've come a long way from slamming down beers at the Trail's End after a climb in Yosemite," Jess said, waving at the view, the expensive furnishings, and the modern art hanging on the few walls that weren't glass.

"While I do apologize for the way I acted toward you, I don't for the way I live. I've worked very hard for everything I have."

"Who would've thought a little gallery in Berkeley would lead to all this."

"I never doubted it for a moment. Business is like rock climbing. The top's the goal. Anything short is only a waste of blood, sweat, and tears."

"That's a Logan saying."

Sarah ran the tip of her finger around the rim of her wine glass. "I still care about Logan. Very much. I was crushed by what happened between us. It took me a long time to get over it."

"Is that why you never remarried?"

"I am married. To Wild Things." She took a sip of wine. "I'm very worried about him."

"Logan's in his element. The bigger the challenge, the happier he is."

"I know, but he's bitten off too much. He's fighting Big Oil. He's fighting a foreign country. He's involved in a murder. I mean, my God, it's horrible."

"Logan says it all boils down to money. Theirs and his. He's hoping he can raise enough to defend Dabo as well as the rainforest."

"Do you think he has any chance stopping CaliCo from winning those leases? The tracts on the Tarani homelands are estimated to hold fifteen million barrels. If the deal includes shipping it directly to their refinery here, CaliCo's annual revenues will go through the roof and stay that way for years."

"You've been doing your homework."

Sarah turned toward the window and its view of the water. "I must've picked that up in *The Wall Street Journal*. Whatever. The important thing is, while Logan and I have had our differences, I certainly don't want to see him get hurt."

"If you're asking me to tell him to stop short of the top and rappel down, forget it. He wouldn't listen."

"How much will it take for him to win?"

"To defend Dabo?"

"That too, but to prevent CaliCo from winning the oil leases."

"Logan's goal is upward of three million to get Dabo freed

and continue his fight to block CaliCo. I assumed you weren't interested in contributing."

"What makes you think that?"

"The feeling I got when I walked in and Logan was talking to you on the phone. He didn't sound very happy. Angry and frustrated, more like it."

"You must've misunderstood. Logan always gets worked up when he talks about money. That's what he was doing, asking me for a contribution. A sizeable one at that."

"Does that mean you'll be attending the big fundraiser he's having?"

"The event Mattie Voss is putting together?" Sarah's nose wrinkled. "Logan hasn't changed. He's always needed a woman's help. There are lots of Matties. Young, beautiful, and bright enough to act not too bright around men like Logan."

"Mattie's plenty bright. And determined. When it comes to orchestrating a campaign, she sees the big picture but doesn't lose sight of the details. She has quite the track record winning political contests. How about your friend, Clare Buckle? Does your description apply to her?"

"That's awfully harsh considering what she's going through."

"I'm not the one who wrote about her in Buckle's obituary. How she went from a junior assistant in CaliCo's marketing department to the wife of the CEO and having a seat on every nonprofit board there is in the Bay Area. Kind of in your league when it comes to supporting the arts."

"If that's supposed to be your idea of a compliment, it's pretty left-handed."

"You invited me over, Sarah. Apology aside, I'm guessing you'd like me to get Logan to stop asking you for a donation. I can ask, but he won't listen. You want my advice? Cut him a check or give him one of those paintings on the wall to auction off."

"Inviting you here to mend fences was a mistake. I see that now. You've never gotten over that I forced you out at Wild Things." She paused. "Or is it that you've never gotten over your boyhood crush on me?"

"I'll tell you what I haven't gotten over. It's something Dabo said when I saw him at Dire Straits earlier today. He said the worst thing was not being able to go outside and breathe fresh air, smell the trees, hear the birds. Without them, he could never be free." Jess waved at the room. "None of your big windows open. You can't smell the water, hear the seagulls. It's no different than a jail cell."

On the drive home, Jess remembered a time from years before. The City of Oakland and the Port Commission had launched a ballot initiative to rezone all of the blocks down by the waterfront. Part of the campaign included taking over buildings through condemnation or eminent domain. When his grandfather got wind of it, he vowed to barricade himself in the boat shop and defend it against all comers.

"The damn developers are to blame, the greedy sons of bitches," he'd said. When Jess tried to explain it was a City of Oakland-backed initiative, the old man scoffed. "It's not the politicians, lad. If you want to know who's really behind the plan, just follow the money."

The memory prompted Jess to make a stop on the way.

It was closing in on nine o'clock when he arrived at the Orbit, a dive popular with bloggers and gamers in West Oakland. Harrison Eight was sitting at the bar playing a game on his phone waiting for someone to respond to his latest post. Popular topics on his blog were conspiracy theories about Bitcoin, NFTs, sovereign debt, and credit derivatives.

Jess took the stool next to him. "Buy you one?" He signaled the bartender and asked her to bring the blogger another cocktail and a beer for himself.

Harrison squinted through owlish, black-framed glasses. "Do I know you?"

"Jess Parks, Search and Rescue. Last year at Del Valle? You got lost on the Haas School of Business reunion hike. Remember?"

"You must have me mistaken."

"No mistake. You lost your glasses and lost your way on the Murietta Falls trail and sprained your ankle. I'm the one who found you in the dead of night and carried you out. We talked a lot on the way."

"Right you are. I remember now, though I do try to forget my more painful embarrassments. What are you doing here?"

"I live nearby. What are you up to these days?"

"Work. Covering cryptocurrencies and how they're fueling a global crime syndicate. Forget James Bond's Spectre. This one's real and well on its way to collapsing the international financial system and taking over the world."

The bartender slid an appletini in front of the blogger. Harrison pulled the slice of green apple from the rim of the glass and took a nibble. "Is this a bribe of some sort? I have to tell you I won't be bought. I cover the truth, no matter how hard people try to cover it up."

"I remember our conversation when we were coming out of Del Valle that night. It seemed to me that you knew everything about every business in the Bay Area."

"I do, why?"

"I need some background."

"On a who or a what?"

"Both. Logan Riggins. Sarah Newton. Wild Things."

Harrison groaned. "That's ancient history."

"I guess you haven't been keeping up about Logan coming back after living in Ecuador to stop CaliCo Energy from bidding on oil lease tracts there. Jim Buckle's murder? Logan was taken in for questioning. His Indigenous friend was arrested for it."

"Of course I know all about that. I meant the divorce and sale of Wild Things. It was seven, eight years ago. That's a lifetime in business. Tech firms? They go through an evolution annually. During the heyday, hundreds of start-ups were bought and sold or flamed out every week."

"What do you remember about the buyout between Sarah and Logan?"

"That I was glad I never got married. Seriously, I worked my ass off trying to nail down that story. It wasn't easy. For starters, the company is privately held. Since it doesn't issue publicly traded stock, it doesn't have to disclose financials."

The blogger chewed the rest of the apple garnish and followed it with a gulp. "A lot of the furniture and home goods companies are like that. They have a hard enough time as it is getting investors because their business model is so flaky. Sales go up and down with the seasons. Twenty-somethings furnishing their first apartments after college deciding what's hot and what's not can make or break a company. A boat bringing in goods from an Asian sweatshop gets delayed by a typhoon and, wham, they miss stocking the shelves for the all-important Christmas rush."

"How much do you think Logan walked away with money-wise?"

"No way it was a lump sum. They wouldn't have structured the deal like that. Too much cash for a company their size to come up with, plus too many tax liabilities for both sides."

"How would they do it?"

"I don't know for sure. I was digging into it, but kept running into Great Walls. When Logan joined the ranks of the disappeared, all of my usual sources suddenly became Sarah Newton cheerleaders."

"But I bet you have a pretty good idea what the terms were."

"All the analysts had Wild Things's market cap pegged at three billion. That's not the same as walkaway money in a sale, mind you."

He pushed his glasses to keep them from sliding off his nose. "Meaning, if Logan and Sarah had sold, they wouldn't get a billion and a half each. You have to calculate assets and revenues against debts. Same if one of them buys the other out. But say they finally get the number they both want. Sarah bought out Logan, but she wouldn't have that kind of cash on hand. She couldn't go out and borrow it either because she'd have to disclose the financials to get a loan, and whoever lent it would want a piece of the pie. She'd be trading one husband for another."

"Then how'd they work it?"

"An up-front lump sum followed by regularly scheduled payouts based on how well the company did each year. Best guess? Twenty percent of his portion of the walkaway with subsequent payments based on a percentage of the annual sales. Logan probably insisted on some kind of collateral to handle the follow-up payments. I'll bet you there wasn't a whole lot of trust between them when they were cutting the deal."

"What kind of collateral?"

"Hard to say. It could have been anything from a big chunk of money put in some kind of special account as a guarantee against future payouts or a bond that would cover the amount in case Sarah defaulted."

"If you had to guess, what do you think he walked with?"

"A hundred million along with a pretty fat check every year."

Jess stared at his beer trying to sort through it all. Logan had told him he put his entire Wild Things's stake down as a nonrefundable surety on the debt-for-nature swap deal. One hundred million dollars was a lot to risk in anybody's book.

"You look confused," Harrison said.

"A little. What do you figure he's getting in terms of the annual payment?"

"It all depends on Wild Things's revenues, but it's not what he expected seven years ago. It's not the same company. Sarah has taken it in a whole new direction. She had to."

"Why's that?"

"She has all sorts of new competition from new companies, new brands, new tastes. At the same time that she's trying to stay a step ahead of them, her costs keep going up and her margins down. Not the easiest position to be in, but, hey, that's the home decorating trade for you."

"Care to explain?"

Harrison pushed his glasses up again. "Margin is the spread between how much it costs to make a bedroom set and what she gets when she sells it. It was one thing when she was selling her own brand through her own stores, but now that she has to move merchandise through big box chains, she has to sell a lot more goods to equal the kind of spread she once made."

"You mean Wal-Mart, Target? Why is she doing that?"

"Because everyone wants a discount. Target may be selling more units for Sarah than she ever did herself, but there's no way she's getting the same markup."

"She doesn't look like she's hurting. You should see her house in Sausalito."

"What do you expect? She's in the appearance business. Image is everything. She has to put up a front even if it's all leveraged to the max so she can stick with her own kind. It's a high price to belong, but worth it. The woman Sarah sits with on the opera board has a partner whose international law firm helps her get a favorable trade agreement with China. A member of her health club heads a transportation firm willing to give her a break on shipping."

"Thanks for the info. I got to go."

The blogger frowned. "You sure? It's early. Have another beer."

"Some other time. If you think of anything else, give me a call."

"Okay, but it'll cost you more than an appletini. I'm thinking dinner at Chez Panisse."

27

The light was flat and skeins of mist snaked between the office towers lining Broadway and floated over the side streets. Despite the gloomy weather, downtown Oakland was pulsating with human energy. Jess could hear the drums and bullhorns, chants and cheers from blocks away. Several hundred demonstrators were gathered in front of Cali-Co's corporate headquarters. Their protest signs and banners were the modern-day equivalent of torches and pitchforks.

Logan Riggins stood on a stepladder and shouted through a megaphone. "What do we want?"

"Justice," the crowd roared back.

"When do we want it?"

"Now."

"What do we want?"

"Justice for Dabo."

"When do we want it?"

"Now."

"What do we want?"

"Save the rainforest."

"When do we want it?"

"Now."

"What do we want?"

"Freedom from Big Oil."

"When do we want it?"

"Now."

Logan raised a clenched fist and the crowd erupted. He jumped off the stepladder and a local rap artist took his place. The crowd cheered again when the heavy thump of bass boomed and his trademark staccato rattled the windows of the office buildings.

Stop the drillin'

Stop the killin'

Who the villain

Big Oil

They come to the jungle and cut all the trees

They take all the oil and do what they please.

They come to the jungle and kill all the birds

They lie to the people, don't listen to their words.

Stop the drillin'

Stop the killin'

Who the villain

Big Oil

The crowd surged forward as they picked up the refrain. OPD patrol cars were parked nearby with lines of cops dressed in riot gear standing by. TV news vans arrived and the video crews began pushing their way through the demonstrators to get to the front of the building.

The presence of the cameras triggered a new round of chanting and shoving. Signs were swaying back and forth like buoys on a windswept sea. A clap of thunder sounded, but it wasn't from stormy weather. Someone had thrown a metal trash can at one of the ground-floor plate glass windows. The explosion sent people running. It also triggered the riot police to charge.

Logan jumped back on the stepladder and urged the crowd to remain calm. His words were lost in the din. He was soon surrounded by cops wielding batons. Logan was pushed off the ladder and belly-flopped on one. That sparked even more pushing, shoving, and shouting.

When it was all over, the members of the riot squad were facing down the crowd. Logan lay on his stomach, his hands pulled behind him by a cop struggling to cuff them while another pinned him to the pavement with his knee. Blood was streaming down his forehead as a TV camera along with a hundred cell phones captured it. By the time he was yanked to his feet and hustled away, the scene logged thousands of views on TikTok, Twitter, and YouTube.

As the cops pushed the people back from the building and down side streets, Logan was shoved into the back seat of a patrol car. Pius Wheedling appeared. He introduced himself to the television crew filming the arrest and said he had an announcement to make. The camera operator turned the lens on him.

"While CaliCo Energy does not condone Mr. Riggins's tactics, and we are dismayed by his disregard for public safety and private property, we do support his right to free speech." He paused for effect. "For that reason, we will not be pressing charges against him. We would like to invite the public to meet with us so that we may engage in a productive exchange of ideas. We all want the same thing—a healthy environment and a reliable source of energy for our families."

The crew got what they needed and moved on.

"Doesn't matter whether you press charges or not," a cop said to Wheedling. "We're taking him to Dire Straits. He assaulted one of us."

"Of course," he said. "Rules are rules and laws must be

enforced. Please keep us apprised of the injured officer's condition and let him know CaliCo will be making a generous contribution to the Police Assistance Fund on his behalf."

Wheedling came up to Jess as the patrol car pulled away. "I see you have returned from Ecuador."

"How did you know I was there?"

"I, uh, must have heard it from someone."

"Who?"

"I cannot recall."

"Had to have been Lyle Hunt. I ran into him down there."

"You did?"

"Yeah."

"When was that?"

"Before he went missing."

"Pardon?"

"OPD told me Homeland Security contacted them, that they're looking into his disappearance."

"They are mistaken. Mr. Hunt is not missing. He requested a few personal days to take in the local sights since he was already there on business."

Jess realized CaliCo was never going to admit what really happened. Acknowledging an attack in the Tarani homelands would generate press, the kind that might interfere with their bid on the oil leases.

"Then he'll have quite a tale to tell when he gets back, especially if he ventured into the rainforest hunting for wildlife. There's nothing quite like seeing a jaguar or caiman up close. All those teeth."

He didn't wait to see Wheedling's reaction, but returned to the boat shop. Two hours later Logan showed up. His expression looked as angry as the puckered split in his scalp did.

"What the hell were you thinking meeting with Sarah? What did you say to her?"

"I didn't think you two were on speaking terms anymore."

"She has a way of letting me know every time she thinks I misstep. Why did you go see her?"

"She invited me. You asked me to find out who killed Jim Buckle and that's what I'm doing."

"Sarah doesn't have anything to do with it."

"You sure about that?"

"What's that supposed to mean?"

"She was at the hotel the night Buckle was killed."

"So were you. So was I. So were lots of people."

"She was also pretty friendly with Buckle and his wife."

"So are lots of people."

"While we're on the subject, what about you? Did you see Buckle after he left the ballroom?"

"You already know the answer to that."

"I thought I did. Tell me again."

"You and Isabella left. Mattie and I were right behind you. I spent the night at her place. End of story."

"You didn't leave and then go back?"

"Why would I?"

"Did you see Sarah on your way out, tell her you were going home with Mattie?"

"You're pissing me off, Sparks. Whose side are you on?"

"Dabo's. Blue Macaw's."

"So am I."

"Then start acting like it."

"I'm doing everything I can. What more do you want me to do?"

"You can start by telling the truth. You told me you were broke. That you'd put everything you got from Wild Things into the debt-for-nature swap."

"And I did. Want to see my receipt for the surety bond?"

"But you didn't mention that you still get a big check from

Wild Things every year. If you're getting so much cash, why all the effort to raise money for Dabo's lawyer? Why not cut a check yourself?"

Logan walked over to a large plastic trash can used as a standup rack for kayak paddles. He pulled one out and held it like a jousting stick.

"We've been friends a long time. Who are you going to trust? The guy that always held your rope, the guy who pulled you back up Lost Arrow when you fell, or an oil company trying to sink my ship?"

Jess didn't answer.

"I don't expect you to like everything I'm doing here. I'm making most of this up as I go. Playing the media, raising money, putting a defense together for Dabo. But you have to trust me. I'm doing the right thing here. I'm trying to save a whole bunch of habitat from a whole bunch of bad people who can outspend, out-lobby, and out-politic me. I don't care if I have to step on a few toes to make this work."

"You didn't answer my question. Did you talk to Sarah after I left the gala? What about Buckle, did you talk to him?"

"No and no."

"What about later? Did you go back that night after you and Mattie left?"

"I already told you. No. What makes you think that anyway?"

"The cops looked at the hotel phone records. Someone called your room from the lobby around the time Buckle was murdered."

"Well, I'd already left so I wouldn't know about that, would I?"

Logan put the paddle back in the trashcan and walked over to the orange kayak resting on the sawhorses. He ran his palm along *Pursuit's* hull.

"I didn't bullshit you about the money. All my cash is tied up in the debt-for-nature deal. And, yeah, I am supposed to get a regular payment from Wild Things as part of the sale agreement. But it's not so regular."

"Is that why you've been calling Sarah?"

He stopped palming the kayak. "Getting divorced is harder than going bankrupt. Sarah's still Sarah. For your sake and mine, keep her out of this."

28

Isabella was scowling while standing in the middle of her loft. Her arms were tightly crossed against the front of a vintage black-and-white Oakland Raiders sweatshirt.

"How's the new piece coming?" Jess said.

"Frustrating. I'm trying to put a modern spin on mai. It's a traditional Japanese dance, but the soundtrack is in need of inspiration. A lot of inspiration."

"Would some sushi help?"

"You read my mind."

They walked to Shigi's. It was the restaurant owner's nickname. He'd been born in Tokyo and raised on American jazz. He liked music like his fish, raw but smooth, and he served up both seven nights a week.

"*Konichiwa,*" he said as Isabella and Jess took seats at the sushi bar. "I haven't seen you for a couple of weeks. What happen, you find another jazz joint that has fresher maguro?"

"I was out of town for a while," Jess said. "Out of the country actually. Ecuador."

Shigi's hands were a blur as he began slicing thumb-sized

pieces of bluefin and yellowtail and placing them on perfectly molded pedestals of rice. "What's the sushi like there?"

"I didn't go to the coast. I was in the Amazon. The fish I ate was cooked. Pirarucu. They can reach two hundred pounds easy."

"That's a lot of sashimi."

Isabella laughed and toasted him with a cup of sake.

Shigi asked if she went too.

"No, I've been busy preparing a piece I'm doing with dance students at Oakland High. We're going to perform it at graduation."

"Break a leg."

"We don't say that in dance. It's bad luck."

"What do you say?"

"*Merde.* That's French for shit."

"I don't get it."

Isabella shrugged. "It's a tradition a lot older than me."

Shigi placed a wooden platter of carefully arranged fish in front of them. The red tuna, orange flying fish roe, and green horseradish paste resembled a painter's palette.

"Who's in the house tonight?" Jess said.

"Stevie Wesson Quartet. They're homegrown talent, but they can kick it. Plus, a little surprise in store."

"Who?"

"Brandon Margolis. He called from LA and asked if he could drop in so he could try a new riff he's working on. He's scheduled to do some private gig tomorrow night, but he's flying up early."

"Must be techies in Silicon Valley. They're the only ones rich enough to hire a Grammy winner for a cocktail party."

"No, it's here in the East Bay. He says it's a favor for an old friend. He played at her wedding up in the wine country before he got famous. I guess he figures he owes her one, especially after what happened."

"What was that?"

"Her husband was murdered."

"Jim Buckle?"

"That's right."

"What kind of party, a wake?"

"Brandon said it has to do with the family business. A reception after the board of directors meeting. Guess they're doing it up big since she's taking his place as chair of the board."

Brandon Margolis sat in with the local quartet and blew until closing, switching between alto and tenor sax. He mixed in his own stuff with some of the standards and then played his newest composition. Its name was "Like Life" and it started off sweet and innocent, followed by a long, energetic riff, and closed sad and soulful.

"That song couldn't've been named any better," Jess said as they walked home. "Like real life itself."

He was still humming it when the freight elevator let Isabella off on her floor and he rode up to his. Despite the sake and sushi, the jazz had left him keyed up. He turned on his laptop and searched the net for C. Jamison and Clare Buckle AND Sarah Newton.

The list of results ran screen after screen: society blogs, newspaper columns, clips from TV, and web pages covering all the galas and opening night parties at the opera, ballet, and symphony the trio had attended. One of the older posts was coverage of the wedding. The writer gushed that the groom had bought the bride a mansion in Piedmont as a wedding gift and the interior and all its furnishings had been designed and provided by one of her oldest and closest friends, Sarah Newton, founder of Wild Things.

Jess turned off the computer and leaned back. It wasn't Brandon Margolis's new song playing in his head. It was what Harrison Eight had said about appearances and sticking together no matter the cost.

lenn E. Dyer Detention Facility was mostly used for booking and detention. Inmates typically spent less than seventy-two hours downtown. Either they sobered up, made bail, or were bussed to Alameda County's Santa Rita Jail to wait for their court appearance. If their sentence was measured in days, not years, they could finish out their time planting tomatoes and zucchinis. Longer jolts earned them a trip to a maximum-security prison. Sociopaths were shipped off to Pelican Bay, a supermax near the Oregon border where the isolation cells were so small there wasn't even enough room to dream.

Dabo had stayed at Dire Straits longer than most, but with no trial date in sight, the court ordered him transferred to Santa Rita. He was loaded into an Alameda County Sheriff's bus with a dozen other inmates for the thirty-minute journey east. Upon arrival, he was assigned a bunk and given a towel along with a Bible. A member of the Aryan Brotherhood jumped him within an hour.

Tyrone Stone called Jess to give him the news. "The other caveboys took their time getting out of the way when the guards tried breaking it up. By the time they got to Dabo, he'd lost a quart of blood, four of his ribs were busted, and his cheekbone crushed."

Jess asked if he was going to survive.

"They put him in ICU. He's on a vent and hooked to a dialysis machine because the shiv cut a kidney. Word is, wait and see."

"Was it random or was he targeted?"

"All joints run on lies and rumor. Santa Rita's no different. Truth gets put in a brown bag along with an inmate's civies when they check in. Transfers from Dire Straits find their reps get there before they do. Dabo's was a case of mistaken identity. Somebody trying to buy himself protection spread the word that Dabo was MS-13. The Brotherhood decided one more Mara was one too many. They launched a preemptive."

"Who else knows about the attack?"

"What you mean is, does the media know. Not yet, but it's only a matter of time. They checked him into Highland under his prison number, but what comes next is what always happens. His name gets leaked from another prisoner trying to trade on it or a special interest group or elected official makes a big announcement trying to trade on it too."

"But you called me first."

"This comes from upstairs. They want you to tell Logan Riggins what went down. No one wants to see it spun as some kind of conspiracy between the oil company and the City."

"And there isn't one?"

"I'm telling you what I know, but you tell me the folks upstairs are wrong thinking how Riggins will play it."

"The same way he does everything—to win. There's nothing I can say that will make Logan dial it down once he hears. He's organizing a defense fund and holding a checkbook rally at the

Fox on Saturday night. News of Dabo being assaulted in jail will make it standing room only."

Logan took the news like Jess knew he would. "The bastards. First they try and kill his sister, now they try and kill him. CaliCo won't be satisfied until they've drained the Amazon. They don't care how many Tarani die in the process."

Jess was calling while driving to Piedmont. He stopped at a red light and waited for Logan to say more. The only way he knew he was still on the line was the muffled voices coming from the war room at Mattie's house.

The light turned green. "You still there, Sparks?"

"I'm here."

"You say Dabo's in ICU on life support?"

"That's what Stone said."

"I wonder if they allow nonfamily visitors."

"They might make an exception for you since he doesn't have any relatives here. It would certainly help lift his spirits. I'll come pick you up. We can go together."

"I meant if they'd permit a camera crew. We can't waste what happened. This is war and Dabo's a soldier who went down in battle. We have to make something of his sacrifice. We upload a deathbed scene and we'll win this thing. I know it. A picture's worth a thousand words. A video's worth a million."

Jess clicked his phone off.

He drove the speed limit through Piedmont and parked in front of the Buckle mansion. Esme answered the front door. "Is the señora expecting you?"

"No, but tell her it's important. It has to do with Sarah Newton."

She closed the door in his face the same as before.

As he waited, he glanced at the front yard. Jim Buckle was dead and buried, but someone was still paying the gardener's bill. The grass was newly mowed and edged. The flowerbeds showed more hues than a crayon box. A pair of goldfinches chirped from a trellis dripping with purple wisteria.

The door opened and Esme led him to the backyard. Clare was sitting at a patio table next to a swimming pool watching two little girls playing in a sandbox.

"I'm not sure why I agreed to see you," she said. "When you were here before, you pretended to be a policeman."

"No, I said I was working with the police to solve your husband's murder. I still am. If you call Detective Tyrone Stone, he'll verify that. Would you like his number?"

She hesitated. "What do you want?"

"First of all, congratulations. I understand CaliCo's board elected you as its chair."

"Thank you, but that's not why you wish to speak to me, is it?"

"Not the only reason, no. Last time you gave the impression that Sarah Newton was a passing acquaintance."

"I don't see what relevance that has on anything."

"It depends."

"On what?"

"The truth. The way you understand it and the way you tell it. Sarah decorated your home here. She attended your wedding. You two have headed the invitation list on every party and every fundraiser that's ever been thrown in the past five years."

"So?"

"She was also a close friend of your husband. Her ex-husband is connected to his murder. She was at the hotel the night he died."

"Everyone already knows that."

"Then why tell me she was only an acquaintance?"

Clare sighed. "Because when all is said and done, that's all she ever really was. I met Sarah at a fundraiser shortly after Jim and I were engaged. I was very intimidated by her. She ran a billion-dollar business. I was the girl who worked in the marketing department and married the boss. At first, I expected she would treat me as a trophy wife like so many others did, but she surprised me and said we should become close friends."

"But that didn't happen?"

"Not for lack of trying on my part, but eventually I realized she was only being nice to me because of her relationship with my husband. She'd known Jim from before. They were both on the Bay Area Business Council and served on boards together. They spoke the same language. Business. You know, return on investment, operating exposure, look-through. They were both very competitive. With others, with themselves."

"Were they having an affair?"

"Oh, they'd had a little fling before I met Jim—he told me—but after we were married, their relationship was strictly business. Who was building the best company, the most successful. Who was gaining market share the fastest. That sort of thing."

Clare picked up a glass of iced tea, but didn't drink. She looked at the two children playing in the sandbox. The older girl was using a red plastic scoop to fill a matching bucket. Her little sister was trying to mimic her.

"My husband loved us very much. He gave us everything we needed. We were his life. I don't doubt that for a minute. But I also know we weren't his only life. His business life was very important to him. It was how he defined himself. Sarah's the same."

"I believe you," Jess said. "But I also believe you weren't being truthful when I asked you about the young woman from Ecuador who cleaned your house. You knew about Blue Macaw. You found her in your bedroom after she shrieked when she saw a photograph of you and your husband. You dismissed her immediately."

"I thought ... I thought the girl was stealing something."

"No you didn't. You told Esme to lie about her when you went out to the hallway to bring her in to talk to me. You knew your husband had brought her up from Ecuador and kept her in an apartment leased by CaliCo."

"How do you know all that?"

"Because I was in Ecuador. I met Blue Macaw."

Clare gasped.

"She told me everything. If you don't believe me, I can describe your husband's, er, fascinations in detail."

She set the glass of iced tea down. "I didn't know her name. I never met her. Not until that day here in the house."

"Did you talk to your husband about it?"

"No. If I had, it would have made it real. Besides, it ended on its own anyway. Those sorts of things always do."

"Are you saying there were other girls like Blue Macaw?"

"I'm quite finished speaking on that matter. Esme will show you out."

Clare picked up her iced tea. The cubes clinked. The sun hit the swimming pool at an angle and sent a shower of sparkles across the water like someone throwing cut glass on a blue tarp.

"Tell me about Jim and Sarah's business dealings together."

"I don't know what you mean."

"What was it? He gave her a loan in exchange for a stake in the company?"

"You make it sound so illegal. Don't you think I know how this kind of thing can get twisted around? How the media will treat it?" She glanced at the sandbox again. Her oldest daughter waved at her. She waved back. "CaliCo wasn't only Jim's company. It belongs to me and the girls too."

"It's all going to come out, one way or the other. I'm not the only one trying to solve your husband's murder."

Clare pursed her lips. "You're making something into a big deal that was nothing. We were at a dinner last year and Sarah mentioned that she was having trouble getting financing for something. I don't remember what. Jim offered to back a corporate bond for her. He said one of these days she'd have to take the company public, and when she did, he expected in on the IPO. It was typical business stuff. You know, financing arrangements, companies helping companies. It's done all the time."

The little sister in the sandbox started to cry. Clare stood abruptly. "There's nothing more I can tell you. Please don't come here again. You frighten the children."

30

Jess was back in his truck when his phone rang.

"I've got something for you," Harrison Eight said. "You owe me a big dinner."

"Sorry, can't do it right now. I'm on my way to something."

"It won't be as important as what I found out."

"What is it?"

The blogger snickered. "'Oh what a tangled web we weave when first we practice to deceive.'"

"Shakespeare?"

"For this, I'm going to order the tasting menu at Chez Panisse."

"Tell me and we'll see."

"I want props too. A quote for my website. 'Greatest financial writer ever. Makes Michael Lewis look like a Little Leaguer.'"

"You haven't told me anything."

"Are you listening? Here it comes. I have a source at Hamble and Schist, the big merger and acquisition firm. He was in on the Wild Things deal."

"What did he tell you?"

"Everything. The amounts, the way the deal was structured between Sarah and Logan, and—wait for it, wait for it—the special holding account."

"What's that?"

"The guarantee Logan got for his annual payoff."

"So?"

"*So?* Is that all you have to say?" Harrison gave an exaggerated moan.

"Okay, here's the CliffsNotes version. The special account is called Rock Solid. It's directly linked to the company's pension plan which has millions of dollars in assets—stocks, bonds, annuities, and mutual funds. Turns out, Logan wasn't the pushover the media made him out to be. In exchange for him giving up any say in company management, he got the right to tap into Rock Solid if Sarah missed making a payment."

"You mean, Logan can call up the brokerage firm and tell him to unload some stock to cover it?"

"No. He can't sell any existing positions because they're all in the company's pension fund—Federal protection laws and all. But here's where I have to hand it to him. He can basically use Rock Solid like it's a credit card."

"What, he can draw on it for what Sarah owes him and she gets stuck paying back the principal plus the interest?"

"Correct, but it's even better than that. He put a loophole in the agreement you could drive a semi-truck through. He has the right to use Rock Solid to buy stock on margin—which is basically taking a loan out from the brokerage firm—and then keep the profits when he sells them."

The blogger took a breath. "Rock Solid has been doing a lot of margin buying lately. I mean a shitload. Millions of dollars worth. Get this. All the buying is in shorts and put options in none other than CaliCo Energy."

When Jess didn't say anything, Harrison blurted, "Don't you

get it? Logan Riggins is using Rock Solid to short CaliCo stock. He's betting the ranch the company's going to take a dive."

The blogger whistled. "I always heard the guy had balls. You know, all that rock climbing stuff. But if the brokerage firm calls that margin and the account gets stuck with all those options and shorts, then look out below. Logan will be living on the streets in a cardboard box and Sarah will be sharing it with him because she'll be on the hook for making up the loss."

"But what if the share price goes down like he's betting? He'll make a bundle, right?"

"An oil company stock that goes down? Come on! As long as they have a license to drill, they have a license to print money. It pumps oil, it makes money. It makes money, its stock goes up."

"What about when Buckle was murdered? Didn't that drop the share price?"

"It took a quarter-point dip intraday, but wound up right back where it started at the close of the bell. On Wall Street, the only reaction traders have when a CEO dies is to put in a buy order for Kleenex. Now, let's talk Chez Panisse. I'm free most every night."

Jess clicked off and broke the speed limit driving to Mattie's.

"Logan left an hour ago," she said. "He needed some space."

"What happened?"

"Oh, nothing. Oh, everything. Oh, I don't know."

"Anything I can do?"

"It's—" Her throat caught and it took her a couple of tries to clear it. "It's been so tense around here. There's so much to do. There's so much at stake. I understand what Logan's going through. He's under so much stress. But we all are."

"What happened?"

Mattie walked over to the window. It faced the west and offered a view of the Berkeley Flats and the Bay beyond.

"It's all the pressure. Logan's going a mile a minute. He isn't sleeping very much and drinks too much. He does that to cope with having to raise money for Dabo's defense. Raise money to buy a home for the Tarani. On top of all that, there's dealing with the media. Dealing with foundations. Dealing with his ex-wife. Sarah calls all the time."

"You mean, she's returning his calls after he's left her messages asking for a donation."

Mattie shook her head. "Other way around."

"You heard something?"

"Accidentally. He had the phone on speaker when he answered and took it in the other room. The door didn't close all the way. Sarah was practically screaming at him about money."

"I'll go talk to Logan," Jess said.

"But you don't even know where he went."

"I know where."

"You do? Okay. I'll see you at the Fox Theater for the fundraiser."

"I'm surprised you're holding it there."

"Why?"

"I thought it'd be at the ballroom at the Grand. It holds more people and I read they're discounting rental fees big time since the murder. It led to a lot of cancelations."

"No, it's too dated, too bourgeois. Logan and I have been planning to do a big event from the start. It's the reason I went to the Arts Foundation gala with him. I wanted to check out the Grand. I had my doubts while we were there, but it wasn't until we went back and I saw the ballroom again with fresh eyes that I realized it'd send the completely wrong message about protecting human rights and the environment."

"You went back that night?"

"Had to. We were halfway to Berkeley when Logan realized he'd left his phone in his room."

"And while he ran in to get it, you checked out the ballroom again and decided big chandeliers and white linen tablecloths didn't exactly go with endangered wildlife and Indigenous people."

"Exactly. I called the Fox the next day and booked the first available date."

"Did Logan agree when you showed him what you meant?"

"Huh?"

"After he retrieved his phone, didn't you call him to tell him to meet you there instead of out at the car?"

Mattie laughed self-consciously. "Must have been all that wine they kept pouring. Leaving phones seemed to be contagious. I'd left mine in the car and so I used the one in the lobby. They'd only connect me to his room, but it didn't matter. He didn't pick up and so I went back to the car. He was already there."

"You're right about the Fox being way better, especially for music. What bands have you lined up?"

"The who's who of Bay Area rock 'n' roll, hip-hop, and reggae. Everyone wants to play. You know how people talk about being at the Fillmore in the sixties? They'll be talking about this like that fifty years from now."

"I bet they will."

31

———

Indian Rock was a ten-minute walk from Mattie's house. The sun was heading for the horizon when Jess got there. Logan was free-soloing the Center Overhang, a technical route that only peaked three stories high above the deck but rated a 5.11 on the climber's difficulty scale of 5.0 to 5.14. He was wearing a tank top and had a red nylon bag filled with powdered chalk hanging from a carabiner clipped to his shorts. His muscles rippled like the folds in the rock.

Logan reached the most difficult section of the pitch, an eave right below the roof that required making a dead point while clinging spread-eagle to the angled underside. With his face kissing the wall and his backside pointing to the ground, he rose up on his toes from a foothold on a narrow ledge and lunged for the next grab, a blind pocket on the top edge of the eave.

Friction and a powerful left-handed grip on a tiny knob kept him from falling backward. When he came up a couple of inches short, Logan didn't panic. In the split second before the bone-breaking pull of gravity took over, he pushed hard on the knob to give himself more height and stretched with all his might.

The veins in his neck and the tendons in his arms bulged. Like a Braille reader, he sensed the pocket before he touched it. He jammed his fingertips into the half-inch deep crevice and caught himself just as his toes slipped off the narrow ledge and his legs swung out beneath him. It left him dangling by one hand.

Executing a deadweight pull, he raised himself high enough so he could get his hand up and over the eave while getting a toehold on the tiny knob. The three-point stick allowed him to raise his head and chest above the roof. He placed his forearms on top to leverage himself the rest of the way up and stood triumphantly.

"You can still bust a move," Jess yelled.

Logan looked down. He was breathing hard, but managed a grin. "This old Class Three? Every hold is a party ledge. I could've done it carrying a case of beer."

He tossed him the chalk bag. Jess had a second to consider the challenge. To take any longer would've meant losing even before he started. He clipped the carabiner to his belt loop and chalked his fingers.

Logan hooted. "Stick it!"

Jess hadn't been on rock since he'd been shot and he hoped the months of rehab had done their job. He took the first pitch fast, using momentum to carry him up the slippery face to the overhang. Needing to prove something, he decided to take the Leonard Leap-of-Faith, a tricky traverse pioneered by a local legend.

After rechalking, he made his move and quickly reached the tiny knob that Logan had used to launch his move up and over the eave. Instead of doing the same thing, he reversed his grip and alternated his toeholds so he was sideways to the wall.

"What do you think you're doing?" Logan said.

Jess was too busy looking across the eight-foot gap to answer.

He spotted his next grab, a banana-sized bump that blended in so well with the rock's slick surface that it was nearly invisible from where he perched. It appeared a lot farther away than he remembered, but there was no turning back.

Sticking out his left arm for balance, he flexed his knees, and pushed off hard, driving his outstretched hands toward the column as he sailed through the air. It took less than a second, but it felt like a minute before his palms slapped the bump and he curled his fingers. As he made the grab, he swung his legs forward, brought his knees up, and planted his toes on a thumb-wide ledge.

From that four-pointer, it was an easy push and reach to the first rung of the ladder. He joined Logan and stood on the roof.

"And people call me crazy," Logan said with a laugh. "I'd forgotten all about the Leap."

"You showed it to me the first time we came here."

Logan's grin melted like the rays of the setting sun. "That was a long time ago. A lot has happened since."

"Tell me about it."

"You knew David Brower grew up right next door, right? He used to climb here as a kid. He and Dick Leonard invented a lot of climbing techniques still used today. People remember Brower as the environmental movement's archdruid because of all his work at the Sierra Club and Friends of the Earth, but he was always a climber at heart. Even in World War II. He was in the army's Tenth Mountain Division. They stopped the Nazis at Riva Ridge. Sure, his division took heavy casualties in the process, but he and the rest of those boys helped end the war."

Logan stared at the horizon. The sun had disappeared beyond the gray edge of the Pacific. "Sometimes you don't have a choice, Sparks. Sometimes it takes a sacrifice."

"I suppose that depends."

"On what?"

"On whether the person who's doing the sacrificing volunteered."

"What do you want here?"

"The truth."

"Why do you care so much?"

"Because Dabo's lying in a hospital bed with more tubes sticking out of him than roots on a redwood. Because Blue Macaw and the Tarani are doomed as soon as CaliCo gets those leases. It's got to be the truth or nothing. There's no other way. Things either are or they aren't."

"Not always."

"Always," Jess said. "You lied to me about being at the hotel that night. You went back."

"I don't know what you're talking about."

"Mattie told me about your phone. Why didn't you answer when she called your room? Where were you?"

Logan started to walk away, but Jess grabbed his wrist.

"Let me go."

"Not until you tell me what happened. You were upstairs the same time Buckle bought it. You weren't in your room. Where were you? Come on, Logan. Let me help you."

Logan batted at Jess's hand. "Let go. I'm warning you."

"I need to know the truth."

"I didn't kill Buckle. That's all you need to know."

"Then tell me who did."

"Why the hell do you think I know?"

"Because you were there at TOD."

"What's that supposed to mean?"

"Time of death."

"Cop talk. Is that what you are now?"

Jess tightened his grip on Logan's wrist. Logan grabbed his.

"Come on, Logan. What happened?"

"And I already told you. I didn't kill Buckle."

"Then quit acting like you did."

They pushed each other in a circle, each trying to control the direction. Logan tightened his hold, cutting off Jess's circulation.

"Why would I want to kill him?" he shouted. "How could I negotiate to stop the lease sale if he was dead?"

"I know about the stock deal. You've been shorting CaliCo."

"What?"

"You've been shorting their stock, betting it will take a big drop."

"What the hell are you talking about?"

"If you can prevent CaliCo from winning its bid to drill in Ecuador, their stock is bound to take a hit. Anybody who had the foresight to sell it short will cash in."

"Since when do you know anything about the stock market? You don't even have a savings account."

"Tell me, Logan. Tell me what's going on."

Logan tried to trip him, but Jess jumped his foot.

"Is that what this is all about, you made yourself a backup plan in case you couldn't talk Buckle out of drilling?"

"You don't know what you're talking about."

"Sure I do. You used to say it yourself. When you're on rock, always leave yourself a backup. You put all those millions down on a debt-for-nature swap and if it goes south, so does your money. But you can make it back shorting CaliCo stock."

Logan crab-walked, pulling Jess with him. "You wouldn't understand even if I explained it."

"Try me."

Logan's eyes narrowed. His jaw tightened.

"Tell me the money you're trying to make is for Dabo. Tell me it's for buying the Tarani homelands."

Logan went limp. The sudden lack of resistance caught Jess off guard. As he stumbled, Logan quickly ducked and flipped him right over his back. Jess hit the rock hard and the darkening sky exploded in bright lights. As quick as they flashed, they began to dim.

"I told you to leave it alone." Logan planted his foot on Jess's shoulder where he'd been shot. "Keep away or you're going to get burned."

"It's too late now."

Jess brought his knees up fast and bucked, twisting and grabbing at Logan's ankle. It threw him off balance. He screamed as he pitched over the side.

Jess rolled onto his stomach and quickly snaked to the eave, certain he'd see Logan's body smashed on the deck below. Instead, he heard fingernails scratching frantically right below him. He stabbed his right hand down and grabbed, locking his grip as soon as his fingers felt flesh and bone.

"Got you!"

As Jess latched on to his wrist, Logan's fingers slipped from the one-handed grab he'd managed to land. The sound of his shoulder popping out of the socket sounded like a bat smacked against the rock wall.

Jess fought the pull of gravity. He jammed his left palm against a bump to halt his slide, plowing his toes to try and find purchase.

"Pull yourself up," he said. "I don't know how much longer I can hold you."

"Can't. My shoulder's dislocated. Again."

"Grab my wrist with your other hand. Hold on."

Logan grunted and Jess felt him clutch his wrist.

"Can you get a toehold?"

"It's too far away."

Jess's arm was burning, his hand shaking. He could feel his own shoulder getting ready to pop.

"Let go, Sparks," Logan said, his voice turning eerily calm. "Let me drop."

"No way. You'll cheese-grater all the way down. You'll die."

"Do it or we both go down."

"Climber's creed. No letting go."

"Don't be stupid. You don't owe me a thing."

"I'm going to slide forward. It'll give us another foot. When I do, I'll swing you toward the wall and let go. The pendulum should throw you pretty close. That section has plenty of knobs and cracks. You're going to have to stick it."

"You do that, you'll slide right off."

"I'll catch myself first."

Logan went silent. Wind whispered through the trees. A crow cawed in the distance.

"Do it," he finally said.

"On three," Jess said.

32

"Now you look like you fell off a bike," Isabella said as she tweezered shards of rhyolite from Jess's knees and elbows.

He pointed to a tube of ointment next to the rolls of tape and gauze in his Search and Rescue Response Pack. "Use that one. It's better against infections."

She held up an IV drip set and inflatable leg splint. "Keep doing what you've been doing and you'll wind up needing these too."

"A little skin's a small price to pay. Logan could've died."

"I guess it all depends on if you think he's still worth it."

"What's that supposed to mean?"

"You have serious doubts about him. It's written all over your face. At least the parts that aren't scraped."

"Things aren't so clear, is all."

"They are if you want them to be." She finished applying the ointment and taped gauze over the deepest scrapes. "Do you know who the killer is?"

"I'm pretty sure."

"Sure enough to tell Detective Stone?"

"If I do that, it changes everything because if I'm wrong, there's no going back."

"But what if you're right?"

"I have to be certain. One hundred percent. Then I'll tell him."

Isabella finished doctoring. "Good as new."

"Good enough to go dancing?"

Her head cocked. "You don't dance."

"I meant you. Tomorrow night. The Rainforest Now! bash at the Fox. They'll be dancing in the aisles. You can show off some of those new moves you've been working on for your Oakland High graduation piece."

"And what will you do?"

"Watch and learn."

The following night, four people dressed as rubber trees stood alongside a green carpet and waggled their limbs hello to Jess and Isabella as they arrived at the Fox Theater. The lobby of the historic movie house-turned-music venue had been transformed into a jungle with towering vases of red anthuriums, stalks of birds-of-paradise, and vines of orchids, bromeliads, and hibiscuses dangling from the ceiling. Live parrots and macaws squawked inside cages. Women wearing bikini tops and floral wraparound skirts glided through the crowd holding aloft trays of tropical drinks.

Some of the attendees wore costumes. Pith helmets were big. So were zebra- and tiger-print dresses. A woman carried a live snake draped around her sleeveless shoulders. A man toted a black leather whip and wooden stool.

Isabella and Jess made their way to a potted rubber tree where a pair of sulphur-crested cockatoos perched on a trapeze.

"Someone should've checked a field guide," Jess said.

"Why's that?" Isabella said.

"Cockatoos are native to Australasia."

Harrison Eight joined them. He clutched a hurricane glass with a purple paper parasol sticking out of it and a plate heaped with fried bananas and coconut-glazed shrimp.

"What a great party," he said.

Jess nodded at his drink. "You're not working?"

The blogger waved his glass at a throng of business executives. "This is work."

"Did you learn anything more about Logan and the Rock Solid account?"

"No, but I found out something even more intriguing. CaliCo was in the process of buying property in Ecuador. A lot of it. Oil companies don't buy the land they plan to drill on. They lease it so when they're through, they don't wind up owning a chunk of worthless dirt they've scraped all the trees off and left covered in toxic goo."

"They didn't go through with it?"

"No, the company withdrew the purchase offer the day after Buckle was killed."

"Do you know if it was in the same area as where the oil tract leases are?"

"Not even close. Weird, huh?"

"Maybe not," Jess said.

He left Harrison talking to Isabella as he went to search for Logan. He found Mattie first.

"Can you believe this turnout?" she said. "All the 'Gramming and TikToking has gone viral. Online donations are snowballing. It's nearly crashing our platform."

"Congratulations. Where's Logan?"

"He's probably talking up a big donor or one of the elected officials who came. If you see him, remind him they're going to open the doors from the lobby into the theater in a few minutes. There'll be a crush. Logan has to be on stage and give his kickoff speech before the music starts."

Jess found Logan thanking a couple of tech titans for their support. When he turned around, he scowled. "What are you doing here?"

"Same as everyone else. Supporting a good cause. Your shoulder looks like it's doing better."

"It's the least of my problems, thanks to you."

"What's that supposed to mean?"

"You talked to the cops. My lawyer tells me they're going to issue me a subpoena because new evidence has surfaced about me returning to the hotel."

"I didn't tell anyone."

"Someone did."

"It wasn't me, but don't underestimate Stone. Be straight with him. You lie to him about one thing, he'll figure you're lying about everything else."

"That's what lawyers are for."

Logan started to push past, but Jess put a palm on his chest to halt him.

"Why didn't you tell me CaliCo was looking to buy land outside the drilling zone? What happened? Did you get Buckle to go along with your debt-for-nature swap after all?"

"I've told you all along to trust me on this. Why can't you do that?"

"I do, but you're on a big wall with no holds and no more pitons in the bag. It's too slick, too steep, too complicated. Stone has the machete. They call that *means*. Now he's put you back at the hotel. That's *opportunity*. How long do you think it'll be before he learns about the CaliCo stock shorting deal? That's *motive*. Your lawyer won't be able to hold him off. You need my help."

"You're way out of your element here."

"Go see Stone. I'll go with you. Talk to him. Tell him what really happened that night. Tell him what you saw."

"And to think I used to rope up with you."

Logan disappeared as the doors from the lobby to the theater opened and a flood of people surged to find their seats. A local comic took the stage and began a manic string of mimics and one-liners.

As the laughter swelled, he crowed, "Let's give it up for the man who brought us here tonight, the man who's doing all the hard work to fight for Indigenous rights, find solutions to climate change, and save our planet. Let's give it up for the one and only Logan Riggins."

Applause thundered as Logan vaulted onto the stage. Stage lights made him squint as he looked out at the jam-packed theater. Someone handed him a microphone.

"Ecuador's a long way from here and a bend on the river in the rainforest where some friends of mine live is even farther," he said without preamble. "They're far away not only in time and miles, but in spiritual ways too. There's a butterfly there with wings the size of an open magazine and colors more beautiful than a painting. I've heard birds in the jungle that sound sweeter than a concerto."

He took a breath. "Ecuador's a long way from here, but right now, right here, seeing all of you, I realize how close it is. It's close to my heart and now I know it's close to yours too."

The applause started up again, but Logan barely paused. "The oil companies want to drill this place that you and I love. If we let them, they'll not only destroy it, but all of us. Oil companies tell us they must go to places like Ecuador to protect our national security. It's a lie. It's not about national security. It's about profits. Theirs. And we're the ones paying for it with our health and our children's health."

Clapping again rocked the room. Logan didn't try to silence it. "Oil companies say they're changing their ways, that they're investing all their profits into clean energy—wind, solar, and other technologies—to reduce carbon and address climate change. It's a lie. This year they'll spend five hundred billion dollars producing new oil and gas supplies, yet invest less than five percent of that on developing clean energy sources."

Outraged groans grew loud.

Logan said, "My friends who live on that bend in the river are pretty simple people. They hunt, they gather. They don't take more than they need. They always leave enough behind so it replenishes. But I tell you this, when it comes to looking at something as complex as oil drilling, they sound pretty smart to me. Here's what they say. 'We don't inherit the rainforest from our ancestors. We only borrow it from our children.'"

The crowd broke into cheers and whistles. The room rocked with clapping that went on and on. Someone pushed up against Jess. He turned, expecting to see Isabella, but found Tyrone Stone with two uniformed officers in tow.

"Man gives quite a speech," the detective said.

"It's not hard when you're telling the truth," Jess said.

"We'll see about that."

"What's going on?"

"Got a warrant."

"You're going to arrest him here? In front of all these people, all those cameras? Come on. Why here? Why now?"

The detective's brow furrowed. "The commissioner, the chief? They're all saying he's a flight risk."

Jess glanced up at the stage. Logan was watching them, a scowl growing on his face.

"You mean the one who's pulling the mayor's and district attorney's strings. Pius Wheedling knows the PR impact arresting him here will have."

"We got proof he was back in the hotel when Buckle was killed. A parking guy who'd gone home to visit his sick mama returned. We were finally able to question him. He remembers

Mattie Voss coming and going twice that night. First time was at the start of the gala. Second time was later that evening. She asked him to let her leave her car near the entrance for a minute. Parking guy made Riggins when we showed him a photo. He said Riggins got out, ran into the hotel, and then came back and they drove off."

Logan pumped his fist and shouted, "Save the rainforest. Save the Tarani. Save Dabo. Thank you for your generous support tonight. Together, you're making a difference. Together, you're saving the world. Now, enough with speeches. It's time to party. Let's rock this joint!"

The curtain behind him drew open as he ran off the stage. Drums began to pound. A horn wailed. A keyboard cried. An electric guitar howled like a wolf. The melody was instantly recognizable and the lead singer's voice that filled the room was as familiar as fog horns on the Golden Gate.

"Damn," Stone said and plunged into the crowd to give chase.

33

"You think he did it?"

Isabella's voice was calm despite Jess grabbing her hand and pulling her along. He was trying not to run people down as he weaved through the crowd for the exit.

"Doesn't matter. The cops do."

"Sure it matters. If it didn't, then why are you hustling me out of here so fast? You're going after him, aren't you?"

They reached the street. "Something doesn't fit. Logan's a lot of things. Self-centered? Definitely. Self-righteous? For sure. But self-destructive? No way. I don't see him risking the gas chamber over negotiating a deal with Buckle."

"Maybe you're not allowing yourself to. Didn't you tell me he once raced to the top of Mount Whitney despite having three broken ribs to win some kind of record? Sounds like he's the kind of man who doesn't like to lose."

"Logan's never given a shit about money. He certainly wouldn't kill for it."

"But what about face? He lost his company. He lost his wife. And now he's losing his fight to save the Tarani homelands? Maybe this is one too many losses."

Jess started to think Isabella might have something there. Logan had always been competitive. It's what made him a top climber when the metric for success was new routes pioneered, summits bagged, and speed to the top. Did he go back to the hotel that night thinking that he'd worked out a deal with Buckle only to discover the land CaliCo was supposedly buying as part of the debt-for-nature swap was all a con? Did Buckle laugh in his face and tell him he'd played him for a sucker?

The only thing Jess knew for certain was Logan ran when he saw Stone. That didn't prove he was guilty, but it did mean he had no intention of giving up or getting caught.

"I have to find him before Stone does," he said. "I owe him that much."

"But then what? He'll know you're there to bring him in." Isabella squeezed his hand. "You are bringing him in, aren't you?"

"I have to. It's the only way to save him because if the cops corner him, he'll try to fight."

"Do you know where he went?"

"I'm betting Mattie's. If he's trying to make a run for Ecuador, he'll need to get his passport."

"You're wrong. He won't be there."

"Where then?"

"Sarah's."

"No way. They hate each other."

"But they also loved each other. They probably can't tell the two apart anymore."

Jess pulled her close and kissed her. "I know the difference right here."

Isabella kissed him back and then pushed away. "Don't get yourself killed, okay?"

As Jess sped to Sausalito, he thought about the times he'd been thrust into the middle of family dramas during search and rescue missions. He'd looked for kids who'd gotten lost on family hikes, pumped on the chest of a father who'd had a heart attack while jogging with his wife and kids, faced the father of a straight-A son who'd driven the family van loaded with his friends into a canal.

Sometimes the situations worked out, a lot of times they didn't. The one thing he could never predict was how people would react when faced with the trauma involving a loved one. Once, a little boy had wandered off at Tilden Park. His team had searched all day and long into the night for him, not knowing if he'd fallen into the lake and drowned, been dragged off by a mountain lion, or snatched by a child molester.

Jess finally found him. The little boy was huddled in the deep underbrush, cold, frightened, and hungry. When he delivered him back to the trailhead, his frantic parents started yelling at him, accusing him of scaring them half to death. Then the mom and dad blamed each other. Insults turned into curses and then slaps. When Jess waded between them to break it up, the little boy ran off. He found him hiding in the same spot, crying that he'd rather stay in the woods than go back home.

Jess didn't know what to expect when he pulled up to Sarah Newton's house. He didn't know if Sarah and Logan still considered themselves a family or not. The thought of walking around and looking in the windows came and went. He knocked on the front door like the old friend he was.

Sarah answered. "What are you doing here?"

Jess brushed past her. "Hey, Logan. It's me. Come on out."

He stopped in the middle of the cavernous living room. The floor-to-ceiling windows that didn't open were unobstructed by drapes. The lights of downtown San Francisco seemed close enough to touch. A hazard beacon flashed atop Alcatraz. In between the cold white bursts, the Rock's brooding hulk loomed. Though the prison had been closed for decades, it still exuded violence.

Logan stepped from a vestibule and blocked the view of Alcatraz. "You took the wrong pitch. Go home before you lose your grip and fall."

"I can't do that. Stone has a warrant. He's like you and me. Turning around isn't on his route map."

Sarah rushed up to Logan. "You fool, you led him here. Go. Get out. Both of you."

When he didn't move, Sarah began pounding on his chest. It might as well have been granite. Logan didn't blink or budge or try to stop her.

"What's it going to be?" Jess said. "Are you going to turn yourself in or am I going to have to?"

"You don't understand."

"Then help me."

Sarah wheeled and hurried out of the room.

"The rainforest," Logan said. "It's always been about the rainforest."

"Has it really?"

"Of course. CaliCo wants to drill there."

"And you'll do anything to stop them."

"Stop them? Stop an oil company as powerful as CaliCo from drilling in a country as hooked on petrodollars as Ecuador? I'd have an easier time trying to stop the rain."

He shook his head. "I've always known I couldn't stop them. All I could do was try to cut the best deal for the Tarani I could. When I couldn't buy the tracts that were being leased for drilling, I looked downriver."

"All the money you put into the surety bond?"

"Gone. Or nearly. I was working out a deal with Buckle to take the land I'd found east of the homelands in exchange for the land in the drilling zone. We'd both walk away with what we needed."

"You trusted him?"

"Buckle was a businessman. He knew a good deal when he saw it. He'd still make money not having to pay for legal and public relations."

Logan glanced over Jess's shoulder. Jess looked at the window behind Logan and saw Sarah's reflection. Her arms were crossed tightly against her chest as if she were hugging herself to keep warm.

"What did Dabo think about giving up their traditional homelands and moving somewhere else?" Jess said.

"He didn't know the whole plan, but I figured in the end he'd accept that half a loaf was better than none."

Jess pictured Blue Macaw, the jaguar shaman, Moipa, Dabo's family, and the other Tarani, both the living and the ones who died because of the captain and Lyle Hunt.

"That's their home you're talking about."

"Do you think they ever stood a chance? Once their land ended up on the wrong side of an exploratory drill bit, they'd lost. The only chance they have is to pick up and move over to the other side of the river."

"Why didn't you tell me before you sent me down there to find Blue Macaw?"

"I couldn't tell anyone. Do you think I could've raised the kind of money we need if donors knew all the details? You think I haven't thought this through? How it's going to be judged when it comes out? How I'm going to be judged? How everybody's going to smear me as some kind of traitor, a sellout, a tool for Big Oil?"

He was breathing hard and his hands kept clenching and unclenching. "But you know what? Screw 'em. A couple years from now, the Tarani will be making chicha and swinging in their hammocks while the tribes who held fast to a world that passed them by will be drinking water full of benzene and watching smoke curl up from where their jungle used to be."

"And Buckle agreed to go along with this, out of the blue, a pirate like him suddenly gets religion and agrees to throw in with you?"

Logan looked down at his feet. It was only for a split second, but it was long enough.

"You did something else to get him to come over, didn't you?" As soon as Jess said it, he knew what it was. He could see her long dark hair, the star cloud orchid behind her ear, smell the first moment after a new rain. "You knew about Blue Macaw all along. You told him."

Logan nodded. "When I was living on the Napo, I'd heard tales of a rich cowori who snatched girls and kept them as souvenirs. Buckle fit the description. When Dabo told me about Mintaka's letter with the Oakland return on the envelope, I knew it was him."

"That's why you had me looking for her. You show Blue Macaw to Buckle, there's no way he won't give you what you want. But then he winds up dead, and there goes your leverage."

When Logan shrugged, it was like the morning in the rainforest when Blue Macaw stepped out of the sunlight.

"You lost your hold on CaliCo because Pius Wheedling stepped in, a guy who doesn't even recycle his newspapers out of principle. He pulled the plug on the deal before Buckle's blood was dry on the hotel carpet. There went your debt-for-nature swap and all your money too."

Logan shrugged again.

As Jess was speaking, he could see Sarah's reflection. She was still hugging herself, rocking back and forth.

"All the money you've been raising for Dabo's defense, there isn't going to be one is there? Now that CaliCo's pulled out, you're going to use all the donations to make up what you planned Buckle to bankroll and buy the land yourself."

Logan jutted his jaw. "Dabo would do the same. He'd want it that way. He's willing to make a sacrifice to save his people."

"Did you go to Highland Hospital and ask him?"

Logan's silence thundered.

"You both have to leave," Sarah shrieked, her voice raw with panic. "Right now. Get out of here."

"And shorting CaliCo stock?" Jess said. "That was your backup plan? If Buckle didn't go along, you counted on being able to stop CaliCo from winning the leases and then cashing in when their stock dropped. If that worked out, you'd get the money another way."

Logan glanced at Sarah. It was like he was standing atop Indian Rock again all those years ago. There was no distracting freeway in the foreground. He could see all the way to the horizon.

"It's like I always said, babe. If it was that easy, everyone would do it."

"Shut up," she screamed. "Don't say another word."

Logan turned his gaze on Jess. "You need to remember there weren't any venture capitalists looking to invest in a start-up home goods company when we grew Wild Things. Back in those days, we were living from order to order. One night, Sarah and I were watching TV. There was this old documentary about the Exxon Valdez oil spill. It had a bit on how people all around the country were so pissed off, they cut up their gas credit cards and were boycotting the company. Exxon's stock took a real hit. I remember saying if someone had known about the spill right before it happened, they could have made a bundle short selling."

His lips puckered from the bittersweet taste of irony. "We were sitting around drinking wine and started going with it, playing it up. How we'd target some big bad company, short its stock, and then do something to make sure it'd take a fall. We'd cash in and use the money for good. Give it away. Play Robin Hood. Of course, when we woke up in the morning and saw how it could never work, well, the whole idea faded faster than our hangovers."

"Only Sarah never really let it go, did she?" Jess said. "When her business started going south and she learned of your plans to block CaliCo, she remembered the short selling scheme and how Wall Street always punishes losers a lot heavier than it rewards winners. The idea of making a killing took hold and so she tapped into the Rock Solid account with its millions of credit available, forging your signature on the shorts and puts orders. She got so far out on margin it made crossing an ice fall without crampons seem safe and sane."

"Logan, make him stop!" Sarah cried.

"Is that what happened?" Jess said.

"I told her about my deal with Buckle. Sarah asked me not to go through with it. She told me if I did, it would ruin us both. If the brokerage called her margins, she'd have to liquidate Wild Things to pay them off and I'd never see another payout."

"But I know you. Saving the rainforest is as much about saving yourself. You didn't back down."

Logan looked past Jess at Sarah. "I'm sorry, babe. I really am."

The rest became as clear to Jess as the light in the rainforest again. Sarah was desperate. At the gala, after Clare went home with a migraine and Buckle said he was spending the night at the Grand, she knew Wheedling would cancel the land swap deal if Buckle was out of the way. That would force Logan to go back and try to stop the lease sale by fighting it.

She went up to Buckle's suite for a nightcap. Maybe she planned to hit him in the head with a lamp and make it look like a robbery. Maybe strangle him and make it look like suicide or a sex act gone wrong. But when he showed her Dabo's machete, she saw a way for someone else to take the fall. The same grit and cool calculations that worked for her rock climbing and starting Wild Things worked for her as she improvised a plan.

There would be blood, a lot of blood, and so Sarah told Buckle to wait, that she needed to use the bathroom. She slipped off her shoes, undressed, and then called from behind the door, telling him to close his eyes, that she had a big surprise for him. When she came out, she picked up the machete. It wasn't so heavy, not for Sarah, not for a woman who could still do fifty pull-ups.

"The next thing you know Buckle's lying on the floor," Jess said as he looked at Logan in front of him and Sarah's reflection in the window. "His blood is draining and so are all your hopes for a land swap. When it's over, Sarah showers, gets dressed, and goes home, leaving behind only a splatter outline of her toes."

Logan's shoulders slumped. "I saw her coming out of Buckle's room that night."

"Shut up!" she screamed. "You didn't see a thing."

"After Mattie and I left the gala, we had to go back to the Grand. I really had left my phone in my room. I got off on the wrong floor by mistake and so I went to take the stairs down to mine. I heard someone in the hall behind me. It was Sarah coming out of Buckle's suite. She was heading toward the elevator and never looked at the stairway, never saw me."

He sucked in his breath. "It's why I couldn't tell the cops I'd gone back. It's why I couldn't tell you. Sarah may be my ex, but I couldn't turn her in. You love someone once, it never really stops, no matter how much time passes, no matter how deep in the rainforest you go."

"You're not running from Stone," Jess said. "You came to warn her."

"Shut up!" Sarah shrieked.

Logan looked past Jess. His eyes widened. "Sparks, rock!"

Jess ducked instinctively at the climber's warning of an object falling from above. The whine of a bullet passed over his head, followed by a sharp crack and an explosion of glass. The sound of more bullets followed as he dove for the floor.

Then the bangs stopped.

Jess looked around. Sarah stood frozen, a chrome semi-automatic dropped from her hand and thudded softly onto the rug. Logan was still standing, the plate glass window behind him shattered, his chest bleeding. He stared at Sarah and Jess. Only he was seeing something far beyond.

It was the hard blue empty.

34

———

Three days later, Jess walked into Hannigan's. Madame Lau glanced up from checking receipts and said, "I told Logan Riggins Miss Better Than Everyone was wrong for him. Now look what she did. You want your regular?"

"I'm meeting somebody," he said.

"This is not a bus stop."

Detective Stone was seated at a window table.

Jess sat across from him. "I thought you didn't eat here anymore."

"I'm making an exception seeing I was on the job all night. Another 187. That makes three murders I caught this week."

"Not counting Logan."

"Yeah, not counting him. That's Marin County. Out of my jurisdiction." He paused. "Condolences for your loss, him being your friend."

"I heard they're only charging Sarah for shooting him. What about killing Buckle?"

"It's taking a back seat for now. The DA figures he can wait until Marin County clears the Riggins shoot, it being easier. Course, Marin is only charging her with Man One."

"Why only manslaughter?"

"They're holding the Attempted on you in their back pocket. I expect they'll charge her with that later. The way they're figuring to play it, they get her to agree she was aiming at you and Riggins was only in the way. You know, call it an accident. Once she signs to that, then they nail her ass for Attempted on you. See, it wouldn't be an accident if she wasn't trying to blow your head off. Both are felony counts."

The waiter slid a plate of stir-fried rice and Mongolian beef in front of Stone.

"But the Buckle killing," Jess said, "Oakland DA's not issuing a hall pass on that, is he?"

Stone used a fork to spear a piece of meat. "He's gonna get around to it, but it's a little tougher. We don't got a witness. We don't got a confession. We're able to put Sarah Newton in the hotel room on your word on account of what Logan said before he bought it, but that doesn't mean she's gonna admit she swung the machete. And even if she did, who's to say it wasn't self-defense. You know, she gets up there and Buckle starts playing unleash the dachshund. She was only protecting her virtue, her doing all that charity work she does. You know how her juice lawyer will play it."

Stone started chewing.

Jess didn't say anything. He'd stopped caring what kind of sentence the system handed her. It wouldn't bring Logan back, and it wouldn't change things in the Amazon either. No matter what the courts decided, it could never come close to the punishment Sarah had already dealt herself. She'd taken the business she loved and destroyed it. In the process, she'd taken the one person who'd ever loved her and destroyed him too. It was something she'd have to live with every day for the rest of her life no matter if she was behind bars or behind the doors of her cold steel and glass mansion in Sausalito.

"So what about you?" Stone said. "What've you been up to?"

"Not much."

He studied Jess for a bit. "You're not finished with this thing, are you?"

"What makes you say that?"

"'Cause you got a soft spot for the Indians. You can't leave it be even if you wanted to."

Jess glanced out the window as a garbage truck rumbled past. "They're holding a memorial service for Logan up at Redwood Park this afternoon. That's all I'm thinking about."

"His version of church, huh?"

"Something like that."

The detective finished his meal. "I got to go. Stay out of trouble, Parks. Buckle may be dead, but that oil company still has a lotta pull in this town. You hear what I'm saying?"

Jess met Isabella at the park. They followed a trail to a small glade that served as an outdoor amphitheater. The bartender from the Altiplano and a group of musicians were standing off to the side playing traditional Quechuan music. They all wore fedoras and alpaca ponchos as soft and gray as mist. The haunting melody of their guitars and pan flutes was as somber as the mood of the people who were seated on rows of rough-hewn wooden benches.

Dabo and Mattie were sitting together. Jess and Isabella sat down next to them. The newly freed Tarani was still covered in bandages.

"I am sorry about Logan," he said, his voice weak and strained. "He was my friend. A friend to all Tarani."

"I'm sorry too," Jess said. "I wish I could've saved him. I also wish I could've saved the Tarani who were killed."

Dabo searched his face. "We are only men. We do what we can. Sometimes it is enough. Sometimes it is not. What is important is we try."

Benny Guerrero and a group of Ohlone people filed in. He gave Dabo a clenched fist against the chest salute and said to Jess, "A'ho, brother. You saved one of us. We won't forget."

Jess listened to the music. He closed his eyes and saw a bend on a languid river that snaked through the flat jungle. He saw Blue Macaw and smelled the moment after a new rain. He saw the jaguar shaman wielding a sharpened stick and Moipa with his bow and arrow, and the last of the Tarani. He saw the looks on their faces when all the birds suddenly took flight and the howler monkeys began to screech as the bubble and gurgle of the river gave way to the thunder of powerful river boats bringing cowori, chainsaws, bulldozers, and greed.

He blinked the images away. "What will you do now?" he asked Dabo.

"Go home. Tarani need me."

"You're going to keep fighting the oil companies."

"With every breath we take, with every spear we have."

Jess put his hand on Dabo's shoulder, taking in his wan complexion, the sunken cheekbones, the tattoos on his face, the feather in his ear. He realized that Logan never had a choice but to do whatever it took to try and help them.

The music ended and the author of environmental best-sellers acclaimed for his lyrical style and exhaustive research walked to the podium. His shock of white hair, piercing eyes, and hooked nose gave him the profile of a bald eagle. A beam of sunlight hit him like a stage light. The rays caught the sterling clasp of his bolo tie, making it shine brighter than a silver dollar.

"People have called Logan Riggins a lot of things," he said, his voice seasoned by campfire smoke and bourbon. "A sinner. A saint. A dreamer. A hero." He paused, letting the moment build. "Logan Riggins was all of those things and more. I'm proud to have known him. Damn proud."

The eulogy went on for twenty minutes, the speaker

extolling Logan's character, sharing anecdotes, likening him to everyone from John Muir to Edward Abbey. Jess tried to follow the words, but stopped listening somewhere between the description of Logan the man he knew and Logan the legend he was now becoming. He realized that's exactly where Logan deserved to be, partly in the real world and partly in the world of his own making. While some people would only remember the good he did and others only the bad, Jess would always judge Logan as a man who'd at least tried.

After the eulogy, Mattie walked to a picnic table and lifted a pale veil of silk that had been draped over a birdcage. A white dove perched inside. She unlatched the cage door and waited expectantly. The bird didn't budge.

"Come on now," she said. "Fly away. That's a pretty bird."

The dove remained motionless. No one said a word. She tried calling to the bird again. She lifted the cage up and gave it a rattle. The bird ruffled its feathers and cooed.

Isabella leaned into Jess. "Go on. Do something."

"It's only an albino pigeon. She lets it out of the cage, a red-tailed hawk will nail it before it clears the park."

"That may be true, but if you don't help, she's going to break its neck for sure. Go on. You know you don't have a choice. Rescue is what you do."

Relief spread across Mattie's face as Jess took the cage from her, held it up, and looked into the dove's frightened eyes. They were the size of BBs and blinked rapidly. He blew softly on its feathers so it could sense the wind and then quietly called. *Oo-roo-coo, oo-roo-coo.* Reaching into the cage slowly, he closed his fingers around the bird's body, careful to keep its head above his thumb and forefinger. He gently removed the dove from the cage, held it up, and felt the beat of its heart.

After giving a nod to the Altiplano bartender, he opened his hand. With a quick flap, the dove took wing, fluttering around his head before circling over the glade. The Quechuan musicians started right up with "El Condor Pasa," the soulful notes from the bamboo pan flutes trailing in the bird's wake as it spiraled up and up.

Jess kept watching until the white dove disappeared over the tops of the green trees and there was nothing left to see but the big blue forever.

35

Spring slid into summer. Jess tried not to think about Logan. He didn't call Stone. He didn't keep up on the case against Sarah. He threw himself into refinishing boats to try to forget what happened to Blue Macaw and Dabo, and what was sure to happen to their home in the rainforest.

One morning before he went downstairs to work on the demasted schooner, the freight elevator door slid open and Isabella glissaded into his loft holding an empty espresso cup in one hand and her phone in the other.

"I'm out of beans," she said.

"I'll make you a cup. How's the new piece coming along?"

"It's coming." She placed her phone on the chart table.

Jess put water and grounds into the moka and turned on a burner. He glanced at her phone. It was logged into a news site. The headline proclaimed, "CaliCo Wins Ecuadorian Drilling Rights." Pius Wheedling was quoted saying, "We are humbled by the trust so many people have placed in us to extract oil responsibly and bring progress and prosperity to their part of the world."

"Kind of burns, doesn't it?" Isabella said. She squared her

shoulders and adopted a deep voice. "You're not going to quit now, are you, Sparks?"

The nickname and tone took him by surprise. "You sound just like Logan."

"Good. I've been practicing. You know, there's a saying in ballet when it comes to difficult moves. Either make them or fake them, but always take them."

"What's that supposed to mean?"

"Once the music starts and the curtain goes up, you dance no matter what. Back when I was in repertoire, a piece called for a grand jeté. It's one of the hardest leaps in ballet, like what you call a dyno—a dynamic. You throw your front leg forward, push off with your back leg, leap as high as you can, do the splits midair while sailing across the stage, and land on your front foot. Right when I started my jeté, something popped in my front ankle. No way I could land on it, and so I did a half-twist after the splits and landed on my back foot. Call it a sleight of foot, but the audience bought it. I can still hear their applause."

"You think I should take up ballet?"

"I think you should do something that will dazzle CaliCo into believing they have no other choice but to give Blue Macaw and Dabo what they need."

Jess looked out the window. The morning sun was chasing away the shadows cast by the cargo cranes. Sparkles were starting to gather atop the Oakland Estuary. It wasn't the Caiman River, but it beckoned to him all the same.

He carried *Pursuit* down to the estuary, slapped water on his face, and started paddling around Alameda Island. Close to shore, he spotted a flash of white in a thick tangle of bulrushes. Two egret chicks peered from a nest tucked among the blades. The current pushed his kayak closer.

The bulrushes suddenly parted in an explosion of white

feathers as the mother shot out, her eyes blazing with fury, her beak poised to inflict maximum damage. The bird was completely undeterred by Jess's size. He quickly back-paddled, but the enraged egret kept coming. When he finally retreated far enough, she veered off and returned to her vigil beside her chicks.

Jess recalled the sapphire and turquoise flowerpiercer doing the same thing when he'd gotten too close to her nest beside the lake in the Tarani homelands. "Mad as a mother hen," he muttered.

Something clicked. He said it again and then whipped the orange kayak around and began paddling home. He paddled hard and *Pursuit* sliced through the water as easily as a machete cutting through skin and bone.

Back at the boat shop, he found the feathers Blue Macaw had given him. He held them in his palm and heard her voice telling him how she'd planned to reclaim power over Jim Buckle. Jess put the two blue feathers in his shirt pocket and began packing. He assembled the climbing gear he hadn't used for months and packed up camping equipment too. As he was loading everything into his truck, Isabella came out.

"What are you doing?" she said.

"I'm going climbing."

"It's about time."

"But I need to do something first."

"What?"

"Take a dyno."

Eyes and lips smiled. "You'll stick it. I know you will. See you when you get home from the mountains."

He drove to CaliCo's headquarters. A skinny man with loose dentures and a baggy rent-a-cop uniform signed him in at the front desk, pointed to the elevators, and told him top floor. When he reached it and the doors slid open, a woman whose expression was as tight as the bun at the back of her head greeted him curtly. "This way, please."

She swiped her plastic ID through a security card reader and a heavy mahogany door swished open. Jess followed her down a thickly carpeted hallway. She pushed open a set of double doors at the end of the hall and ushered him into a large conference room.

Clare Buckle stood primly at the head of a long table. She was dressed in a dark blue suit over a silk blouse the color of the moon. Pius Wheedling stood to her right.

"Please be brief," he said. "Mrs. Buckle has a very busy schedule today and we really have no time—"

"My assistant says you have something of my husband's you wish to give me," Clare said brusquely.

"I do. Remember the first time we met at your home? You showed me a video he'd made for your wedding anniversary. Your husband had a thing for making home movies, didn't he? Trouble is, not everything he recorded was G-rated."

Wheedling shot his hand up. "That is quite enough. I am calling security." He reached for a phone on the conference table.

Jess pulled a flash drive from his pocket and placed it on the table. "Don't let me stop you."

"What is that?"

"A video sent to me by a priest named Father Banana."

"Father what? Is this some kind of joke?"

Jess kept watching Clare. "Father Banana runs a mission near where your company just won drilling rights."

Wheedling groaned. "Let me guess. It is an expose showing how poor Indians are suffering at the hands of the big bad energy companies. Do you know what I would like to see? A video showing how environmentalists are keeping people locked in the Stone Age because of their trust fund vision of paradise. They should be regulated for polluting savages' minds with things that can never be."

"Not this one, Pius. It actually stars Jim himself. Turns out he liked to set up a camera in the corner of the bedroom and make movies of himself with little girls. This one features a Tarani he snatched in Ecuador and smuggled home on the CaliCo jet and set up in a company-owned apartment beside Lake Merritt. You know who I'm talking about, don't you, Mrs. Buckle? Mintaka. Blue Macaw. She cleaned your house. You threw her out."

Clare's lips pursed. "You asked me about her before. I told you then, I'll tell you now. She never stepped foot in my house. I never heard of her."

"But she did and you do remember her because when I told you then she was from Ecuador, you said you didn't know an Indian girl from the Amazon. Why did you pick the Amazon? Lots of Ecuador's Indigenous tribes don't live there. The Amazon makes up less than half the country. But it was where your husband spent a lot of time. And he wasn't only searching for oil, was he?"

Clare's stare remained focused on the drive.

"When Blue Macaw finally escaped from the apartment, she took a flash drive your husband had loaded with his selfie movies raping her. The video became her scarlet letter. She couldn't throw it away, nor could she ever forget it. She took it with her everywhere she went, even after her brother was falsely accused of murdering your husband and she had to run for her life.

"Once she got to the Amazon, she went to the mission to beg forgiveness. Father Banana listened to her confession. All the guilt she'd been carrying came pouring out. She confessed what happened to her on the Caiman River years ago, how her abuser flew her to Oakland, why she disappeared, and why she never returned home. The priest absolved her and then told her to give him the drive, that he'd destroy it, and she'd be free."

Jess gripped the edge of the conference table. "But before Father Banana had a chance to do that, a bunch of mercenaries in the pay of your company came gunning for Blue Macaw because they knew she could alibi her brother and tell the world what your husband did to her. Lyle Hunt, Pius's personal pit bull, was with them and led the charge. Because of him, many Tarani were murdered."

Wheedling slapped the table. "He is lying. If he has a video of what he says, why has he waited so long to come forward?"

"Three-toed sloths aren't the only things that move slow in the jungle," Jess said. "Mail there still travels by dugout. It takes days, weeks."

"Do not believe him! It is a lie."

Jess held the drive out to Clare. "Let's see who's telling the truth. I'm sure there's a laptop handy we can plug this into. You can either watch it here or wait until it airs on YouTube."

The flash drive transfixed Clare the way a candle draws a moth. "What is it you want?"

"Your husband was planning to buy land for the Tarani beyond the drilling zone in a deal he made with Logan Riggins. The plan died when Jim did. Pius here killed it. Put it back in play. You have your greenlight to drill for oil. Now give the surviving Tarani a safe place to live."

"That is extortion!" Wheedling shouted. "The board of directors will never allow such an expenditure. The shareholders would have their heads. I will never approve it."

Clare turned to him. "You won't approve it? You? You're not the chair of the board of this company. I am."

"I meant you, of course. I would strongly advise you not to."

"Think of your own daughters and what their lives would be like if a man took them and did the things your husband did to her," Jess said. "Do the right thing here. Help all the other Blue Macaws."

"We already won," Wheedling said. "We have the drilling rights. The only obligation we have now is to our shareholders."

"Be silent," Clare hissed.

"I cannot let you jeopardize the company that I have devoted my life to."

"That is quite enough. Leave us."

"Leave? Who do you think you are? Who do you think runs this company?"

Anger spotted her cheeks. "If you're not out of this room this instant, I will call Detective Stone and have you arrested. Go. Now!"

Wheedling glowered and stalked out.

Clare inhaled sharply and straightened her shoulders. "If what you say is true, why do you think I'd do anything to protect my husband's reputation? After all, he was murdered by another woman, and in a hotel room at that. You can imagine what people already think. His death hasn't hurt the company any, nor will a tawdry revelation about his private life."

"Nature's way. The same as a bird will guard her nest, you'll do whatever it takes to protect your chicks, even if it means covering up what their father did so they can grow up without ever knowing the truth and burdening the shame."

She began toying with her pearl necklace. "My husband was an exemplary father to his daughters. They love and worship him still."

"But will they continue to when they find out what he did to Blue Macaw and who knows how many other young girls?"

Clare bunched the necklace in her fist. "If they find out, they find out. It will help them grow up and make them stronger. Children can't be shielded from the real world forever. Now, get out. But know this: if you show your sad little movie to anyone, I will do everything in my considerable power not only to destroy you, but the Tarani as well."

Jess realized one jump wasn't enough. It was going to take two—a double dyno. He picked up the flash drive and leapt again.

"Remember what you told me beside your swimming pool? CaliCo isn't only your husband's company; it belongs to you and your daughters too."

"So?"

"So, maybe your migraine wasn't a migraine the night of the gala but a convenient excuse to be home with an alibi. Maybe you and Sarah Newton were closer friends than you let on. Maybe you both had something to gain by your husband's death."

"How dare you insinuate that! I'll sue you for slander."

Jess felt himself sailing through the air, reaching for a grab. "No you won't. If you do, your daughters will hear about it and always wonder if it's true. Finding out their father was a rapist is one thing, but wondering if their mother is a murderer?"

Clare's eyes burned with fury as she stared at him, but finally she blinked and let go of her pearl necklace. "How do I know that video is what you say it is?"

"You don't, but you know it could be."

"And if I were to authorize money for this land deal, what about the drive? How do I know you won't release it anyway? How do I know you won't spread rumors about my husband's death?"

"You don't, but you know I will if you don't do what's right for the Tarani."

She took a deep breath and exhaled slowly. "Very well. You have my word that I'll do it as long as I have yours the video will never be shown and this conversation never happened."

Jess's fingers touched rock and he grabbed hold with both

hands as his feet landed as light as the blue macaw feathers in his pocket.

Back down on the street, he got in his truck, tossed the empty flash drive on the seat, and drove out of Oakland. If he was lucky, the freeway wouldn't be too jammed and he'd be in Yosemite in three hours. If he climbed fast and took the most direct pitch no matter how dangerous, he could summit Lost Arrow before sunset and look south and imagine being back on the Caiman River where blue macaws flew and jaguars ran free and waterfalls splashed in the moonlight.

But if traffic was bad, well, it was like Logan Riggins had taught him. Sometimes the route you pick doesn't work out. In that case, you need a backup. And if that doesn't work out either, then you need to keep on climbing and make it up as you go because, once you start, there's no turning back. Not ever.

ABOUT THE AUTHOR

Dwight Holing is the award-winning author of twenty books, including two popular mystery series: the acclaimed Nick Drake Novels and the witty Jack McCoul Capers.

His genre-spanning work includes stand-alone novels, short story collections, and books on natural history, conservation, wildlife, and outdoor travel. He lives beside a coastal river in California with his wife and two dogs who'd rather swim than walk.

ALSO BY DWIGHT HOLING

The Nick Drake Novels

The Sorrow Hand (Book 1)

The Pity Heart (Book 2)

The Shaming Eyes (Book 3)

The Whisper Soul (Book 4)

The Nowhere Bones (Book 5)

The Forever Feet (Book 6)

The Demon Skin (Book 7)

The Jack McCoul Capers

A Boatload (Book 1)

Bad Karma (Book 2)

Baby Blue (Book 3)

Shake City (Book 4)

Short Story Collections

California Works

Over Our Heads Under Our Feet

GET A FREE BOOK

Sign up for Dwight Holing's newsletter to get a free book and be the first to learn about the next Nick Drake Novel as well as receive news about crime fiction and special deals.

Visit dwightholing.com/free-book. You can unsubscribe at any time.